Saddam's Parrot

Jim Currie

Agnes Publishing

Honolulu, HI, USA
2017

Published in the USA by Aignos Publishing
an imprint of Savant Books and Publications
2630 Kapiolani Blvd #1601
Honolulu, HI 96826
http://www.aignospublishing.com

Printed in the USA

Edited by Karen Grimshaw
Cover Images, Artwork and Design by author
(see "Permissions and Attributions")

13-digit ISBN/EAN: 978-0-9970020-4-1

Dedication

To Blessed Elephants, Bernie Sanders and Our Revolution.

Acknowledgements

Thanks to the following for shepherding the book through the myriad editing steps and eventually to finished product: Karen Grimshaw, editor; Dan Janik, publisher.

The following offered indispensable artistic feedback and stirred imagination: Myra Zylstra, Holly Alderman, F.J. Bear, Gigi.

Others who were especially supportive: Satish Kumar, Betsy Gould, Alan Bomser, Phil Aaberg, Darrell and Donna Duffey, Joe Steiner, Dagmar Galleithner-Steiner, Peggy Wortman, Teresa Bledsoe, Colby Chester, Dick Kelley, Katherine Connor (Boon Lott's Elephant Sanctuary), Carol Buckley (Elephant Aid International), several college classmates, and various elephant and parrot spirits who constantly reminded me of why the book needed to be published.

Permissions and Attributions

Cover image of the flying parrot is by licensing agreement from Dreamstime.

Cover image of the White House is from a photo by the artist, Holly Alderman, with permission.

Cover image of Saddam (face only) is in the public domain (https://commons.wikimedia.org/wiki/File:Field_Marshal_Saddam _Hussein.jpg).

Interior image of Alex on Saddam's shoulder is a composite of the Wiki Commons photo of Saddam and a Creative Commons photo of the bird, available at Creative Commons Zero and Maxpixel (http://maxpixel.freegreatpicture.com/Parrot-Perch-Cucumber-Afri can-Grey-Eating-Bird-85585).

The story in the Introduction, and chapters 10, 11 and 16 about the rediscovery of the Sarasvati River and the importance of elephant fossils in the find is largely taken from a 2 December 2002 BBC article by Narayan Bareth, "Fossil Hints at India's Mythical River."

The story of the "Big Gulp" in Chapter 15 comes from multiple newspaper articles on research regarding the effects of climate change, water withdrawals and earthquakes on the Sacramento River.

The story in Chapter 30 and Epilogue of the feats of messenger pigeons and the accomplishments of the US Army 279th Pigeoneers are described in materials published by the US Army. In particular, see the informative 2012 film, *Pigeons in Combat* (http://www.pigeonsincombat.com/Historical Office).

The stories in the book about the card skills and underground activism of Red Bill are a fictionalization of the actual life of William Callison, as related by his family through personal communication.

BD Harmsworth is an entirely fictional character, but origins of shock and awe are drawn from *The Shock Doctrine* by Naomi Klein (Random House, 2007), James Risen's *Pay Any Price*, (Houghton Mifflin, 2014), and various works about the life of P.T. Barnum.

The story in chapters 34, 35 and 40 of the twin elephants is an adaptation of a story related orally by a vet in upstate New York about the twins born to a dairy cow and her subterfuge to protect a chosen calf.

The story in Chapter 39 of the Hamsa Swans of Srinagar comes from multiple sources about the mythology of the white swans of Dal Lake and their annual migration over the Himalayas.

The story in Chapter 32 of the return of grateful elephants to the grave of a human protector is mainly taken from *The Elephant Whisperer* by Lawrence Anthony (Tom Dunne, 2009). Other similar stories can be found in the lore of elephants.

The cognitive feats of Alex the Parrot described in multiple chapters are drawn from the story about the remarkable, real parrot, Alex, as related by Irene Pepperberg in *Alex & Me: How a Scientist and a Parrot Discovered a Hidden World of Animal Intelligence* (Harper Collins, 2008).

Learning to fly, but I ain't got wings,
Coming down is the hardest thing.

- Tom Petty and the Heartbreakers

Preliminaries - Notes from Pankaz

Ms. Betty McClain
Editor, *The Barb Online*

Dear Betty,

Enclosed is the promised article, "The Jig Is Up"—the story of Saddam's parrot, Alex, whom I have written about in other, shorter articles for *The Barb*, dating back to 2013. No problem publishing it now.

Following this is the story in 51 chapters and three parts of all the mischief caused by Alex, aka Ali, and the people whose lives he affected after his fly-in three years ago from Telegraph Hill.

More than a few missing pieces of the puzzle are revealed that trace to the beloved Marianne, friend and patron saint of both elephants and parrots, whose shoulder Alex landed on. Marianne taught us all much about graceful flight, indomitable spirit and wonder of the natural world, and hopefully I've captured some of that.

Please refrain from publishing the manuscript until 2017—just because of recriminations that might be exacted against Alex and Marianne's San Francisco family, myself included. By then, enough time should have passed so that no one is likely to be in danger, or we will already be domiciled at Guantanamo.

Sincerely,

Pankaz

Saddam and His Beloved Alex

The Jig Is Up
Special to *The Barb Online*
On the Performing Parrot Named Alex
By Pankaz Panday

In another life, Saddam Hussein might have been a stand-up comic. In the next reincarnation, Saddam's parrot, Ali, aka Alex, might be headlining in Vegas.

Dating back to childhood in his hometown of Tikrit, Saddam loved to tell jokes and compose stories. But this, of course, presented a problem for the mature dictator who had outconnived, plotted against and gutted his enemies over 40 years to become the feared *Butcher of Baghdad*. Always there was a lingering uncertainty over whether his gallows humor about camel drivers, George Bush and Osama bin Laden, was really funny, or the audience was simply humoring him because they feared that if they didn't, gallows nooses would soon be draped around their necks.

As Nabila Al-Jabouri, Saddam's personal maid, candidly explained, "Saddam doesn't die on stage; his audience does."

If anyone would know, it would be Al-Jabouri, who had been with Saddam since his early days in Tikrit. She had risen to the position of semi-trusted confidante because Saddam was a level-five germaphobe. This has been well established by all the credible biographies.

Nabila's mission going on 40 years was to keep unwanted dust and bugs of all sorts from terrifying the hypersensitive dictator, whether he was spending the night in the Baghdad Presidential Palace or holed up in Tharthar outside of Tikrit on the Tigris.

Because of this special dependency, Saddam began to ask her for more than just advice about ring-around-the-toilet and how to eradicate troublesome blood stains. On occasion, it would be her opinion of his jokes and eventually his self-amusing plans to be-devil George W. Bush, the CIA, and those obsessed about whether he, Saddam, was cooking up a new 9-11 attack with Osama bin Laden or hiding WMD (weapons of mass destruction) in the Baghdad Zoo.

His most common question to Nabila, roughly-translated from Arabic: "Do you think it's really funny, Nabila? Maybe it's just me."

"What do I know?" she would reply, "I'm no funny person and definitely not a politician."

When his pleas for reaction rose to the level of nagging, she would eventually blurt out, "Look, Sad-dam, you really need to get yourself a pet. Animals will never lie to you."

"I am already surrounded by terrified parrots," he answered.

"Get yourself a real parrot."

"Parrots are dirty animals."

"Not if someone cleans up for them. Humans can be pretty dirty too."

Saddam had to agree.

The next day she gave him an article from the Baghdad Times about a remarkable African grey parrot from the Al-Ghazal Bird Market that had been under study at the Baghdad University Animal Communica-tions Lab. His name was Ali (aka Alex in English), and he had been wowing researchers with his command of English and Arabic, his memory and cognitive skills. Beyond all this, he was clearly a performer and his own repertoire included dance and song.

Two days later, Ali became Saddam's personal pet, fully-fledged confidant, partner in musical comedy and political chicanery, relieving Nabila of the one aspect of Presidential dirt management that she most disliked. She also agreed to clean Alex's cage and developed her own bond with the precocious bird.

The relationship between Saddam and Ali seems to have been a near-perfect marriage and something that gave Saddam much joy even during the pre-invasion bombardment. The best part of it for Saddam was that Ali, when truly amused by a ditty, joke or something of his own design, would execute a special jig, compleat with a powerful squawk. This would send Saddam into a joyful guffaw, knowing that he must have dialed into something truly funny.

Frequently he rewarded Ali with cucumbers or Doritos, one of Saddam's favorite snacks, and a treat that Ali enjoyed playing with as much as eating.

April 1, 2003 was the last day that Saddam was together with both Nabila and Ali. With bombs falling everywhere on the Tigris-Euphrates floodplain, and Saddam readying himself for a dash to a Tikrit safe house, he escaped his worry to try out his latest comedy routine on Ali. According to Nabila, on this day he brought along a jumbo bag of Doritos for Ali who seemed to sense that something dire was afoot. Nabila recalls the following by Saddam:

"...So this fat camel driver, walks into this Baghdad Bar where George Bush is sitting with Osama at the front. The waitress, Marilyn Monroe, is dressed in a skimpy dress showing her cleavage. She approaches seductively asking if they would like a drink. In awe at the sight, Osama replies, "Praise Allah for this gift.' Then Bush declares, 'Forget about Allah, praise her lovely mother and praise the USA.'"

According to Nabila, at this point Ali declared,

"Bush is a camel's ass," which caused Saddam to laugh brightly and shower Ali with more chips.

But then Saddam's assistant burst into the room, exclaiming that American tanks had entered the out-skirts of the city, and Saddam had to get out immedi-ately.

"Dear Ali, my friend, I fear the jig is up," declared Saddam, dropping the jumbo bag of Doritos on the floor and racing for the door.

"It was a terrible mess," stated Nabila.

Little did Ali know that this was the last he would see of Saddam and that he would soon end up in the White House with George Bush, Saddam's arch-nemesis, and the butt of most of his jokes.

There would be no Doritos for Ali in his new home.

Introduction

Before Alex's surprise fly-in and landing on Marianne's shoulder, I had little experience with parrots or any other talking, precocious birds. I never had one as a pet, nor did any of my friends. From Hindu mythology, which I got doses of from my upbringing in India, I knew that gods rode them through the heavens and took to heart their spouts. I do recall that my poetic mother, Amita, mentioned a very smart parrot in a poem by Tagore, or was it Rumi?

The parrot in that story, much like Alex, realized that singing and performing was probably a bad idea if you wanted to be a free bird. Too bad I didn't exactly recall what Amita had said about that bird's clever escape strategy. If so, I might have pieced together more quickly the story of what happened to Alex in his days in the White House, and how he ended up with the Wild Parrots of Telegraph Hill.

Elephants, not parrots, were the *vehana* of my family—the animal carriers of divine wisdom to which my sister, mother, and especially my father, most often turned in dealing with the confusions of *maya* and earthly travails. They also gave instruction on virtue.

My father, Dinesh, was a *mahout*, or elephant caretaker. His beloved elephant was a gentle female named Deli. Dinesh loved almost everything about that elephant—the way she sauntered, the way she adroitly used her tactile trunk, how quickly she learned, and how loving she could be. Sometimes, she seemed so smart she was actually holding up a mirror so that all of us could see what we were capable of.

Born in the city of Prayag and growing up in Uttar Pradesh, my first panoramic view of India came at age 10 at the edge of the Yamuna River where Dinesh placed me on top of Deli's broad back. Unbeknownst to my father but immediately triggering notice from Deli, there was sugarcane in my pocket that I had pilfered from an Allahabad market. While Deli reached back with her trunk and tried to pick my pocket, my father pointed off into the distance and explained that three sacred rivers came together at Prayag. Each represented a divine spirit in Hindu myth. One of these, the Sarasvati, had mysteriously vanished 4000 years ago and left behind a dry bed.

"According to myth, or at least his version of it, the Sarasvati represented the gift of knowledge and abundance. She blessed the land with luxuriance that led to the rise of Vedic civilization. But she was also elusive and chimerical and dove underground when the natural balance was disturbed."

Elephants, explained Dinesh, played an important role in the story of India. "They are the guardians of creation," he declared. "It is reflected in their love of water and rain and a unique ability to locate hidden sources."

Fortunately, my hidden stash was no longer of interest to Deli. She was focused on a large lotus flowering in the muck at the edge of the river.

"They are also the carriers of memory, observing all the insults and abuses of wretched humans on the Great Vedic floodplain."

"If the Sarasvati is finally rediscovered, or at least its underground channels, elephants will point the way. And you can be sure that a great elephant spirit knows exactly what provoked the disappearance of the Sarasvati."

I might have easily let this go in my relief in not being exposed for the sugar thief I was, but a part of me not fully flowered found it interesting that rivers could mysteriously dive underground, and that a knowing creature like an elephant might pick up on this and even trumpet a re-eruption. I suppose a part of me also took note of the fact that Deli had achieved more virtue in my father's eyes than his only son—definitely something to work on if I were ever going to win his approval.

Only much, much later in my life in the United States as a journalist, did the full force of this hit me. In my own right, I had become a sleuth of hidden, subterranean dramas, interested in divining disturbances and insults on the human floodplain, and ferreting out those responsible.

In fact, the basic idea of floodplain disturbance pretty well describes the series of articles I've recently been writing for *The Barb*—in this case everything from political chicanery by arrogant people in power, to the origins of *Shock and Awe* and extensions of the Patriot Act. I've even taken to writing about rivers drying up because of climate change and what this might do to the State of California and the American economy.

I know all of this might seem pretty far afield from a fly-in by Saddam's Parrot, but I'll do my best to make the connections. At times it may appear that I've succumbed to a bizarre form of mental disintegration, leading you off into many dead-end channels involving parrots and elephant whisperers, pie-throwers, and practitioners of torture. Rest assured that the separate streams will eventually converge and maybe in the process offer a clarifying, panoramic insight, much like the one gained on Deli's back at the edge of the Yamuna.

There is one other elephant story in the river-flow of childhood that really deserves initial mention. It too involved Deli who frequently had nightmares that I remember well. A few hours after dark I would often hear her in her stable trumpeting anxiously or banging into the walls. My father was convinced that this had something to do with abuse she had suffered in her early years as a beaten, working-elephant clearing timber.

My father's remedy for this was music and, in particular, music from his own *bansuri*, a simple bamboo flute that my father played well. It had a calming, somnolent effect on her, first causing her to slow her thrashing, then fall into the rhythm of the music, swaying to and fro while her trunk swept back and forth like a giant metronome. Her eyes would glass over, and she seemed to have left the premises.

At the tail end of one of these musical rescues in which Deli had already escaped to elephant Nirvana, Dinesh declared to me with a smile, "The Indian Elephant is the one great and majestic creature in the animal kingdom that is truly harmless—especially when soothed by music."

At that moment she did look pretty harmless, but I wouldn't want to be around her if that nightmare returned.

Less than a month later, the *Dingaling Circus* bought Deli from her owner, requiring that my father deliver Deli to the Port of Calcutta where she was scheduled for transport to the circus training center in Florida. Right away, Deli sensed that some something was up. By the time we reached the Calcutta waterfront, she was wet from stress. She spooked on the Calcutta dock and accidentally crushed my father like a cheap tin can.

The trauma of that event left a powerful footprint on my view of the world—suddenly I realized just how precarious life could be and the hazard of assuming that anything in life was benign or harmless—especially when spooked. I was also tattooed with distrust for circuses of all types. I'm sure it only amplified my curiosity about human and animal dramas seemingly benign or headed for Nirvana, but ripe to take an abrupt dive into a dark netherworld.

Jim Currie

Part 1 - Flux and the Flood on the River of Blessed Sacrament

Chapter 1
Strange Fly-Ins

Last June in the middle of an unseasonal hot spell, I made my way to *The Offshore Cafe* from my apartment a half-mile way away. Breakfast at *The Offshore* had long been my morning routine before work at *The Barb*. It was now nine years since the fall of Baghdad, and though I wasn't yet aware of it, the presentation of Alex by the 3rd Marine Division to George Bush as a spoil of war.

Though it was only 7:00 AM, the temperature was over 80 degrees F., unusual for San Francisco at any time of year and probably close to what it was in Baghdad. In the Sacramento Valley, it already had to be 90 and headed for 120. Records were being set throughout California, and more than a few atmospheric scientists were convinced that this and reduced water supply were caused by climate change, which I had written a short article on for *The Barb*.

I had been gathering information to do another but wasn't quite ready. I came to a favored newsstand owned by an old Nez Pierce Indian, named Truman Jefferson. Truman often appears half-asleep, but he is taking in way more than you can imagine,

13

particularly about the state of the planet and topics he says I should be writing about.

"Sweltering out there, Mr. Panday. People and animals having a hard time." He nodded toward the morning *Chronicle* whose banner read, *Temperatures Soar; Water Supply Down at Hetch Hetchy.* I gave him a buck; he smiled and handed me the paper, watching as I scanned it.

I knew the reporter, a friend I sometimes compared notes with, and I wondered if he had said anything about research I had been tracking on reduced rainfall and snowpack.

I raced through it quickly: no, it mostly covered how people were dealing with the discomfort, including water rationing. He did, however, mention that summer water levels at the Hetch Hetchy reservoir were at an all-time low.

"Scientists are worried about saltwater in the Delta," declared Truman. "Bad for fish and critters."

"At this rate, we'll need to call out the elephants to save us," I murmured.

"What's that, Mr. Panday?"

"Elephants to divine for fresh water," I declared.

"This would be a very good idea," he answered in perfect deadpan. It brought a grin to my face. It was my first pleasant thought about elephants in years.

I stashed the paper in my pack and rounded the corner onto Columbus. In less than a minute, I was passing through the door of *The Offshore Cafe,* a modest 50's-style diner located near the intersection of Columbus and Broadway and a lesser-known hangout of artists, writers, old radicals and waterfront folks. Its signature aroma is fresh java and steaming hash, whose vapors seem to gather around an historical photo of a San Francisco steamship mounted on the back bar. The diner still possesses an old, wooden phone booth where longshoreman used to get work calls.

Marianne, the spritely 35-year-old waitress, flashed me a bright smile as she hustled delivery of a 'special' across the reflective checkerboard floor. It spiked my heartbeat and fixed my attention: she was wearing a tight, white waitress-dress accessorized by a coffee stain where the hem met her shapely left leg. Her short, sandy-colored hair was slightly disheveled, testament to the fact that she was handling orders for most of the diner. I knew also that she had been doing volunteer work for the elephants at the zoo. She had to be running on empty.

At a booth next to the window I could hear Tony the Pigeon-man, gruffly spouting to Roger, Darrell and Alex the parrot, who was perched on the sill of a partially-opened window. We all called him Alex—Marianne's idea—because he seemed to cock his head knowingly when she called him that.

Her own history with the bird was only a month old. She and Tony often took walks before her morning shift, and on one of these occasions a fringe member of the Telegraph Hill Flock, an African grey, seemed to hear her singing and landed on a tree not far away.

> *Like a bird on the wire,*
> *Like a drunk in a midnight choir*
> *I have tried in my way to be free.*
>
> *Oh like a bird on the wire,*
> *Like a drunk in a midnight choir*
> *I have tried in my way to be free.*

He promptly circled her, landed a few feet away and answered her singing with squawks, knowing head nods and feather ruffling, apparently intended to demonstrate his worthiness as a mate. Within a few minutes he landed on her shoulder, showing no apprehension.

He repeated this a few days later and was soon following her to *The Offshore*, a half-mile away. Once there he would perch on the sill within earshot of the booth where our group takes breakfast together and argues about the state of the world. Our loud, theatrical banter didn't seem to bother him. His attention was fixed on Marianne.

Most of the group might be called "circus performers," a queer conference of eccentrics, young and old, stricken with an inability to hold down an ordinary job for more than a few months before getting canned. Each has a favored animal affection or a significant animal-other. I guess in the case of Alex that would be human-other, albeit Marianne. The bird obviously had a crush on Marianne.

Tony is the senior in the group—an 80-plus pigeon trainer who earns occasional money in the clubs and on the street by getting his birds to perform. As far as I know, he has no family—certainly none that he openly talks about.

Darrell is an unmarried 32-year-old impressionist who sometimes plays Vegas. He specializes in imitating animals, celebrities and American Presidents. He can incarnate as 50 different characters, including Richard Nixon, whom he bears an uncanny resemblance to.

Big Roger is a 46-year-old Black, former defensive tackle for the 49ers, alienated from his family for being gay, who now sings

R and B in the local clubs. He's currently looking for a slobbering Saint Bernhard, big and strong enough to knock him off his feet.

"I don't care what they say; it's global warming," declared Tony the Pigeonman, paying no attention to my arrival.

"Could be," replied Roger, "but these heat waves come and go. I remember in the late seventies we had a drought, and no one was flushing their toilets. That was brutal."

Tony had turned his attention to Alex who was focused on Marianne.

"This ain't no ordinary bird," he declared. "Sometimes I think he knows exactly what we are talking about. He's taking it all in."

"Just because he finally spouted," replied Roger.

"He spouted?" I declared. "Let me guess—Alex wants a cracker?"

Roger piped up: "Alex wants a cool glass of water?"

"No," answered the Pigeonman with a smile, "Some kind of foreign language."

"C'mon," answered Darrell. "I heard it better than you did. It was gibberish."

"Tony's right," replied Marianne arriving with coffee, looking radiant with a splatter on her apron. "Sounded like Arabic to me."

"Better tell him to shut his mouth," added Tony, "or he'll get a call from the FBI. Right, Pankaz?"

"Yeah, end up on five watch-lists and find his bank account frozen," I declared. They all knew that one of the stories I was working on for *The Barb* was proposed additions to the Patriot Act.

"How about you?" answered Marianne. "I'm worried about a knock on your door, especially after what you wrote about in your article." She really did look concerned.

"Which one?" I answered trying to deflect, not wanting to worry her.

"Yeah," answered Tony, "He's pissing off everyone, especially the Bushies."

He was referring to my recent article on James Mee, the infamous lawyer who had written the opinion that enabled the Bush administration to get away with torture. Since 2004, he had been a law professor at Berkeley's Boalt Hall Law School, lying fairly low but apparently unrepentant about all the Constitutional abuse he had unleashed. Now he was involved behind the scenes in a revision of the Patriot Act.

"Vincent, my lawyer, says I'm too small a fish for anyone to care about."

Marianne didn't look convinced: "Just be careful." She reached inside her apron and handed me a sealed envelope, then dexterously refilled everyone's coffee cups.

I was pretty sure I knew who this was from—one of my underground sources, a fellow named Red Bill who had been making drops for me about James Mee and the Patriot Act cabal.

The note said that Mee had decided to participate in an upcoming symposium to be hosted by Boalt Hall. It probably wouldn't be open to the general public. No date and time had been set but Bill would keep me posted. He was pretty sure that other ex-members of the Bush administration would be there, "including a shadow figure named BD Harmsworth. They might be having pie for dessert," Bill had written.

"Hmm," I answered, "sounds like a little guerrilla theatre in the making. I think I need to be there if banana cream is flying."

"Pie?" declared Darrell. "Good idea. What have you got

Marianne?"

"Pies—let me see—blackberry, strawberry…"

At that moment, Alex flew through the window and landed on Marianne's shoulder.

I was caught off-balance, as was Tony. Marianne simply smiled and declared, "What have you to say for yourself, sweet one?"

Alex inspected her closely, cocked his head and sang out, "Let's have another piece of pie."

"Where did that come from?" I declared.

"I don't know," smiled Marianne, "but I had a feeling he wanted to get something off his chest."

Jim Currie

Chapter 2
Book of Elephant

A few days after Alex's spout, I was again at *The Offshore*, but this time alone inspecting an unopened package from Lucknow, India sent to me by extended family. I wasn't sure I wanted to open it. I couldn't remember any past letters or parcels from India that didn't contain bad news.

Marianne caught me inspecting it and shot me a curious glance.

"Anything coming from India is usually a tragic story or a plea for money."

On her next circuit of the cafe she found me looking at *The Book of Elephant*. It was my father's lifelong project to describe the behavior of the animals that he had more or less devoted his life too as a professional mahout.

Although it wasn't immediately obvious that it was a manuscript about elephants, Marianne, part elephant that she is, picked up the scent, and I was soon explaining how my father first managed Deli as a forest-clearing elephant and then as a performer. Before long, some kind of alien force was controlling my mouth, and I was narrating passages from the book, including stories about Airavata, the white, flying elephant that carried the God, Indra. I even gave Marianne the story of how my father put me on Deli's back at the edge of the Yamuna and explained how the Sarasvati

River had suddenly vanished underground.

"So your father sent this to you?' she asked.

"No, he's gone. It came from an uncle who just croaked."

"Hmm. Seems a little strange that something like this wouldn't go to you right away, "I sighed. "It's a long story. Elephants are a sore spot."

"How could that be?" she answered with a look of perfect innocence.

I shrugged and then, to my complete surprise, blurted out an abridged, casualized version of the Calcutta crushing.

"I guess I didn't want much to do with elephants after that," I smiled.

"You held it against Deli?"

I heaved a sigh. "Not really. She was a good elephant. She didn't know."

She nodded, and I chuckled at this strange experience of candor: "It's funny. I think this is the first time I've said anything about India in fifteen years."

Actually it was eighteen. Only a couple of people, and no one in the US, knew the story of "Deli and the Tin Can"—not even my ex, who in our first year of marriage had tried but failed to get me to open up about my upbringing in India. Without elaboration I told her it was deleted. I never again wanted to think about or consider in the abstract all the foul drinking water, the insufferable congestion, the phony gurus, abject poverty, horrific chemical spills, and seemingly weekly train disasters. But above all, I never wanted to return to the trauma visited on my family after the death of my father.

In any case, Marianne didn't seem ready to let my dismissal

go: "Want to do something really important to help the elephants at the Golden Gate Zoo?"

Under the influence of normal brain chemistry, I would have replied, "No, never," or something to the effect that I still considered elephants to be dangerous, but instead, perhaps because of Marianne's emotive emerald eyes or maybe that form-fitting, white, splattered dress, all I could come up with was the feeble response, "I'm working on that symposium over at Berkeley—the one involving James Mee and torture."

"No you're not, that's still a week or so away."

I sighed. "Geez... You're the hardest person to lie to."

She must have taken this as an indication that she had won me over.

"The elephants have been losing their babies to a virus, and we're trying to liberate them to a sanctuary. You don't even have to take sides—just give the story some press."

"You would have to set it up..."

"I'll talk to the director today about an interview, say next Friday? Okay?"

I sighed and she knew she had won.

"I'll give you the confirmed time and provide you with all the questions that need to be asked."

I rolled my eyes.

Jim Currie

Chapter 3
Music for Elephants

The following Friday, as I turned off I-99 toward the zoo, I realized that Marianne was working the same magic on me that she had on Alex.

For me there was no *Bird on a Wire,* but I had to admit I was close to being smitten and finding it harder and harder to refrain from landing on Marianne's shoulder and spouting song.

Here I was at 42, and a veteran of more than a few disillusioning relationships, including one brief marriage to a very smart woman who quickly reached the conclusion that I wasn't the sort of person interested in either nesting or disclosing anything too emotional.

In any case, since then I really had little interest in ever getting involved with any creature of the opposite sex. My job was pretty much my life and nothing I was apologizing for. I genuinely enjoyed the chase and challenge of investigative reporting, preferably of a Fortune 500 CEO committing fraud or embezzlement; hedge-fund swindlers; BP, Halliburton, and Exxon colluding to emasculate environmental regulation or fix prices; judges signing off on torture and illegal wiretap to make good on their political appointments; the Croak Brothers funding a new museum while working behind the scenes to fossilize a hundred endangered species. The sleazier and more craven, the better, and if a little danger or personal threat were added to the mix—perfect.

So the truth was that lack of time as much as disinterest in entanglement explained my lack of significant other or any kind of mating activity. It seemed pretty much the same for Marianne, except that her *raison d'être* wasn't reporting dire and corrupt events on the human floodplain so much as safeguarding the sentinel elephants that had been left behind to protect creation.

When I arrived at the zoo, a loud demonstration was underway. Roughly 60 people were parading in front of the zoo administration building, hoisting signs and chanting "Free the elephants." The leader of the group was a 20-something woman I had seen at other animal rights demonstrations in the Bay Area—Julie Jensen from Eugene, Oregon.

Off on the perimeter, shadowed by an elm tree, was a large fellow I recognized from old-growth rallies, the activist Willy Davis, who had gotten into trouble for spiking Giant Sequoias in the Siuslaw National Forest. Last I heard, he was wanted for questioning about the torching of an SUV lot in Medford. He was hard to miss—weighing over 350 pounds, which was why he had earned the nickname, Jolly Green Giant.

From my perspective, the best part of the demonstration was that it was colorful and dramatic and a good photo-op. A zoo employee was engaged in heated argument with a fellow in a papier mache elephant head. Neither of them was backing down.

"Never argue with an elephant," popped into my head. It was a phrase my father used. I hadn't thought of that in 30 years.

I managed to snap a picture of the staff member grabbing the demonstrator by the tusks and pushing him away. I was sure my editor would like it.

I had to show my press credentials to a security guard at the front of the administration building who for some reason decided to frisk me. It seemed pretty extreme. After that I was ushered into the office of the director, Dr. Sa'id Shipp. Marianne was already present, seated across from Dr. Shipp. She was wearing a powder-blue jump suit and her face was slightly smudged from elephant caretaking. She smiled warmly at me.

Shipp wasted no time in making his point: "I want to address the 'misconceptions' in some of the reporting about our elephants. I'm not sure the press or public realizes the lengths we go to in providing for them. We spend more on them than any other animals. Frankly, we treat them like royalty."

Marianne couldn't let this go. "What you spend isn't the issue," she smiled sweetly. "A lot of it is on the illnesses they contract, plus all the ridiculous artificial insemination. These are stressed, highly intelligent social animals living in unnatural conditions. With all due respect, they don't belong here."

"I'm not sure how stressed they are, but consider the habitat we have created for them—two adult females with a full two acres to themselves, along with lots of shade and a large mud hole that you can see they much enjoy."

"Yes, but you know they are migratory animals and are used to living in large families, especially the females."

"Some elephants in the wild, Marianne, but these elephants all come from a circus where you can be sure they were habituated."

"Elephants don't live in twos in the wild," replied Marianne authoritatively. It was hard to get the better of Marianne in any discussion about elephants. Shipp seemed to realize it.

"We know that four adults would be a better number and are working on that," he answered.

"You should be subtracting by three, not adding," she replied firmly.

I couldn't help but chuckle. Her conviction was firm but with no hard edges, and that made it even more compelling. It wasn't like anything I had seen in America—much more reminiscent of a *sadhu* or *sādhvī* in India practicing ahimsa with a smile. Yes, one of those Jain monks who sometimes blessed Deli.

I decided to bring up the disease issue which Marianne had given me notes on: "You now have another sick newborn, baby Hansa. If I'm not mistaken, she's the third of Gigi's babies that's gotten sick. The others died. Doesn't this suggest that you shouldn't be breeding elephants until you've gotten to the bottom of this?"

He fidgeted in his seat, "We're really concerned about this. As Marianne knows, we've brought in some great public health folks and followed their recommendations to identify and control the sources of microbes."

"Yes," answered Marianne, "But this is the problem, isn't it? There really isn't a good way for cooped up and stressed elephants to fight off infection, and the microbes are pretty much every-where. The only way to really deal with the problem is to move the poor elephants to a more natural habitat—a sanctuary."

Shipp shook his head: "This is extreme. We need to be scientific about this. We're confident that there are solutions." He turned back toward me, "Maybe we can show you some of the things we are doing."

A few minutes later we were at The Elephant House, a barn where the elephants took cover on cold days and where they were fed. Shipp and an assistant were quick to show that the zoo keepers and volunteers, Marianne included, were keeping the barn clean and separating food from waste. It was more hygienic than I expected, but then again, Shipp knew we were coming. He added that special attention was devoted to checking the elephants for foot sores that could lead to infections.

I asked to see the germ-free quarantine room where baby Hansa was being treated for a mystery infection, and he led the way. I wasn't allowed to enter but could see through the glass that she was being closely attended by a vet's assistant. At that point, Shipp left, and Marianne and I exited a door that led to an adjacent yard where Gigi and Sari huddled inside a fence. They didn't look happy, especially Gigi.

I knew all of the signs. They had all been recorded in *The Book of Elephant*—secreting profusely from temporal glands, erratic pacing, abrupt and alarmed eruptions from her throat, flared ears. This was the kind of stress that could turn something or someone into a tin can. People didn't tolerate violent elephants, even if they were just scared. I could see why Marianne was so concerned.

"They've both been like this since Hansa was taken away," declared Marianne. "They both know she is inside and want to get to her."

Marianne let go with an impressive rumble, then trumpet, causing both Gigi and Sari to turn toward us. Gigi turned back to focus on the doorway to the quarantine room, but Sari came bounding toward Marianne and reached out to her with her trunk.

"Yes, sweetie, you tell Gigi that I saw Hansa, and she is fighting very hard. We're doing our best for all three of you. We'll survive all this and then I'm going to get all of you out of here to a sanctuary." Her lips were pursed defiantly, but her tone was calming and melodic.

Sari nuzzled Marianne for a minute more and then ran off to see Gigi. I had no doubt that Sari had passed word to Gigi that Marianne had seen Hansa and was helping. Marianne approached Gigi along the fence line, singing to her, lullaby-like though I didn't recognize the tune—something very comforting that would put to sleep all the earthly worry an elephant mama would feel when her beloved babe was sick. You could tell from Gigi's ears that she heard. I couldn't help but think of my father on the Calcutta dock doing his best to calm his beloved elephant.

In the hour before Deli spooked on the Calcutta gangplank, my father recognized that she was nervous and resistant. She knew that this was no ordinary day of clearing trees, toting logs or performing. Something very strange was up that she wanted no part of.

My father reached for his *bansuri*, figuring this would calm her, but she shook her head as if rejecting the fraud. She even threw out her trunk and caused my father to drop his flute.

I was ordered to remain behind on the dock when they continued on toward the awaiting ship. I wasn't there at the gangplank when Deli rampaged. All I heard were her frantic screams, and then the cries of those who witnessed the crushing.

What I did see and find on my own was the other casualty of that event that lay only a few yards away from me—my father's crushed *bansuri*. It was broken in half and flattened like an abandoned serving of naan bread. There was no way the most skilled craftsman was ever going to repair it, and no way it was ever again going to make sweet music to elephants.

"Oh my gosh," Marianne blurted out. At first, I thought something had happened in the yard.

"I forgot to tell you—Red Bill left a message for you this morning—you are supposed to be in Berkeley by 2 PM for that symposium on wiretap and torture. What time is it? Can you still make it?"

"Yeah, but I gotta go." I waved goodbye and raced for my car.

Jim Currie

Chapter 4
Flying Banana Cream at Boalt Hall

My message drops from Red Bill at *The Offshore* were originally anonymous and dated back several years. In fact, this is how I first came to the cafe—to pick up an envelope he had left with Marianne about the infamous meeting between oil company executives and Bush's Vice President. I wasn't sure how he knew Marianne. What mattered to me most at the time was that his information was reliable and precise.

Subsequent drops documented instances of Administration zealots smearing and scapegoating luckless generals and admirals, including the poor female general who ran Abu Ghraib Prison and took the fall for the CIA contractors.

I soon deduced Bill's identity. In Berkeley he was a borderline folk hero for clever activism dating back to the early 1980's. On more than a few occasions he had made the FBI look like Yosemite Sam trying to nail Wily Coyote.

He had first gained notice as a young Stanford whiz kid with a photographic memory who had gone to Vegas and, using a combination of legerdemain and probability theory, stung two of the largest casinos. After that he was banned.

Then he started showing up at anti-apartheid, anti-imperialist rallies in the early 1980's, especially targeting the CIA for supporting the Nicaraguan Contras. His speeches were fiery, supposedly inciting demonstrators to assault Monsanto and Union Carbide recruiters on the Berkeley campus. Warrants were issued for his arrest, but he had eluded all attempts to capture him.

What interested me most in this latest tip was the possibility that BD Harmsworth might be going public or at least attending the symposium. Red Bill believed that Harmsworth was the unpublicized mastermind of Reagan and Bush Administration campaigns of shock and awe dating back to the overthrow of Allende in Chile. It would be a reporting coup if I could get a photo of him.

When I arrived at Boalt Hall, two university policemen were standing in the foyer making sure that all cameras and cellphones were checked by attendees. They also inspected bags and packs. They took my smart phone but missed my mini camera.

I seated myself in the middle section of the lecture theatre and seconds later a note arrived from my right. It was from Bill. I read it quickly—apparently, the fellow four rows ahead of me on an aisle was BD Harmsworth, incognito.

I pointed my camera at him and took my first shot. He was queer-looking fellow with a strange, angular, stooped-over posture. He wore a thin moustache and crooked smile. He gave the appearance of someone supremely self-assured and amused by himself.

The Dean of the Law School, Dr. Manfred Schmoot, promptly introduced members of the panel who, to my surprise included David Badminton along with Mee, plus Dr. Cheswick Bowles, a silver-haired Berkeley professor emeritus of constitutional law who looked bloated and about to tip over.

"Let me be clear here," declared Dean Schmoot. "This is intended to be a civil exploration of the constitutional issues involved in controlling terrorism and protecting national security. We will examine the limits and extent of Presidential authority regarding detention and what special measures might be justified in a state of war. According to rules negotiated in advance, there will be no interruptions of speakers by the audience and no tolerance for outbursts or demonstrations; no filming, taping and no cellphones...We're all here for reasoned discourse."

The dean must have been smoking dope to believe that he could get away with such restrictions in the Socialist Republic of Berkeley.

For 45 minutes Schmoot managed to prevent all interruptions as Badminton and Mee regurgitated their standing arguments without much resistance that the President possessed war powers to contravene both the Geneva Convention and the 1984 Convention on Torture.

Mee rattled off the names of notorious terrorists he claimed would never have been captured but for the torture of Khalid Sheik Mohammed—'the 19th hijacker.' "What we witnessed over the succeeding years is the return to a coddling, nanny culture that will leave our country, our pillars of industry and out best people in all fields subject to attack and terror. You need only scan the newspaper headlines to understand that our business people and way of life are under open attack."

I could only suppose that he was referring to a recent kidnapping of two American businessmen in Bhopal who ran a dirty chemical plant. Fox was giving it around-the clock coverage and intermittently editorializing that it demonstrated the laxness of our response to international terrorism.

Dean Schmoot allowed each of the participants a summary statement, and Mee closed by asking the audience to consider the higher morality "that the only way terror can be stopped is with superior counterforce—inaugurate special protections for key scientists, military leaders and even entrepreneurs; and to go after all the evil-doers preemptively."

"Now for a limited number of questions," declared Schmoot.

A young law student rose and tried to corner Mee on what he meant by "special protections." Mee simply answered that this was something that he would leave to security professionals who were studying the issue, "advising Congress and the President."

Across the room a gray-haired fellow in khaki turned toward Badminton and asked, "Do you deny that even high-level generals and admirals said you were legitimating torture—the same torture used by Japanese interrogators in WW II and what the Chinese did to American POW's in North Korea?"

Now I recognized the voice—it was Red Bill. I trained my camera on Badminton.

"Yes, of course I deny it. Enhanced measures which some people try to label as torture are not torture, precisely because they were applied within limits and justified by the imperative to protect innocents. Ends do, on occasion, justify the means."

"Haven't tyrants and demagogues spouted that time and again over the course of human history? Maybe we should consider the graphic horror of what you legalized in the name of the greater good," declared Red Bill.

Suddenly the room went dark and a projector clicked on. A video was instantly projecting the most horrific images from Abu Ghraib and Guantanamo. I was pretty sure that this was new footage. I pointed my camera toward the projection and selected video.

Four different captives were shown being water-boarded, and

another administered something up his rectum by a female interrogator. For a moment I had to look away. I had seen graphic pictures of some pretty horrendous torture by Nicaraguan Contras, but never anything like this. It was enough to spook every sentinel elephant on the floodplain.

Several prisoners were shown nude wearing dog collars, being forced to bark and beg; others were being suspended by ropes to stress positions. The interrogators were remorseless and derisive.

The screen turned blank and the words appeared:

"To this day members of the Bush administration who legalized torture have escaped trial for war crimes. A June 2006 report by The Council of Europe estimated 100 people were kidnapped by the CIA on EU territory and rendered to other countries. In 2007, according to the EU Parliament, the CIA conducted 1,245 rendition flights transporting prisoners to places where they could be tortured in violation of article 3 of the United Nations Convention on Torture."

A picture faded in of Don Haney. His confident monotone filled the lecture hall: "A lot of what needs to be done here will need to be done quietly, without any discussion...it's going to be necessary to use any means at our disposal, basically, to achieve our objectives..."

This gave way to a dark frame showing only a figure in silhouette. The caption was "BD Harmsworth, Author of Shock and Awe." Once again audio filled the room:

"Our mission here will be to execute an age-old theatre to paralyze and disable our enemies. Only by convincing them that they are confronted by a superior, more powerful God-force—that of fantastic guided missiles, satellite-directed warheads and psy-ops—will they capitulate—capitulate in the same manner that the Aztecs shuddered before the Spanish Conquistadors and the Gauls quaked at the thunder of Caesar's legions."

When the lights came on, I focused immediately on Harmsworth. Strangely, he looked pleased.

Suddenly, pandemonium struck. From both corners of the stage, demonstrators appeared with pies and raced toward Mee and Badminton. Both were hit at point-blank range. Professor Schmoot was also wounded and began dripping banana glop.

The university police rushed forward to apprehend the demonstrators, but were blocked by several students, possibly abettors. In the chaos and confusion, Red Bill and friends raced backstage in the direction of an exit to Bancroft Way.

I turned again toward Harmsworth and was surprised that he was even more amused than before. Now it seemed that he was even whistling. Yes, no doubt about it:

So let's have another cup o' coffee
And let's have another piece o' pie!

It was the same tune that Alex had sung three days earlier.

I was up all night writing both my article about the elephants and about what had happened at Berkeley.

The next day frames from Red Bill's slide show arrived by special delivery at *The Barb*. These ornamented and graced my scoop that was picked up by all the wire services and went international.

Yippies Back from the Dead?
Mee, Badminton Creamed by Radicals
by Pankaz Panday

Today an underground group calling itself *The Banana Cream Liberation Front* claimed responsibility for the pieing of James Mee and David Badminton, the notorious architects of Bush torture policy. The crust and cream bombs were launched at a semi-public meeting at Boalt Hall, UC Berkeley, sponsored by the law school. Mee and Badminton are believed to have survived the attack.

The "assault" occurred after a hacked, previously undisclosed Pentagon video was released of CIA torture of detained and suspected terrorists between 2002 and 2004. According to a University Police spokesman, a person of interest is Red Bill Callison, aka William Callison, the storied Berkeley militant who has revived the Yippie tactics of the 1960's.

In the audience but avoiding assault was BD Harmsworth, the notorious author of Shock and Awe who worked for several Republican administrations and was a close associate of Don Haney and Karl Rove. Harmsworth seemed amused rather than outraged by the pieings.

Another seemingly synchronized attack occurred on the East Coast at Harvard's Sanders Theatre. This followed the same basic MO. The victims there were William Kristol, well known NeoCon, Alan Greenspan, ex-Chairman of the Federal Reserve, and George Will, syndicated columnist. The *Lemon Meringue Liberation Front* claimed credit for this attack.

Homeland Security and the FBI have orchestrated a wide-ranging search for the perpetrators who they believe are Neo-Yippies, followers of the reconstituted Youth International Party.

The original Yippies were prominent in the 1968 demonstration outside the Chicago Democratic Convention against the Vietnam War. They gained both fame and notoriety for pieing defenders of the war and prominent conservatives and reactionaries, including William F. Buckley, Jr., Phyllis Schlafly, ex-CIA Chief, William Colby, and Senator Daniel Moynihan.

Maybe their most famous action was a stunt in 1968 when they invaded the New York Stock Exchange and showered hundred dollar bills from the balcony, causing a greedy stampede on the floor of the exchange.

Yippies reemerged in 2002 when Don Haney was non-fatally hit by pie in mid-town Manhattan, producing a spike in banana cream sales. In 2007, shoeing began when an Iraqi reporter, Muntadhar al-Zaidi, tossed a dirty sandal at George Bush during a Baghdad press conference.

My editor said it was a smash based on the web-hits and downloads of the accompanying video. She wanted more. I didn't mention to her the coincidence that Harmsworth and a parrot that had flown in from Telegraph Hill had both sung the same tune.

Chapter 5
Sorting Out Strange Coincidences

Two mornings later, Truman realized I was running late when I arrived at the newsstand and handed me my copy of the *Chronicle*. I only had time to read the headlines—the kidnapping in Bhopal had provoked Congress to pass a new law providing the President with wide-ranging powers to protect American businessmen. It was called the Private Enterprise Protection Act (PERP).

This was surely what James Mee had been advocating in his monologue at the law school.

Truman sent me off with his own summation: "They'll be a lot of pie flying now, Mr. Panday."

When I arrived at the café, the pieing and the appearance of Harmsworth was the main topic of conversation among the elephant herd. I related the fact that Harmsworth had whistled the exact same tune as Alex.

"Pretty weird coincidence," I added.

"He's a plagiarizer," answered Tony. "He's got to be stealing Alex's material."

"Consider the probability—this has to approach lottery magnitude."

"I'm not surprised at all," declared Marianne. "Synchronicity comes in bunches. The universe is a trickster." Marianne made an abracadabra gesture with her hand accented by a "poof". I loved it.

41

"A mere conversion of energy into matter. Dance of Shiva," I declared. "Of course, you might want to look at what Sai Baba or the Bhagwan is hiding behind his back."

"What's that?" inquired Marianne.

"Sorry, just an old discharge," I replied.

"No, I like to hear these stories about India."

"That makes one of us," I answered.

"Boo hoo," she answered, pretending to be gravely disappointed.

"Maybe there's no coincidence in Alex's spout," declared Darrell.

We all looked at him strangely.

"I'm just saying it's a common tune. Maybe they both heard it on the radio."

"First of all," declared Roger, "I don't think Alex is listening to the radio. The bird be trippin' with the cherry conures at the Coit Tower."

Marianne sounded a whistle in the direction of Alex to see what he might have to say, but he was focused on another bird—a big crow not particularly pleased by the invasion of his territory by this fellow with the curved beak and strange markings. Alex seemed ready to hold his ground.

"You think you've got a guy paying attention to you and then suddenly his mind is elsewhere," added Marianne shaking her head. "What's a girl got to do to keep a boy-bird on the hook?"

"Show more cleavage," added Darrell.

"That could be tough," answered Marianne, cupping her own small breasts, trying to get them to bulge and perk.

It shocked me and then brought a smile to my face. She

seemed to be searching me for an opinion.

"Looks good to me," I blurted out.

I looked over at Alex—Marianne's words had gotten his attention. It seemed to be the word, "cleavage"—or maybe the gesture used by Marianne to describe it.

"Are you going to pay attention or flirt?" declared Tony.

"I'm putting my money on some non-Voodoo connection between Alex and BD," declared Roger. "Either he was Harmsworth's bird, or the bird of someone they both knew."

"It makes me even more curious about this Harmsworth guy," I answered.

"I might be able to find out something about this bird," added Tony. "I got this pigeon-racing friend, Rollie the Racer...runs an exotic pet store."

"Rollie the Racer?" I answered. "Everybody you know's got a bizarre name."

"Jailhouse buddies," declared Darrell.

"Beg your pardon," corrected Tony, pretending to be hurt. "He's a pigeon racer—actually thinks he's better than me. By the way, Pankaz, I thought you were going to do an article about me and my racers. You know I almost copped the Florida International—one of the jewels of pigeon racing."

"It's a good story but it's down the queue—just below the story about Marianne's mission to create the African Free State of Mastodonia and the infernal California water crisis."

"Mastodonia should be highest priority," declared Marianne, "but we'll try to be patient."

"Yeah, you should do another story on the elies first," added Tony sympathetically. "We've got to get those elies out of that zoo."

Marianne's eyes met mine, interrogating me in irresistible ultramarine for a reaction.

"My editor has a say in what I cover."

It was a feeble response. We both knew that I exercised a lot of discretion in what I covered and wrote. The truth was that I really had no interest in further reminders about my history with elephants.

Marianne seemed to read my mind. "Pankaz will come around, " she declared confidently. She rushed off to serve another customer, and I didn't see her again until I was leaving.

She was alone at the counter calculating a tab. "Just a word, Marianne. You need to be careful in passing me information. There seems to be a clamp-down coming on people like Red Bill. You could get in a lot of trouble."

"I'm not worried. As far as I'm concerned it's all related to what's going on with the elephants. I'm with Alex, Red Bill and the Yippies—let's have another piece of pie—pie in the face. These guys deserve it—that and some hard jail time."

Her reaction caught me off-guard. I had never heard her voice a strong opinion about anything other than circuses and zoos, and even then, no suggestion that she was planning to take to the barricades with a red, black or green flag.

As I passed onto the sidewalk, the thought occurred that I had stumbled onto the really "bad girl"—Patty Hearst or Bernadine Dorn with red bandana ready to make a statement on behalf of the Symbionnese Elephant Army. Was it possible?

I did like the absurdity of it: ever-so-sweet and caring Marianne using the waitressing as a cover. The main mission was to recruit an 80-year-old pigeon trainer and radicalize the rest of us. Her conspiratorial interest in me was obvious—a five-eight reporter from India with a weak chin and a receding hairline who could not only concoct useful disinformation but cause Homeland Security to break out in laughter.

Too bad I wasn't working for the *Enquirer*. I could weave this together with a story that Elvis was in the building and had taken a bite out of Mama Cass's ham sandwich.

That night I filed my report on the plight of Gigi and her baby. I mentioned the problem with viruses, the plight of Gigi's baby and included most of the facts that Marianne had fed to me.

The day after it posted to the web Marianne sent me a handmade card expressing her deep appreciation. She even included a cartoonish picture of Alex on Gigi's shoulder. Out of his mouth were pouring lines of music, and you could see he was very proud of himself.

Jim Currie

Chapter 6
Betty Crocker and the Yippies

Five days after the Mee-pieing, I learned from email that the police conducted a raid against *Pope Pie-Us III*, a café in Berkeley believed to be the source of pies used in the attack on James Mee. This was apparently based on detailed forensics comparing the cream on Mee's clothing and pies being sold at *Pope Pie-US III.*

The owner of *Pope Pie-Us III,* 69-year-old Ivan Bochinsky, a past consort of Callison in public theatre, was being represented by the flamboyant and well-known defense lawyer Vincent Berlioti, author of the best seller, *The Prosecution of Don Haney for War Crimes.*

That same evening, Cable Channel 347, which garners a .002 percent of the Bay Area TV market, mostly featuring ferret rescue stories with a decidedly "Leninist slant," interviewed Bochinsky. He appeared in an all-black uniform wearing wrap-around dark glasses that accessorized a Bakunin-like manner or at least something reminiscent of Dan Akroyd and John Belushi. The questioner didn't waste any time popping the germane question: "Do you think you will go to jail for this?"

Stated Bochinsky, "Look, I'm a legitimate arms dealer, protected under the first and second amendments—the right to bear arms, arm bears, toss pies, whatever. I really don't care who does what with my pies—eat them, accessorize sex, weaponize them. If they are used for self-defense, launched against the NSA, Hamas or the IDF—makes no matter whatsoever to me. I would like to add that our *Scud II*, which I believe was used at Boalt Hall, is one of our most popular pies and ballistically very advanced compared to the weaponized pies of the 1960's.

"Just remember us if you've got a gripe with Halliburton, Trump Industries, election fraud, or are worked up by something at Area 51. We've supplied insurgents from Uzbekistan to Gaza and accept all credit cards. Our motto is "Banana and whip, let it rip!"

Early the next morning, even before my coffee at *The Off-shore*, I discovered that Ivan Bochinsky had gone public on the web with the *Pope Pie-Us III* recipe for banana cream pie:

Pope Pie-Us III Recipe for the Scud II

Ingredients
3/4 cup white sugar
1/3 cup all-purpose flour
1/4 teaspoon salt
2 cups milk
3 egg yolks, beaten
2 tablespoons butter
1 1/4 teaspoons vanilla extract
1 (9 inch) pie crust, baked
4 bananas, sliced

Preparation
1. In a saucepan, combine the sugar, flour, and salt. Add milk in gradually while stirring gently. Cook over medium heat, stirring constantly, until the mixture is bubbly. Keep stirring and cook for about 2 more minutes, and then remove from the

burner.

2. Stir a small quantity of the hot mixture into the beaten egg yolks, and immediately add egg yolk mixture to the rest of the hot mixture. Cook for 2 more minutes; remember to keep stirring. Remove the mixture from the stove, and add butter and vanilla. Stir until the whole thing has a smooth consistency.

3. Slice bananas into the cooled, baked pastry shell. Top with pudding mixture.

4. Bake at 350 degrees F (175 degrees C) for 12 to 15 minutes. Chill for an hour.

He offered the following qualifications: "The *Scud II* is a short-range ballistic pie. For long-distance strikes, we recommend the *Scud III* which contains dreaded corn fructose. This prevents fragmentation on the front end and holds the potential for collateral nutritional damage."

Serving Instructions

Here there are many options. We generally recommend a short-armed Stooges delivery with the pie placed in the outstretched palm and thrust forward without spin.

Spin may cause the pie to drop and curve, thereby missing the strike zone. Only the most skilled pitchers should attempt the side-arm Frisbee technique—and harder still the Sandy Koufax, three-quarter motion with a high leg kick which is never advised with the *Scud II* but has been successfully employed with the *Scud III*.

Whichever delivery is used should be gauged to the athleticism and nimbility of the target.

This was clearly someone I had to get in touch with immediately, someone who possessed serious feature appeal. Hopefully I could interview him and take pictures of him baking a *Scud*. On my way to *The Offshore*, I dialed up *Pope Pie-Us III* but got only the following recording: "This is B. Check back later, we are experiencing an untimely disruption of ..." And then not only did the message abort, but my ear drums were insulted by a sound that had to approximate what people must have heard in Japan at 8:15 AM on August 6, 1945 if they had been on the line to someone in Hiroshima.

Chapter 7
Haplessly Seeking Balance

When Hiroshima was followed by Nagasaki in trying to reach Ivan by phone at *Pope Pie-Us III*, I decided to make an in-person visit. I was surprised to discover that the roof had collapsed. Literally.

I found Ivan inside, dressed in anarchist black, down to his wrap-around *Noir* glasses, shaking his head. In the back of the store were two firemen, discussing the damage with an insurance man.

"Did you get bombed?" I asked. I showed Ivan my press pass.

"No. The roof fell in—I don't get it."

"What do you mean?"

"I mean I'm doing my best to make a goddam living, and I finally make a payment on the damn store, and the roof collapses. Go figure."

"From what?"

"That's what I'm trying to figure out. Berkeley Fire says there was a 3.2 tremor on the San Andreas this morning. But what the fuck is that? A good orgasm is a 3.5."

"You got insurance, right?"

"They're telling me that it's only partial. Partial? Supposedly it's in fine print that I've got to pay 50 percent on natural disasters.

Think about that—natural disasters are not okay but unnatural disasters are covered? So a lightning fire isn't covered but if your aunt Batty in the attic takes to playing with matches, everything's just fine. I just don't get this system. How's an ordinary guy gonna make it? Everything's about fine print and avoiding predators. The one-percenters have got everything rigged. It's not like I'm not trying. I finally get this pie thing going and wam—rebuked by the goddam universe."

He removed his glasses and stared me in the eye with exasperation. "I hate these damn glasses."

"I thought they were all part of the uniform—Sacco and Vanzetti and all that?"

"No, man, I've got a goddam Th1 disease."

"What's that?"

"Yur damn immune system goes berserk, and you're all out of balance. Suddenly joints, gut and everything are on fire."

"I've never heard of this."

"Supposedly it's all caused by some exotic stealthy bug that confuses 'yur immune system. Only way to get rid of the bugs is to cut back on sunlight and dose 'yurself yellow with antibiotics."

"No way."

"No, I'm serious. T-cells and B-cells get jammed up and 'yur whole system goes haywire." He shook his head disparagingly and put his glasses back on.

"I'd like to talk longer but I gotta move my car—new city parking regulations, for Chrissake. I can't afford another ticket."

He headed out the door, and I followed closely. He had just entered the sidewalk when he spotted a cop attaching a boot to his wheel.

"Oh geez, don't do that," he cried out with despair, realizing he was too late.

He turned back and shook his head woefully. "Man, I gotta get back in balance. These goddamn bacteria are killing me."

Jim Currie

Chapter 8
Masters of Deceit

I took a few pictures of Ivan and *Pope Pie-Us III* and dropped into a nearby café to upload them to my laptop. The best image showed poor Ivan a few seconds after realizing he had been booted. As I studied the picture, it occurred to me that that this was a perfect replication of "dissolute and disoriented" in *The Book of Elephant*. My father had used it to show the confusion of a herd that was leaderless or unable to make sense of new surroundings. Ivan only needed a dragging, hang-dog trunk.

I decided to connect to the web and browse for something that might explain BD Harmsworth and, in particular, his smug whistling after the banana-cream pandemonium. Before I started *Googling* I learned the new national security bill (PERP) had been signed by the President.

I was still puzzling over the key words to guide my search when a flashing notice crossed my computer screen: "Congratulations Pankaz, you've just won a free pass to the Greatest Show on Earth."

WTF?

I clicked on the image and read the following: "*Masters of Deceit* was the title of BD Harmsworth's graduate thesis at Graceland College. It explored the uses of magic and deception in the art of war. It was quasi-psychological, investigating how conquistadors and generals dating back to Genghis Khan and Sun Tzu preyed on the superstitions and fears of their adversaries to defeat them. All of this came together in a theory about shock and awe that was quickly taken to heart by folks up at the University of Chicago in love with Leo Strauss and Milton Friedman. On the basis of that he was hired as high-level advisor to Don Haney and George W. Bush."

Out of nowhere, came the voice, "You're probably wondering where you can find Harmsworth's thesis."

I looked up and met the eyes and grin of Red Bill.

"Try Bancroft Library."

"How did you do this?"

He chuckled. "Nothing to it, really. No encryption. You should see my real magic tricks."

"And how did you get away? I was sure you were dead meat."

"Once I got out the exit, I was home free. On Bancroft Avenue there are people who look more like me than I do." He broke into a grin. "I would love to chat but here's the word—I'm pretty sure this Harmsworth guy is behind this PERP business."

"I haven't been following this as closely as I should have."

"Private Enterprise Protection Act. Plug in. Consider the timeline here—the bill is in trouble and suddenly two businessmen with intelligence community ties get kidnapped. And then all of a sudden, it slides through like a greased pig. It's important to find out more about this Harmsworth guy."

"Where do you suggest I look?"

"Maybe Graceland College, his alma mater. Also, I think he's interested in magic tricks and probability, which is something I've long been involved with. I'm trying to figure out if we've crossed paths. I might have something on this later."

"How will I reach you?"

"I'll reach you."

He smiled confidently, tossed his backpack over his shoulder, and turned toward the door.

"Hey, one last thing." I declared. "Right after the pieing, BD Harmsworth started whistling 'Let's have another piece of pie.' Any significance to that? Marianne's parrot sang the exact same tune ten days ago when he started spouting."

"Really? No answers off the top of my head, but I'll give it some thought."

As he slipped out the door and crossed over to an alley on the other side of the street, it occurred to me that he was the ultimate performer. I had interviewed fugitives and criminals on many occasions but no one like him. He seemed to view what he was doing as art and himself as a practitioner of high-tech Dada. Maybe this, as much as radical politics, explained his connection to Marianne—most everyone in her circle was some kind of a performer with a dream of more than working in a phone bank or greeting shoppers at Walmart.

Ten minutes later I was at the Bancroft Library on campus reading a copy of the semi-redacted graduate thesis of BD Harmsworth.

I spent two hours studying it. It was a rambling tome of 500 pages that traveled into the history of warfare to describe how Caesar, Spanish Conquistadors, German storm-troopers and even the US Air Cavalry paralyzed their enemies with shock techniques designed to convince them that it was not only futile to resist, but that they were up against a dark God-force with magical powers.

Parts were interesting. Harmsworth described how deceit, magic and war-making were woven together in Greek myth, including the stories of the Trojan Horse, the deceptions of Odysseus and the Chimera. He focused on Caesar's blitzkrieg in Gaul and the crossing of the Rubicon; he made much of the way the Air Cavalry planted aces of spades on the dead bodies of VC in Vietnam.

The thrust of it seemed to be that all great empires depended on the manipulation of people's worst fears to induce passivity, compliance and surrender: "We repeatedly trick ourselves into believing that horrors of the underworld will erupt from our nightmares and punish us. The agile conqueror takes advantage of this:

> *The straying dreams of men*
> *May bring them ghosts of joy*
> *But as they drowse,*
> *The waking embers burn them.*

The thesis focused as much on fire-and-brimstone preachers as conquerors. An entire chapter was devoted to Pentecostal snake handlers and the cheap magic tricks of traveling evangelists. "The goal of evangelist, like that of the conquerors, is to paralyze self-agency and belief in the individual's ability to control destiny in both life and afterlife. All of this is facilitated and inspired by dazzle, shock and awe."

The dissertation made long, heavy-handed digressions into the power of illusionists and magicians; it discussed the mesmerizing effects of the "The Greatest Show on Earth" devised by P.T. Barnum that would activate "archaic centers" of the brain wired for enchantment and "authoritarian" direction.

A few hours later as I passed over the Bay Bridge toward San

Francisco, it occurred that an alternate title for the thesis might have been, "Prince II: Guide to Managing Fear on the Human Floodplain." About all that was missing were suggestions for silencing those pesky, trumpeting elephants.

The day after my session in the library, I wrote a short article for *The Barb*, entitled, "BD Harmsworth, Master of Deceit, Surfaces in Berkeley." It was only a few column inches, mostly regurgitating what I had read in the *Washington Post* article and in Harmsworth's own thesis. The more I considered what I had written, the more dissatisfied I became. I really didn't understand this character and hadn't done a very good job of describing him. Was he some kind of cold sociopath, intellectual nihilist, self-absorbed narcissist, or maybe some combination of them? And then there was the question of why, about which I had no real clue except this obvious interest in Pentecostal snake-handling.

Jim Currie

Chapter 9
Darjeeling Tea with Marianne

That evening I called Marianne at her apartment, asking if she might help me unpuzzle some of my questions about Harmsworth. It was the first time I had dialed her up, and I probably wouldn't have done it if I hadn't noticed that she seemed to be inviting more connection with me.

She said she would love to help "though I'm a little brain-dead from work. Why don't you come over for an hour or two?"

My appearance in her doorway caused Alex to fly the sill where he had been perched. "He's a quirky bird," Marianne declared. "He comes and goes on whim. Sometimes he'll fly in and sit on my shoulder. Sometimes he even watches TV. And then all of a sudden he's gone, back to Telegraph Hill."

"I can relate—probably worried someone will put him in a cage."

"Yup," she answered, suggesting that he had come to the right sill and that her windows would always remain open for entry or escape by any living thing.

While she boiled water for tea, I decided that I would make sure the conversation focused on Harmsworth and not my own family history. She handed me a cup and I declared, "I've never run into anyone quite like this Harmsworth. I read his thesis at the library."

"Spooky?"

"Yeah, *sangfroid*—no hint of empathy—Machiavelli on steroids."

"And this interests you because…"

"Just a curiosity about what drives people to extreme beliefs."

"I'm sure there's some kind of payoff in it for him," she answered.

"Well, you can be sure he was paid well for his services."

"I wasn't thinking money."

"Then what?"

"You said he seemed happy to see his buddies get nailed by the pie-throwers."

"Exactly."

"Sounds like someone working on a case of bitterness—petty bitterness."

"Yeah, that certainly fits."

"And probably someone in the market for confirmation."

"Confirmation of what?"

"Meanness."

"As in life is brutal; get over it?"

"Exactly, along with survival of the fittest."

"I like this. I think you're onto something."

"So my guess is that behind it all is something unhealed and festering. Got any ideas?"

She sipped from her cup and studied me for a reaction. Suddenly I felt exposed. It was as if she was talking about me and possibly the flattened bansuri on the Calcutta dock.

Alex suddenly landed on the sill and announced himself with

a bright squawk.

"That's his I'm-a-person-worth-paying-attention-to message. Come here, pretty bird."

Alex blew through the frame and landed on Marianne's shoulder.

"Which brings me to my other question: there's got to be some connection between Harmsworth and Alex. How would we find out if Alex knows him?"

"We could ask him."

"Harmsworth?"

"No, Alex."

"Come on."

"No. Seriously. We do it in parrot terms—we show him a good picture and see if he reacts."

She could see that I was skeptical.

"Better idea: did you take video and audio of Harmsworth singing the tune when you were at the lecture?"

"Yeah, as a matter of fact I got it on flash."

I knew what she had in mind. I fumbled through my pocket and produced the stick. In a few seconds we were loading it onto Marianne's computer, then downloading freeware so that I could play it, complete with the sound track.

"Got it," I announced.

Marianne approached the computer with Alex on her shoulder. I made sure that I had the audio on max so Alex could hear every note, including the coffee and pie verse that Harmsworth had whistled.

Alex only blinked vacantly.

"I'll rewind and play it again."

I did and this time he only pecked at Marianne's ear. She shed a look of disappointment.

I rewound it and the whistled verse had barely ended when Alex sounded with Dolby clarity: "Asshole dumbfuchs."

Marianne was gleeful: "Sounds like confirmation to me."

"Me, too—had to come from Harmsworth and his degenerate buds. See, this is why I need your help on all my animal stories."

"Everyone needs help from a bird-brain," she declared. She puckered as if about to plant a kiss on Alex's beak and held the pose. It was a precious freeze-frame, capturing her playful, irresistible spirit. At once it melted all intellect. The only thought streaming through my smitten brain was how do I get rid of the bird and spend the night with her?

She read my disturbance and flashed me a quizzical look that said, "Are you okay?"

"It's nothing—wandering mind—I get a bad case of that when I'm working on so many different stories."

It was a silly thing to say, borderline gibberish, but at least I had unfrozen my mouth. She waited for an elaboration that didn't come and then turned toward Alex, let him find her finger, and pointed him toward the window. He flew to the sill, gave her back a quick glance and then was airborne in the direction of the Coit Tower.

I took this as a cue for my own exit before another brain-lock set in.

"Okay, enough of this babble—thanks again."

I started for the door but she stopped me with a kiss to the cheek. I had no idea what it meant, only that it was something between a sisterly kiss and an invitation to press against her and not let go. I was paralyzed until she disengaged. Determined not to be exposed, I turned toward the door and escaped.

Back in my apartment an hour later, prostrate on my bed and inspecting the ceiling, all my dialogue with Marianne streamed back to me. Below the surface I wasn't sure what she was telling me—more intimacy or this is where the boundaries are. It could have been either one. It was no more clear whether the line about old wounds was about me or Harmsworth.

Then her words came back to me about survival imperatives, meanness and extinction of empathy. I decided to down a glass of water and finished it at my kitchen table while paging through *The Book of Elephant*.

My father had said a lot of about the unique ways that elephants coped and failed to cope with environmental stresses. Their adaptations were genetic as well as behavioral. Chapter 4 caught my attention, particularly because of how it explained elephant empathy and cooperation:

Adaptability of *Elephas Indicus* and *Elephas Africanus*
(From Chapter 4 of *The Book of Elephant* by *Dinesh Panday*)

Twenty-five million years or so after the dinosaurs became extinct, the first proboscides appeared that could easily be recognized as prehistoric elephants. Few things in natural history are as confusing as the difference between mammoths and mastodons. Mammoths emerged on the historical scene much later than mastodons, arriving in the fossil record about two million years ago and, like mastodons, surviving well into the last Ice Age.

Mammoths and mastodons share the fact that both survived well into historical times (as late as 10,000 to 4,000 B.C.), and both were hunted to extinction by early humans.

Modern Elephants and Survival Repertoire

Trunk, tusks, body size, foot design, thick skin and large, floppy ears are distinguishing characteristics of modern elephants that in one way or another are responses to evolutionary challenges.

The trunk is elongated and specialized to become the elephant's most important and versatile appendage. It contains up to 150,000 separate muscle bundles, no bone and little fat. Elephant trunks have multiple functions, including breathing, smell, touch, grasp and sound production. The animal's sense of smell may be four times as sensitive as a bloodhound. The trunk's ability to make powerful twisting and coiling movements allow it to collect food, and lift up to 350 kg (770 lb).

It can also be used for delicate tasks, such as wiping an eye. With its trunk, an elephant can reach food at heights up to 7 m (23 ft) and deep into mud or sand for water. It can suck up water both to drink and to spray on itself. An adult Asian elephant is capable of holding 8.5 liters of water in its trunk.

An elephant is forever fighting a battle with heat and high temperature. Though its thick skin protects it from the savagery of tigers and other large cats, it dries easily. An elephant is constantly on the lookout for places and ways to keep it wet and packed with protective mud. An elephant also lacks sweat glands, but its wrinkly skin and big flapping ears help it to get rid of excess heat.

Ability to Find Water

Elephants are among the most skilled water diviners in the animal kingdom, able to sense and find shallow wells, pools and even underground streams. One of the great mysteries of nature is the paradox that they are so dependent on water but also inhabit deserts where it is scarce. This has sometimes been attributed to their acute sense of smell, but surely it also relates to their great memory and ability to communicate with other elephants.

In Africa they have long been known to save villages suffering from drought. Tuskers will use their ivory as pick and shovel to dig and create pools and even find streams that have vanished. Because of this, some tribes will follow elephants closely and rely on them to survive a water crisis. One oddity no one has quite explained is that elephants don't seem at all selfish about protecting their water sources from other animals.

Cooperation and Society

A great achievement of elephants perhaps exceeding that of any other herd animal is their empathy and regard for one another. Females will take delight in the birth of babies that aren't even their own. The spirits of all the elephants are enlivened when the new baby arrives, and all the females will help in bringing it to its feet.

One of the common traumas they face is lifting stuck babies out of mud holes. Females will gather and trumpet advice and opinions about what needs to be done. It may involve nudging or offering helping trunks from different angles.

I turned another page to my father's description of how an elephant matriarch would watch over young females losing their virginity to overly aggressive males. If a bull became too dangerous and overpowering, the matriarch or the other females might rush him, chastise him and even force him away.

I read the last section again, falling into deeper comparisons between the social impulse and empathy of elephants and the apparent absence of this in Harmsworth and the people he traveled with. Marianne had to be right—his cold bloodedness had to be a survival response to something very painful. Deep down there was some kind of formative and defining trauma, probably as significant in its own right as Deli and the Tin Can.

In a few seconds I had booked a next-day flight to Chicago for closer investigation of BD Harmsworth's past and what might have turned him cold and callous.

The next morning on my way to the airport, I slipped a copy of Chapter 4 into an envelope and sent it to Marianne. My note was simple and casual: "Just thought this might be of interest. Fits with what you said about survival and how elephants care for each other. I 'm sure you know all this, but it's a beautiful thing."

Chapter 10
Pentacostal Snake Handlers

At Graceland College, there was faint memory of BD Harmsworth. I was about to leave when an administrative assistant well into her 70's intercepted me and said she remembered BD—said he was a pretty eccentric kid—very serious. She paused and said she thought he came from Cairo, Illinois. She fished through old files and confirmed it.

I headed for Cairo in my rented car and decided to check in at a local barber shop to see if anyone knew the family. There a fellow named Brody told me that the family ran *Harmsworth Pig Rendering and Sausage,* but it had long ago shut down. As far as he knew, the family had passed on. I was about to leave when he recalled that Harmy had a buddy named Jake Cloppits whose family "ran the old Flying A. Of course, that's gone too, but Jake has the 7-11 that replaced it." He gave me directions and I was there in five minutes.

Jake was amiably serving up slurpees and warmed-up hotdogs when I came through the door. I told him my interest and he didn't hesitate: "Yeah, I knew Harmy and family. *Pork and Sausage* supplied everyone in town until the health department did a number on them for e-coli."

"What about BD or Harmy?"

"We were friends in grade school, then things sort of went

south."

"What do you mean?"

He chuckled, "Harmy didn't have too many friends—he was sort of a nerd. But he got this magic set that he saved up for and tried to use it to make friends. He called himself, Harmy the Magnificent. Trouble was, he was all thumbs and would botch all the tricks. His rabbit wouldn't come out of the hat, and whenever he tried to make something disappear, you could see exactly where it went. His real problem was that he couldn't make his dad disappear. He was a real SOB and beat the hell out of Harmy."

"For what?"

"Almost anything. Scared me to death, which is why I quit going over there."

I checked into a hotel that night and discovered that I had inadvertently turned off my cell. All kinds of voice mail and text had piled up. My editor wanted to know what I was up to; I had messages from Vincent, my lawyer, that we needed to talk about PERP and what he had heard about pressure being put on the press; plus Marianne had left a message. Hers was the voice I wanted to hear. I turned the volume up to max:

"I got your chapter from the book, and it was wonderful. Your dad was more perceptive than you gave him credit for. He really did understand elephants and why they are important to civilization. Fits perfectly with the story of the Sarasvati River diving underground and knowing elephants standing as observers of all the abuse on the floodplain. I found something on this that I think might interest you and sent it to your apartment. Great synchronicity.

"I feel honored that you would ask for my opinion about

Harmsworth. He strikes me as very tragic as well as dangerous. Be careful."

The next day I made stops in town at the local high school, two orphanages, a half-way house, and finally, a Walmart where I spoke to a greeter named Waldon Frum who was Harmy's last-known teacher. I cobbled together what I learned in the following article for *The Barb* that I submitted electronically to my editor the day before my return to San Francisco. I decided to send a copy to Marianne.

Shadow Character Harmsworth Reappears
Overcame Snake Fear to Join Bushies
by Pankaz Panday

BD Harmsworth was a young boy in Cairo, Illinois, and the son of an uneducated pig butcher and sausage maker. Each year from the time Harmy turned 10, Harmy Senior, a man of God and faith, would take his son to the Cairo fairgrounds for the outdoor performance of Ebenezer Jehosavat, the traveling Pentecostal snake handler. Jehosavat dazzled the gathered throng by reaching into a bag of rattlers, typically holding a large one up to his nose, staring it in the eye with perfect faith in Jesus, and somehow avoiding the snake's fangs.

"Praise the lord," Ebenezer would declare, causing Senior to blurt out, "Get down on your knees with me and pray, Little Harmy." Harmy notes that Senior wore the same hapless expiring gaze of the pigs in the split second after receiving a slice to the carotid.

"Glaze and daze" akin to "shock and awe" always lasted well into the passing of the collection

71

plate during which Ebenezer's beautiful young assistants would relieve Senior and others of their pork and bacon money.

Young Harmy didn't forget the lessons of forced prayer and obedience to his dumbstruck father, and would later refer to such folk as "wdf's", which friends said stood for white "devout Christians" or "dumbfuchs".

Those who knew Harmsworth as a boy and adolescent suggest that his contempt didn't arrest a gathering curiosity regarding the many ways that people as well as pigs are dumbstruck and herded to slaughter.

Harmy ran away three times from his family before age 15. Each time he was tracked down by his angry father and tasted the rod of disobedience. Finally, he escaped but ended up in the Sandusky Home for Wayward Boys, an institution not noted for its healthy effects on young men.

Somehow, against all the odds, he earned a GED and matriculated at Graceland College where he eventually earned a master's degree in 1972 with a rambling, undisciplined but occasionally insightful thesis entitled *Masters of Deceit: Snake Charming, Magic and the Winning of the American Mind.*

The local barber in town, who knew the family, commented that "It confirms the old saw that even the son of a blind pig butcher occasionally stumbles upon an acorn."

Despite its failings in scholarship, it was a timely study that did not go unnoticed by Republican thinkers up at the University of Chicago who were already hard at work trying to figure out a formula that might forever roll back the programs of FDR, rid Latin America of unionists, open up markets to transnational corporations, and just maybe reclaim the rights to the untapped oil fields in the Middle East.

On my return-flight home, I couldn't help but wonder whether Harmsworth would have turned so cold and cynical if he had a family like mine, particularly a mother like my own Amita and my sister, Arundhati.

There was no safety net for any of us after my father died. His income as a mahout and his meager veteran's pension had made it possible for my family to live in a decent but modest house removed from the deprivations and insults to human dignity that come from abject Indian poverty.

That was all gone. There was no life insurance policy, no mahout survivor's benefits, no gratefully received charity to us to make up for the loss of my father's income. My mother, Amita, also knew that her chances of finding another husband were diminishingly small. Extended family was barely better off than we were and could only be counted on for blessings.

All at once we were in serious danger of slipping into the Great Indian Cesspool that no team of elephants could ever drag us out of.

The first casualty was the house which we could no longer afford to make payments on from my mom's meager wages as a tailor's assistant.

We soon moved from our then home in Faizabad to the outskirts of Lucknow after which my mom soon got a job in a ratty textile factory working 12 hours a day and 6 days a week. She was grateful to find any kind of work.

My mom was a rare gem of a woman who always considered

herself blessed to have us as children—we happened to be twins—and my father as a devoted and hard-working husband.

My sister was the first-born, 12 minutes ahead of me, and the two of us always laughed that it was because she had to get out and turn over rocks and figure things out.

Arundhati was far more curious and quicker than I when it came to school and any kind of puzzle-solving. In playful exploration, we would climb trees and race across pastures, looking for strange bugs, unusual flycatchers, or rodents in thicket or copse. Almost always she spotted them first and was soon investigating what made them tick, fly or burrow and not get caught.

That wasn't enough, either. She had to convey their masterful ways to her dull unobserving brother, always a few steps behind and a little slow on the up-take. Perhaps just to make me feel better, she would declare, "You, Pankaz, are the one with words who can tell the stories of all that we find together." She never grew impatient and I tried not to let her down.

The second casualty, of Deli's rampage was Arundhati's education. Arundhati had always been the better candidate for college. She had always done better in school and was always at the head of her class. Teachers thought she had a chance of some day becoming a scientist or doctor.

One day soon after Amita began her new job, she appeared when Arundhati was helping me with my homework. I could see that she was dog-tired.

"Come here my lovelies." First, she poured us tea and then after stroking our foreheads declared, "Unfortunately, our rent has been raised and I will not be getting as much as I thought at the factory."

"I'm so sorry, my sweets, but there is only one who will be able to go to school now, and that must be Pankaz." She kissed my sister on the cheek and held her tight. "We will live through him and sacrifice so that he can go to college." My sister raised no protest—she even smiled, angel that she was.

"Yes," she answered. "I know that Pankaz can make it." She wrapped her arm around me.

"Pankaz will carry our dreams."

"With God's help he will succeed, and then he will come back for you, Arundhati." With that we all fell together in a crying hug.

I was determined that I would not fail, and as soon as I made any kind of money, I would help my sister realize her own dream to go to college. I would also rescue my mom from her backbreaking job at *Lucknow Textile and Clothing*.

The following week my sister got a job in my mom's factory at minimum wage. She never went back to school.

Jim Currie

Chapter 11
Dulary

When I returned to San Francisco and arrived at my apartment, I was delighted to discover the promised letter in my mail box from Marianne.

The note was brief: "I found this on one of my favorite elephant web sites—M"

Elephant Fossils Help Scientists
Locate Chimerical Saravati River
by A. A. Kumar, *Jaipur Daily Times*

Indian geologists reported today that they have found an elephant fossil in the Thar desert of Rajasthan, supporting speculative theories that 5000 years ago the vast desert was once the verdant floodplain of the mythical Sarasvati River, described in ancient Vedic texts.

The search for the Sarasvati has been a Holy Grail for over 1000 years and more recently has consumed millions of rupees in sophisticated hydrological, and paleontological research. Senior geologist JS Singh said the elephant fossil was discovered in a village in Nagaur district, about 300 kilometres from the state capital of Jaipur, during gypsum mining.

Professor Singh, who is the head of the geology department at the Allahabad University, termed the find a "mammoth discovery for Indian science, reinforcing the age-old marriage between rivers and elephants."

According to Singh, the fossils were found embedded in a gypsum layer little more than two metres from the surface and belonged to an elephant or its ancestor known as *Stegolophodon*. The fossil is a 61-centimeter femur, a vertebral bone, and a metatarsus.

Singh added that sudden climate change probably caused the river to disappear, "with the effect that the area turned arid with a few small remnant lakes that were salty and inhospitable to most life. Another possibility might be the shifting of tectonic plates that altered drainage patterns."

I couldn't help but think that my father would be smiling. I could picture him declaring, "Most certainly, that's what happened. And yes, the elephants were bound to point the way."

My sister and mother would have loved it as well, especially Arundhati with her unquenchable desire to get to the bottom of natural mysteries.

Marianne was as glad to see me as I was her when we rendezvoused late the following day on Marine Drive near the Golden Gate. She often took walks there at sunset to see the sun marry the ocean and leave behind a brilliant preternatural light. There at the vista, watching the waves roll in from the other side of the earth, I told her of the sacrifice by Arundhati and Amita for the chosen son.

She fastened on the words with pursed lips and knowing eyes. I didn't want or need her to tell me that I did the wrong or right thing in acceding to my mother's wishes. What meant more was the understanding and sympathy in the way she squeezed my hand and pressed against me with her slim hips, the nonverbal expression of wonder that I would be lucky enough to have a sister and mother who loved me so, and that I, in turn, would be so committed to coming back for them when I could.

A few hours later at her apartment, after we had walked all the way back to North Beach, she brought me a cup of Tulsi tea with squeezed lemon juice. The cup itself was precious: its handle the trunk of an Indian elie. I'm sure Dinesh and probably Marianne knew whether it was from India or Sri Lanka or just the handiwork of an artist relying on imagination.

We named the elephant Dulary—an Indian term of endearment reserved for someone much beloved—and decided she had loaned her trunk to thirsty dreamers divining underground pools; and then I kissed Marianne for the first time.

It was as sweet as I could have imagined and our lovemaking probably would have gone on until sunrise, but both of us were wearied by the walk back from the Presidio. We fell asleep in a tight curl that I was sure was close to the embrace between Arundhati and me before she decided to push herself out onto the floodplain of natural wonder.

Marianne awakened first—not sure by how many minutes—and must have crossed to a chair on padded elephant feet to reach her clothes and get dressed. I might not have even known she was leaving except for the soft imprint of her sweetness on my cheek.

Jim Currie

Chapter 12
I Might Have Made a Big Mistake

The night after my sleep-over with Marianne, I struggled with insomnia and decided the best soporific might be television. I switched on my set and after a bit of surfing landed on the PBS station and the re-airing of an old NOVA special on animal communication.

I had actually seen it a year earlier, but that was before the arrival of Alex. Besides addressing the intelligence and language abilities of parrots, it focused on the research of experts studying the communication of elephants at African waterholes. All kinds of equipment had been set up at a forest waterhole in central Africa as well as a wetland in the Okavango in Southeast Africa where elephant families met after long migrations across the drought-ravaged savannah.

One of the researcher admitted that they hadn't cracked the code, but she was pretty sure that the elephants communicated about territorial threats, water and possibly food supply, "and maybe even information about families and subfamilies."

The footage was even more suggestive. In the background were two females from the same extended family but different herds, who apparently hadn't seen each other in years. They were chatting like sisters at a family reunion, and I was pretty sure it was about more than the poachers in Tanzania or lush grasses at Zambezi Sip. It wasn't hard to imagine Rachel passing on rumbles to Polly about Lucy and Rex finally getting together last month when Rex was in musth. He was a clumsy lover and could improve his foreplay. I chuckled and fell back into slumber.

If I had given the special any further thought after my night with Marianne, it might have occurred to me that rumbles might already be emanating from the bush about something that had occurred between Matriarch Marianne and the diminutive Indian bull in musth.

I knew that the herd had already picked up on my increased interest in Marianne, so it wasn't as if they weren't alert to signs and signals that endocrine-induced liaisons might be taking place. Of course, they were all males and weren't quite so skilled and attentive to the low-frequency rumbles and meta-communication as females.

When I dropped into the booth next to Alex's window, nothing seemed different. Marianne was busy behind the counter. When she passed by the booth, I made no extraordinary eye contact, nor did she. *So far so good.* A few minutes later she arrived at the booth with our orders.

When she nearly spilled coffee on me, I thought my retort was perfect:

"Careful, you almost neutered me."

"That might be a benefit to the species," she replied dismissively. Clearly, she recognized the danger of accidental transmission.

And then without thinking I produced Dulary for her to fill to the brim, and she did so with no particular notice. It was grievous error by both of us. The previously unbedded Matriarch- Marianne would surely have said something immediately about Dulary.

"Nice cup," she answered way too late.

"Yeah, I thought you would like it. Dulary is her name."

Tony was quick to respond. "You've named your cup?"

I held it up, figuring display would turn suspicion to comment on its artistry. No, they were scanning Marianne.

"You don't name elephant cups," declared Roger. "Only one person in this group would do that."

"I think I've seen this cup before," replied Tony turning toward Marianne. "I know—at your apartment…"

Marianne ripened like a crab apple.

"You slept together?" declared Tony. "That's it, isn't it?"

"What?" I protested sarcastically.

Marianne scoffed derisively, as if to reply, "Gimme a break—sleep with Pankaz?"

"You pathetic liars!" declared Tony. "That's exactly what happened."

"Jeez," declared Darrell.

"And now you're going to fuck everything up," added Tony. "We've all got this nice herd thing going and you jeopardize it by diddling each other."

I realized that denial was no longer an option and drew my rapier.

"Well, if I may say so, I think it was worth it."

Simultaneously Marianne turned to face the heel-nipping hyenas. "Ain't going to be any changes. I guarantee you."

"Fat chance," replied Tony. "We all know what happens next."

"And exactly what is that?" declared Marianne in full confrontational mode.

"Mooning, doting and other inanities," answered Roger.

"Really?" she scoffed.

"Yeah, " added Darrell. "How was your day, sweetie pie?"

"Yeah," added Roger. "The full vomitoria."

"Check your meds," answered Marianne sarcastically.

"You've already named his coffee cup," answered Darrell.

"Gonna get yourself some nice new duds, Pankaz?" declared Roger. "How about a hair transplant—you're looking a little thin up there if you want to get diddled again. What about you, Marianne? Get yourself a new dress?"

"New bra and panties," fired back Marianne. "Want a look?"

"So are the two of you going to be dating now?" shot back Roger.

"No dating," I answered.

"What?" replied Marianne. "You promised me wine and roses."

"Oh yeah, I guess I did."

"Look," replied Tony. "If I need to get myself a new family, I need way more advance notice. And let me say, I think Marianne may have endangered her relationship with Alex, adulterous two-timing wench that she is. You know, parrots can be pretty vindictive."

I checked the sill. Alex was there paying no attention to any of us, fixed on the one crow that he didn't particularly like. He was staring daggers at him.

Roger piped up: "I move that we place our philandering matriarch and omega male on probation."

"No problem," answered Marianne. "This herd of lost little

boys is way too much work and responsibility. I never signed on to be a baby sitter."

She turned and headed off to deal with the more mature members of civilized society.

Without her wit, I knew I was going to be in trouble with the heel-nippers, so I decided to make my escape back to my apartment to work on my stories. This provoked cat-calls which I answered with a French salute.

All the way back I mulled the serious issue behind the farce: exactly how was this night together going to change my relationship with Marianne? I wasn't sure. I did know that I was dealing with a very strong female, maybe even an alpha female. Any sign of clinging and I was out the door.

I suppose I could bring this up with her, but talking about it seemed apt to convince her that more maintenance might be required in our relationship than she had time for or interest in. The main relationship she seemed committed to was her elies.

It made more sense just to let it all work out naturally and not convey the idea that I needed clarification. Let her bring it up if she wanted. Yes, that made way more sense.

Jim Currie

Chapter 13
G-Men at the Door

I had just returned to my apartment and had almost arrested any internal debate about Marianne, when I was startled by a loud knock on my door.

Suddenly, before me were two men in suits, the larger one declaring, "Are you, Mr. Panday? We would like to have a word with you." The larger one flashed Homeland Security credentials. "Can we come in?"

"It might be better if you stayed where you are unless you can produce a warrant."

"We can easily get one but we're really just here to talk. Your article in *The Barb* suggests that you have been consorting with known terrorists. This could make life very difficult for you—felony difficult."

I decided to force the issue. "In what way would I be consorting?"

"Did it occur to you that your sources might be on a terrorist watch-list?"

"You mean like the pie-maker, Ivan Bochinsky?"

The larger fellow chuckled. He knew whom I was talking about. I decided to pursue this.

"I hope you didn't have anything to do with his problems."

This seemed to resonate with the larger one whose snarky

grin deepened.

"The man's got bugs," he blurted out. "Probably needs to be fumigated."

The smaller one didn't crack a smile. "We're not arresting you at this point, just warning you and asking for some cooperation. It's really in your own best interest to identify sources who might be involved in terrorism."

"Last I heard, there was something called the First Amendment. This sounds like something all three of us should discuss with Mr. Berlioti, my lawyer."

The larger fellow added, "We would appreciate a suggestion as to the whereabouts of William Callison?"

"He's your known terrorist?"

"There are felony warrants out for his arrest."

"For something that happened when Ronnie was drawing a blank over guns for hostages?"

No recognition whatsoever. Damn. What a waste. Maybe they were too young to get it.

"By the way, can you supply me with the watch-list you're working off of? A lot of people are getting a little confused about who the enemy is these days and amendments one and four of the Constitution."

"We're not playing games here, Panday."

"Mind if I also take a picture of you?" I answered, reaching for my smart phone.

"We would prefer that you didn't."

As soon as my visitors were gone I fell into puzzlement—*hadn't protection of sources been resolved in favor of the press in the days of Richard Nixon? Why would they even bother to lean on me? Did the new terrorism law change this? Clearly, I needed to talk to Vincent about this.*

I headed for his office later that afternoon. He worked on his own out of an elegant Victorian, gingerbread house in Pacific Heights. It was always as much entertainment as business in meeting with him.

He was in fine form and costume, immediately stirring comparisons to John Kenneth Galbraith, who had been the flamboyant ambassador to India in the early 60's.

Vincent was about the same height—approaching gantry elevation—with lofty diction to match. He was quick to declare that my visit by the G-Men was probably authorized by an assistant US attorney general or even a Federal judge who felt that new, wide-ranging powers over "enemy combatants" and "threats to the United States" had been authorized under the Private Enterprise Protection Act (PERP).

"The language of the act potentially gives the President broad powers to protect 'national assets' from attack or even threat. This could mean threat against any CEO on the Fortune 500 List."

"Pieing?"

"The new act talks about 'bodily threat, incitement and material support."

I puzzled over this. "So if I've got this right, even if you are an American citizen and you are not in Chechnya or Mogadishu or the Khyber Pass, and you do anything to incite, insult or present a threat, you could get your lights dimmed?"

"The way I understand it is that you don't have to be taking up arms. You could be taking up shoe the way that one poor guy did who tossed a dirty sandal at George Bush back in 2002."

"But he was a foreigner."

"Right, this is about American citizens."

"American citizens on a watch-list just for throwing a pie or shoe?"

"If you throw the first shoe you probably get yourself on the list. The second shoe, especially if it's a steel, work boot, might get you a free vacation to Leavenworth-on-the-Missouri or maybe Guantanamo."

"What about abetting—say you drop five bucks into the wrong collection plate?"

"Bad idea, especially if you've previously made a cream-filled demonstration of antipathy toward the wrong person."

"This sounds flimsy as hell."

He shook his head with rueful admiration. "The legal machinations here are masterful—they've stitched together the Enemy Combatants Law, FISA, The Military Commissions Act, The National Emergency Act, The Defense Authorization Act of 2007 and the Patriot Act. It really is a thing of breathtaking beauty."

"You think it could actually work?"

"It never ceases to amaze me how the law and the Constitution can be twisted by these right-wingers. All you need is repeated doses of fear, a few friends like James Mee, sympathetic committee chairmen, and a few wacko judges taking their lead from John Roberts."

"But they can't pick me up—this is 1st Amendment territory, right?"

"Right now that's the stretch, and they know it, which is why they made it a "friendly visit." They won't want to fight that battle until they can make the 'domestic terrorist' concept fly—that and this strange definition of national asset."

He paused thoughtfully. "I need to do some digging here and see if I can figure out what is going on behind the scenes. Someone in Congress or one of the FISA judges has got to know something. In the mean time, you should be extremely discreet and probably assume that everything you say and do is being bugged."

"Just my luck, and I'll end up in black like Ivan."

Thinking about this further, my concern shifted to Marianne. She didn't seem to appreciate the trouble she could get into by running her messenger service. She couldn't claim any press privileges. If Homeland Security knew my address, they had probably tailed me to *The Offshore* to see if that was where I was getting my information.

Jim Currie

Chapter 14
Shooting 8-Ball with Betty McClain

A few hours later I arrived at *The Barb* to meet with my editor and publisher, a no-nonsense 65-year-old Black female named, Betty McClain, who possessed a roto-tilled brow and a Brooklyn edge. She was just the kind of person you would want as a partner in a game of eight-ball at a sleazy bar in West Oakland. It was because of her that *The Barb* had risen to prominence as a savvy, on-line investigative mag.

We had a good rapport. It had taken awhile to work out the terms of our unwritten contract: I could run with whatever stories that felt right as long as I checked in every so often, made my drops on time, and delivered an occasional article from her own list. She appreciated the fact that I was quick and could find the emotional appeal in the stories I wrote.

My problem was that I hadn't delivered too many stories of late and hadn't really cleared my expenses for the trip to Chicago.

I saw my expense sheet on the desk and decided to preempt that discussion by giving her a report on my meeting with Vincent. She knew exactly what I was up to.

"Okay, okay, but I need something more on the zoo story if you've got it, and we're getting killed on this heat-wave business. I thought you had some contacts and were going to do something on that—what did you call it?"

"The Big Gulp."

"Big Gulp, right—has to do with the Sacramento River and the Bay, right? Where's that at?"

My cell saved me. "It's from Vincent," I declared.

"Take it," she answered.

I put it on speaker-phone.

In short order he informed me that he had learned from "sources" that Republican members of the House Terrorism Sub-committee, working with a friendly Assistant Attorney General, had drafted regulations implementing PERP that were as insulting to the Constitution as anything conceived by Mee and Badminton during Bush Administration II.

The regs authorized a "Class-A Terrorist List" that would link directly to PERP. If elected to the list, you wouldn't want to breathe on anyone considered a national-security asset.

"What's the timetable here?'

"My source says that the list has been *de facto* for some time. The new regs just codify it and link it to PERP."

"I'll bet William Callison and Ivan Bochinsky are on that list and probably lots of militant, animal-rights activists."

"My source tells me that Lassie is on it, along with Ed, the talking horse," he answered.

I had a pretty good idea that this was his way of telling me that both Bochinsky and Callison were on the list and that he had a copy of it. He knew the dangers of wiretap.

He ended the call with Betty nodding. She knew what he was saying as well.

"Somehow I think this Harmsworth guy has something to do with all this," I declared starting for the door.

"Let me know if you decide to book a Gulfstream for your next junket," interjected Betty. "And I need that 'Gulp' story by next Tuesday—if you don't mind mussin' your hair."

I worked away at *The Barb* all afternoon, mainly because I could use a hardwire web connection that allowed for encryption. Following a hunch that Harmsworth might not have lost his interest in magic, I ran a web search and learned of a magic society blog out of Las Vegas where a fellow name *HarmyMag* had been corresponding. The fellow seemed particularly interested in some of the recent Vegas magic acts. He had also offered past comments on mistakes by Roy Horn of Siegfried and Roy leading up to the overly friendly bite in 2003 by Roy's 7-year-old tiger, Montecore.

I decided to contact the society's president to see if I could ferret out contact information for HarmyMag. I represented myself as a reporter for *Magic and Illusion Magazine,* and said I was hoping to interview the fellow who knew so much about Siegfried and Roy.

While waiting for a return call, I decided to dial up Marianne. I was pretty sure it was her day off and that she was probably at the zoo with the elies. I was surprised when she answered. I could hear Alex talking up a storm in the background.

"I didn't think you would be there. I was going to leave a message."

"I was just headed out the door."

She seemed impatient. I needed to get out my message fast about the knock on my door. At once it occurred to me that if either of our phones were bugged any kind of a direct warning might implicate her.

"Just wanted to make sure you were doing okay."

"Of course. Fine."

"Well, I'm still picking out poisoned barbs from Tony, Roger and Darrell."

"They don't have anything to worry about. You've got your life and I've got mine."

"Right. And mine grows a bit more complicated."

"What do you mean?"

I decided to give her the warning in code. "'Got a surprise visit today from some unfriendly Feds agents squeezing me about sources. There's lot of political wrangling going on right now about national security and freedom of the press. Expanded wiretaps; trouble for the press and especially for stringers helping them."

Did she get it?

"Sounds wicked. Gotta go now."

When she hung up I tried to deconstruct what she had said, inspecting her tone for comprehension.

No doubt she had picked up the warning, but she might have dropped her own coded message that she wanted more space. I needed to be careful.

I started to replay the dialogue but was interrupted by my phone. It was the call-back from the Magic Society president, informing me that Mr. Harmsworth had agreed to meet with me the following weekend at his Las Vegas condo.

I quickly answered that I would be there at the designated place and time.

There was a problem, however: my promise to Betty regarding my article on The Big Gulp.

Immediately I rang up a hydrology professor at UC Davis, Rich Norgaard, who had been leading much of the California research on climate change and water supply and had written a journal article describing the Gulp in terms of a catastrophic event affecting the Sacramento River and the Central Valley.

When I explained to him my time crunch, he said he would give it to me simple and sweet: "Modeling indicates that low snowpack in the northern Sierras is only going to get worse from climate change. There is already evidence of this from monitoring by the USGS. Shortages will be magnified by increased population and land development in the Central Valley, Contra Costa and Sonoma counties.

"Something will have to give, especially if people care at all about protecting the Delta." He was referring to the entire lower reach and estuary of the river from the northern end of San Francisco Bay to Sacramento. The area supported a diversity of riparian animals and migratory birds and despite ongoing impacts was still considered a national treasure.

"There's also a scarier problem—sea-level rise. The delta channels of the Sacramento River are skirted with 1100 miles of levees that are forever blowing out in floods. Now with increased storm intensity and the sea rising, they are more vulnerable, especially if the area is hit by a major earthquake."

"And this is The Big Gulp, right"

"Exactly," he replied. "It would begin with a breach of critical levees. This would cause a massive intrusion of seawater from the bay that would press upriver from Suisun Bay toward Sacramento, not only wrecking havoc on the ecology of the estuary, but salinating the rich delta farmland and contaminating the fresh water withdrawals for the cities and towns throughout the Central Valley.

"Perhaps the most devastating effect would be the contamination of irrigation water, relied on by growers in much of California."

He expected losses to exceed $40 billion: "It will be a colossal catastrophe that will make the current crisis look like minor inconvenience."

"What size quake would do it?" I asked.

"About 6.5, as near as I can tell. Of course, it depends on tides and storm surges. If you get a perfect storm surge, it would take a lot less."

He would be glad to fill me in and show me the vulnerable locations if I were up for a quick field trip.

"Sounds great," I answered. "I can gang this with a trip to Vegas. "Any chance we could do this tomorrow?"

"Perfect."

I would rendezvous with him outside of Rio Vista that lay on the river, around midway between Suisun Bay and Sacramento. After the field trip I would continue on to Vegas and meet with Harmsworth the following morning. I decided to take a rental car. I would drop it off in Vegas and return to San Francisco by shuttle flight.

Chapter 15
The Big Gulp

It was sweltering out the following day as I drove from the East Bay through the gap in the Coastal Range at Concord, and then began to descend into the delta. At a turn in the highway, I got a panoramic view of the delta that jogged my memory of viewing the Yamuna on the back of Deli.

Actually this was more impressive. I had never realized just how expansive, beautiful and enchanted were the braided sloughs, side channels and wetlands of the Sacramento. It made perfect sense to me that the early Spanish explorers before any of the diversions and channelization would have described this as a "great inland sea and the River of Blessed Sacrament."

Unfortunately, the air conditioner in my rental wasn't working and the engine itself seemed to be giving in to the insufferable heat. When I crossed the Rio Vista Bridge, I was sure the temperature outside had reached 115 degrees F. I was sweating profusely and now wished that I had brought along a large bottle of water.

I arrived at the landing fifteen minute later and noticed Dr. Norgaard up ahead on top of the levee. I approached him and he motioned for me to be quiet. With his eyes he pointed off toward the edge of the river where I could see a very large fish just beneath the surface. A swish of its large tail provoked an impressive cyclone.

"It's a green sturgeon," he whispered. "Of all my years out here, I've never seen one this big."

It had to be an eight-footer. I raised my camera but the fish seemed to sense danger and spooked, diving toward deeper water.

"I love this place," he declared. "You can imagine what it must have been like in the days when the river wasn't channeled and depleted by all the withdrawals. Almost 500,000 acres have been converted to farmland. He pointed landward to remnants of old meanders and oxbow lakes. He even offered dates when they were probably formed and cut off from the main channel. It was a dramatic picture painted by a fellow who loved water and hydrology in the same way that my father loved elephants.

"I sometimes fantasize about prehistoric times here," he mused. "This would have to be one of the world's great estuaries and gathering places for macro fauna. Back in the Pleistocene, California was wetter and far more forested."

"Any mastodons?"

"I wouldn't be surprised, based on the remains they found at Diamond Lake in Southern California. They call that area 'The Valley of the Mastodons.' They found woolly mammoth fossils as well."

He proceeded to give me a whirl-wind tour of the levees and showed me the many spots where levees had blown out in the past or were weak because of underlying peat. He also described the effects of saltwater intrusion as more and more land was falling below sea level. With climate change this would only be getting worse.

Realizing that my time was short, he smiled and turned his truck back toward our rendezvous point. When he came to a stop, he handed me a newly minted monograph he had written about hydrology, climate change and the Delta.

"Call me if you need anything more or have trouble with any of the technical jargon."

I shook his hand, thanked him, and headed for my rental car.

I turned the key, but the starter only emitted a series of clicks. A tried again and the clicks gave way to silence. *Damn. Friggin battery was dead.*

I reached for my cell to call for help, but incredibly, I had forgotten to charge it and it too was dead.

Do it to me.

Now I had no recourse but to trek all the way to Rio Vista which was at least three miles away.

I began walking east beneath the assault of the unfiltered California sun, and my overactive, overheated brain began churning out images of huge prehistoric fish, a catastrophic earthquake turning into The Big Gulp, and interludes of a Cairo evangelist delivering God to true believers by way of rattlesnakes. I hoped I wouldn't miss my appointment with Harmsworth. I needed to make sure that I reached Vegas by midnight, or I might have trouble keeping my hotel room.

I dabbed my brow and images of Shiva came back to me from my days as a schoolboy in Allahabad—Shiva the destroyer and purifier, Shiva the god with five faces, the master of deception, the observer of the cosmos with a third eye. I focused ahead on the dike road and noticed a cloud of dust kicked up by the breeze.

Emerging from the dust was a human form, a tall brown-skinned man wearing a white *dhothi* and sandals and carrying a long stick. Next to him was a formidable, adult female elephant.

I could see right away that the fellow was a mahout, uncannily similar in appearance and dress to my own father when we traveled to the edge of the Yamuna and he told me the story of the Sarasvati. The man noticed me and declared something in Sanskrit but realized immediately that I didn't understand and switched over to English.

"It's fine day to be out in nature, don't you think, young one?"

"A little hot, I would say."

The elephant reached out to me with its trunk but stopped just short of my face.

"Don't worry about her; she's just a little curious. Very gentle, wouldn't hurt a mouse."

"What are you doing here? What are a mahout and elephant doing at the edge of the Sacramento River?"

"I'm afraid you are confused, my small friend. This is the Yamuna, and my elephant friend and I are dousing for a hidden confluence."

"A confluence?"

"Yes, the confluence with the Sarasvati. If you are looking for hidden water, you can't do better than to have a good elephant for your partner. We will find it and then we will woo it back to the surface."

"Woo it back?"

"My friend here is quite a singer." The elephant clearly realized we were talking about her and issued forth a bright trumpet.

"She will sing the *Sama-veda* mantras to it in the same way that they were sung to her when she emerged from the great cosmic egg. That should do it, as long as Shiva, the Destroyer, does not have it under his power. Then it could be a bit more difficult."

The elephant trumpeted, but this time sounding an alarm with flared ears as she set sight on something in the river. I turned just in time to spot another sturgeon, but this one monstrously large, menacing and hideous.

It actually seemed to be watching us, which didn't set well with the elephant, whose body language indicated that she was about to charge it, if only she could figure out how to negotiate the steep levee.

The fish seemed to realize it might be in trouble and instantly dove, creating a large whirlpool. Instead of dissipating, it began to grow, emitting a violent sucking sound as more and more river water rushed into the Charybdis. The entire river seemed to be falling into the cavernous vortex, as if swallowed in a massive gulp by an insatiable underground demon. I wondered if the levee was soon to follow.

The death spiral ended as suddenly as it formed, and I turned back to see the reaction of the mahout and his elephant. To my surprise, they too had vanished, leaving not even a set of elephant prints on the dusty dirt road.

An hour later with the benefit of a kindly farmer in a pickup truck, I reached a small grocery story outside of Davis. Here I called the car rental company, and they replied that they would pick me up and make sure I had a reliable full-size car with air conditioning that worked.

Jim Currie

Chapter 16
Driving Curiosities

When I was finally on my way to Vegas in the rental, I replayed the mirage-induced images of my father and Deli at the edge of the Sacramento River. Lines from the *Rig Veda* ingrained as a schoolboy upwelled from an inner vault:

...Sarasvati with fostering current comes forth, our sure defence, our fort of iron. As on a chariot the flood flows on, surpassing in majesty and might all other waters. Pure in her course from mountains to the ocean, alone of streams Sarasvati hath listened. Thing of wealth and the great world of creatures, she poured for Nahusa her milk and fatness.

I could even remember some of the Sanskrit that was part of my elementary school recitation. Would Marianne be interested in such a geyser or had the sleepover stilled her fascination with India and Vedic mythology?

There were many ways in which Marianne and my twin sister were alike. They possessed the same willfulness and indomitability and many of the same soft edges. Curiosities were a bit different.

As early as 10 or 11, Arundhati was driven to understand the way everything worked. She loved science. When she heard the story of the Sarasvati, her compulsion was to unpuzzle exactly what had happened and why. For her, whys were about science and not the spite, wrath or jealousy of some Hindu god or goddess.

Dinesh was of little help. He was out of his element unless talking about elephants. About all that he could tell us was that earthquakes had something to do with the vanishing river. Of course that wasn't going to satisfy Arundhati. A little exasperated and feeling cornered, Dinesh added that "the ground began to shake and crumble the way it might after the rampage of a thousand elephants."

Arundhati's nose crinkled and eyes narrowed. It was an expression akin to the response that Marianne gave Dr. Shipp when he tried to tell us that the elies at the zoo were well cared for.

Arundhati was soon off to a library to figure out the answers to her own questions. The next thing I knew, she was carrying a pile of books through the door and explaining that she had come across a theory that climate had changed 5000 years ago and this had provoked the river to disappear. This in turn led to other voyages of discovery to figure out how climate worked.

When she thought she had figured most of it out, she had to impart the breakthrough to her dull-witted, unscientific brother.

"It's all determined by heat, water, and the spin of the earth, " she exclaimed excitedly. "The sun is the great heat engine, " she declared. This part I sort of understood. But then she blurted out something about a strange spinning force called coriolus, and that befuddled me.

She was soon creating a map and offering diagrams showing cyclones and typhoons full of ocean water headed toward the Great Himalayan Wall. This came with swooshes and sucking sounds and then her own impersonation of storms dumping rain and snow on the Hindu Kush.

My eyes were glassed over with confusion. "Clouds rise

when they hit the mountains?"

"Yes, of course. Remember how I explained this to you?"

"And this relates to the missing river?"

"Don't you see, Pankaz? This is where the Sarasvati got its water. All of that must have changed. Something changed the winds and clouds or the moisture they were carrying."

And then her eyes brightened and her voice quickened. "Of course, maybe the water was still there in the clouds, but there was less snow and more rain. I guess that could change the amount of water in the Sarasvati. I suppose heat could change as well." With that she raced over to the library to figure out missing pieces of the puzzle.

Arundhati would have been fascinated by what Dr. Norgaard had to say about the Big Gulp. I was sure she would have been equally curious about the possibility that something similar to what happened to the Sarasvati might already be in the works for California and the River of Blessed Sacrament.

I never realized just how much I appreciated those confusing lessons in science until Arundhati was gone.

Now, just for the sake of Arundhati, I really needed to figure out some of the missing links in this idea that what happened to the Sarasvati could also befall the Sacramento. Perhaps Dr. Norgaard would set me straight.

Jim Currie

Chapter 17
Circus Maximus

Harmsworth lived in the 44-story Hegelian Arms Condo-miniums about a mile from the Vegas Strip. It was the tallest residential structure in Vegas. The complex was designed by the famous German architect, Ulrich Von Scharnhorst, who had gained fame for functional, highly-secure steel and glass boxes for upper-level party members in East Germany before the wall came down. I had to be buzzed through two sets of security doors before I reached the spacious elevator that streaked like a V-2 to the penthouse where Harmsworth lived.

He answered the door of an expensive residence graced with black marble floors and high windows that observed the old and recently humanized desert at 360 degrees.

My first thought was that this was the sort of panoramic vantage point that The Prince might choose to keep track of climate change and other events on the Human Floodplain. My eyes met the intense, emotionless gaze of Harmsworth as he forced a slight smile and shook my hand. He turned and ushered me into a study, asking if I wanted something to drink. I replied that jasmine tea would be fine if he had it.

While he prepared it, my second thought percolated: there were no female touches here—no flowers or soft edges; no lacey curtains; nothing but primary colors and maybe most telling, no personal photographs of family.

Books were ubiquitous. I drew closer to inspect the titles. Most were on psychology and history and particularly the history of warfare. A photo in the living room showed him on what looked like a safari in Africa. Another showed him with Don Haney on a charter fishing boat—they were proudly hoisting monstrous ling cod.

There was art on the walls but not anything classical or modern—mostly *trompe de l'oeil* and framed pictures of WWI camouflaged naval vessels and a Potemkin Village of sorts, circa 1942. Harmsworth arrived with a teapot and caught me staring.

"As indicated in my message, I thought you might be the one to talk to about magic tricks."

"For your article—*Magic and Illusion Magazine*, I believe?"

"Yes."

He poured me tea, and I noticed that he was wearing an expensive ring with an insignia I had never seen before.

"It's something I've given some analytical attention to."

"Great pictures, you've got."

"Yes, that one was at Derbyshire—positively convincing from 10,000 ft. It drove the Luftwaffe crazy."

"Actually I'm interested in the more shocking illusions."

"Oh really—such as?"

"Those that trigger fear—SS thunderbolts, buzz-bombs, P-51's with Tiger's Teeth."

I couldn't take my eyes off that ring. They showed a gold crest apparently warding off a thunderbolt. The shield was diamond-studded.

"So you reveal a bit of deceit of your own—you're not really a reporter for *Illusion*—you're that fellow who shot a picture of me at Boalt Hall."

"Yes, I wanted to understand a bit more about your theories. I read your thesis—quite interesting, though some parts were strangely redacted."

"So what did you find interesting about it—Pankaz Panday, right?"

"Yes."

"Indian or Pakistani? Muslim—should I be worried?" He didn't look worried.

"Indian. In fact, my ethnic background plays into this a bit."

"Really?"

"Yes, son of a mahout and somewhat superstitious Hindu who saw *maya* everywhere."

"Fascinating, especially the elephant angle. I've always felt they were second only to tigers as a circus draw. Of course, with the tigers you need a fearless trainer willing to insert his head into the jaws, or better yet a busty blonde-bimbo. P.T. Barnum realized this and he was the modern master, unless you want to give credit to the Pope and the Elmer Gantry's of the world. By the way, did you know that Pompey slaughtered elephants to impress the masses?"

"Yes, I read that in your dissertation. Was it effective?"

"On the soma scale, actually pretty inept. It did cost him in his contest with Caesar. In my view, the elephant card was played best by Hannibal—wreaked havoc on the legions. Can you imagine the fear that rampaging, mounted elephants must have inspired—comparable to Guderian unleashing Panzers against the hapless French."

He could see that I was processing his every word, and he seemed delighted by this. It took me a second to realize that Guderian was a *Wehrmacht* general and one of the originators of *Blitzkrieg*.

I had clearly engaged him.

"Animal sacrifices probably raised the heartbeat a bit at *Circus Maximus* but not enough to engender a *chthonic* response."

"I don't know that word."

"From the underworld—primitive and archaic. That's what we're talking about here—activating the archaic centers of the brain. You know, the cerebral cortex isn't all it's cracked up to be," he grinned. "Once the chthonic is activated, reason runs and hides like a scared little girl."

"For example, when a Pentecostal snake handler stupefies white dumbfuchs?" This seemed to catch him off-balance. He recovered quickly and spouted a grin, as if discovering that I was a worthy chess player.

"I see you've been doing some homework on me. Very good. The truth is that most of the people in my early childhood, including family—well, sadly, were easily manipulated fools. It took me a long time to realize that even the limited ones can make an important social contribution. Every Caesar or Panzer commander needs some devoted, indoctrinated foot soldiers ready to make a sacrifice. Ant colonies require that some ants lay down their lives to create bridges for the others."

"That's an interesting way of putting it."

"I've got a treat for you. Are you afraid of snakes?"

"No less than any other sane person." I was lying. I had had any number of bad experiences in my childhood with cobras. Deli hated them.

"I'll show you my beauties, if you are interested."

I hesitated and he read my fear, breaking into a grin.

"I promise you, there will be no danger. Besides—these are stranglers, not biters. Human babies might be a problem but you're somewhat too large."

"Somewhat?"

He led me to a back room where the stench was overwhelming. It seemed to be emanating from stacked cages of panicky, terrified mice. Nearby in larger metallic cages were two boa constrictors—both of them motionless but coming to attention and focusing on Harmsworth.

"They know it's dinner time and have made the association from my appearance. I actually think they view me as a friend in a quite primitive sense. Do you think animals are capable of higher fidelity?"

"Which animals—Homo sapiens, NeoCons?"

He lifted one of the boas out of the cage and draped it around his neck.

"They actually have personality. Do you believe it?"

"I'll believe whatever you want me to believe."

"This is Franny and that's Zooey. Franny is the sweet one— she strangles gently."

"I can see that they seem quite relaxed at the moment."

"Back inside Franny; supper will be soon enough." I had never before seen anyone with such an affection for snakes. What would Marianne have made of Franny and Zooey? Was her love of animals so great that she was willing to include them in her circle of those deserving affection and sacrifice? Deli seemed to know when they were about and would go out of her way to stomp on them.

Harmsworth led me back to the study and was clearly fortified by his demonstration—or perhaps my intimidation. He immediately reached for a silver dollar on his desk and began finger-rolling it from his pinkie to his index finger and then back. He dropped it, then picked it up.

"Tell me something, Pankaz? Do you know this Red Bill?"

I shrugged. "I know some things about him."

"Are you aware of his accomplishments in the realm of card tricks and magic?"

"I'm aware that he stung the casinos and got barred."

"I've actually seen him in action…at the time I was a rather serious student of magic and legerdemain."

"Including the ways of snake handlers?"

"His skill was quite impressive. There is an important shuffling trick in cardsharpery called the faro. It involves cutting and interweaving a deck perfectly. With eight perfect faros you can bring a deck back to its original order. Consider how difficult this is. It holds the key to any number of stupefying magic tricks. Bill was the best at this of anyone I ever saw, which along with phenomenal memory explains how he could beat the casinos."

"I didn't know this."

"There's actually more to it than meets the eye. The tricks he developed were highly mathematical. You might even say that he changed the face of card magic by mathematizing it. And then, somewhat unfortunately, he turned his attention to a different kind of theatre."

"Why would that be unfortunate?"

"Because of excellence. He achieved mastery. It's sad to see that wasted. If I had such abilities I believe I would have kept pushing the envelope. Unfortunately, I didn't have his memory or dexterity."

"It seems that you've pushed envelopes of your own. I have a question for you—I noticed you are a pretty good whistler. What was that tune you whistled when you were in the lecture hall? Sounds familiar."

"Oh, that," he answered with amusement." He let fly with the whistle "Let's have another piece of pie." I picked it up in child-hood. It's a happy tune, a celebratory tune. I think I got it from my father. He whistled it while he worked."

"As a butcher?"

"Yes, one large pig meant a nice slice of pie."

"So he whistled this when he did them in?"

"While I held them for him and cringed."

"Have any pets when you were young or old besides the snakes?"

"I once tried to save a sow that I grew quite fond of, but she was turned into pepperoni."

"Did that bother you?"

He looked at me queerly like a master chess player observing the aggressive ploy of a rank amateur. "Yes, I suppose it did. I got over it, however."

"I can't imagine being around all that gore."

"It wasn't Auschwitz." He paused contemplatively as I searched for signs of pain. "I guess curiosity saved me. It's about turning your fear into something to understand and master."

"Snakes, masters of deceit?"

"Are you aware that death by cobra venom was considered an admirable way to go by the Romans who lost out in the fratricidal wars?"

"Painful?"

"No doubt, but duration of suffering should be taken into account."

"Interesting—wasn't that part of James Mee's defense?"

He seemed amused by my pivot.

"Very good. What I've learned over many decades is that it isn't death that is to be feared but suffering, and the worst of that is probably a life of banal mediocrity. In fact, it's the understanding of this which probably separates the most artful warriors like Caesar, Genghis and Alexander from the common thugs."

"Haney and Rumsfeld?"

"Skilled and bright exemplars of will to power—and not the devils that they have been caricatured as. People don't understand that they are extremely moral, moral to the point that they understand that hard choices always need to be made if civilization is to survive and the true barbarians kept at bay. This is something that the bleeding hearts will never accept."

"I'm not sure that the bleeding hearts accept the frame. They view it as a convenient distortion and rationalization by the privileged to do almost anything for self-defense while padding their own bank accounts."

"You know, this torture business was exaggerated. There is no comparison between what the Nazis did, and what our skilled interrogators did."

"Did you work in the White House?"

"People availed themselves of my advice and because of it

lives were saved."

"In Iraq, Afghanistan?"

"And a few other places less well-known. Artfully, for the most part."

"I'm having trouble imagining artful waterboarding."

He shrugged. "Sometimes you need to accent and reinforce the perception in order for it to stick. This is where the true art comes in. The evil-doers need to appreciate the fact that you can deliver—that the snake has fangs and will bite; that Sherman is ready and willing to burn his way to Savannah."

"One last question—I'm an animal guy—well non-reptilian animals. Were there any exotic pets in the White House when you were there?"

"Hmm. Just the President's dog, Barney. Might have been a couple of others—a parrot as I recall."

"A parrot? They tend to be pretty noisy. I can't imagine that would be easy to deal with."

"The one I remember was pretty quiet, I daresay retarded."

He seemed to have tired of the interview and was speeding up the rolling of the gold coin in his right hand.

"I'll be interested in reading your article." With that he ushered me to the door into the insufferable heat. It felt like walking directly into Dante's inferno out of the pig locker at *Harmsworth Pig Rendering and Sausage.*

Jim Currie

Chapter 18
Dollars for Details

On my return to San Francisco, my resolution to enforce the firewall with Marianne that separated our interests was still intact but weakening. I really did want to talk to her about the recent monsoon of images and all I had experienced on the river and in Vegas. But as much as anything, I missed watching her dance across the checkerboard floor of *The Offshore* precariously balancing all those orders in that tight, white dress.

Because of this, I decided to brave the abuse I might be subjected to from the other members of the herd at *The Offshore*.

When I arrived, I learned that she had changed shifts in order to help out at the zoo where Hansa had taken a turn for the worse. It didn't bother me that she hadn't mentioned this in any kind of note, but it wasn't lost on me that she wasn't adjusting her priorities or focus just because of our night together.

I thought briefly about leaving her a note, letting her know that I was ready to help out if there was anything she wanted me to do, but quickly abandoned the thought as a probable violation of her space and territory.

Now that I had completed my priority stories on climate change and national security, I was beginning to get pressure again from Betty for something new. She even asked about any new developments at the zoo, but I told her I thought I had a story about the Telegraph Hill parrots that might be more interesting.

The story had long been a favorite since the popular documentary, *The Wild Parrots of Telegraph Hill,* aired by public television. I told her there might be one new parrot—"a very smart one that no one knows anything about who might have some connection to Mee and Harmsworth, and maybe Haney and Bush."

She jumped on it: "This is what I want. Get to work."

The next day I caught up with Tony at the intersection of Filbert and Broadway near Truman's newsstand.

Pankaz, "I talked to Rollie the Racer. He says he lost an African Gray about a year ago. Says he was selling it for someone back East."

"Have you got a phone number?"

"The place is called *Top Flight.* Be forewarned—he'll clip you if he can."

Later that afternoon I visited Rollie at *Top Flight.* The noise from parakeets, mynahs and garrulous parrots imitated the deep Amazon at daybreak. Rollie possessed the physique of a refrigerator and the voice of a castrato. At first he was reticent.

"Tony says you're a pigeon-racer just like him."

"Just like him? Hardly. He's a low flyer. He thinks that just because he got lucky at the Queen's Cup, he can beat me. My bird Maggie would have smoked his, but she got nailed by a sparrow hawk."

He pointed to the wall where he had framed the pictures of the champions he had trained. I trained my eye on the one in prime space.

"That was Beatrix. She was better than anything he ever had. Those were the days when Tony's only pigeons were stoolies in

Cell Block 3 at San Quentin."

"I never heard what he did time for."

"Ha! He didn't tell you about the babies he trained to pick off diamond earrings?"

"You mean steal jewelry?"

"From wedding parties and fancy Nob Hill balls where rich broads parade around with fancy bling. His birds would take off an earring and leave an old bag bleeding to death."

"Sounds like the two of you got a little feud going on."

"Nah—he's alright, just a little puffed up about his abilities."

I produced a picture of Alex on a phone wire and he studied it closely. "Yeah, that was one of mine. My girl assistant got a little careless and he escaped."

"You sure?"

"Positive. I was selling him on consignment for this rich broad who got him back East."

"Where, back East?"

He took a drag on a nearby cigarette, seemingly contemplating a sticker price for any further revelations.

"It would be worth a Hamilton just to find out if the bird spent any time in the White House." I placed the 20 on the table.

"Twenty doesn't go very far these days. And people get pretty private about where they get their birds with all this Endangered Species stuff going on."

"Let's make it 80, but I need to know whether the bird was in the White House and what the connections were."

Rollie grabbed the bills and reached for the phone.

In a few minutes he was talking to a pet store owner in DC who provided the bird to his lady client. The message was clear:

some young staffer working in the White House had brought it in; "Bush got the bird as a gift but it wouldn't talk or perform, and they decided to get rid of it."

My hand was on the front doorknob when he added, "You tell Tony that I know all about the juvenile he's been grooming for the Vegas Cup. My Gwenny will fly circles around her."

Chapter 19
Al-Ghazal Bird Market

My next stop was Vincent's law office where I told him of my meeting with Harmsworth and the puzzle that was coming together about Alex. He seemed more interested in the bird story and asked for details over lunch at his favorite deli in the Heights. Here, over a bottle of pricey cab, tasty bruschetta and exquisite calamari, we covered everything from Alex's various spouts to what Harmsworth had said about the "retarded bird" in the White House.

"Ever consider the possibility that he might have been Saddam's parrot?"

I shot him a doubting glance.

"No, seriously. I think these Iraqis are fond of parrots. Maybe Bush nabbed him when Saddam headed for the hills."

At first I thought it was absurd, but after only few seconds, I began to think he might be onto something—Marianne thought the bird's first spoken words were in Arabic.

The check arrived and I inspected the damage. *This was going to be a problem.*

"Think about it," he declared. "Some Ranger captain breaks into Saddam's Palace and finds the bird. He tells his general and the general tries to make some points with Bush and Haney."

"It sort of fits..." I mentioned the bird's first spout on the window sill of the diner.

"There you go."

"If this is right, you're a genius."

"Genius?." With theatrical aplomb worthy of a Broadway thespian, he reached into thin air and appeared to pluck a note from the ether.

"Groucho's bird says that the magic word is 'genius', so away goes the check." With that he swiped it from my grasp.

Less than an hour later, I learned that Baghdad's Al-Ghazal Bird Market was a major source of exotic parrots before the American invasion. A Google search revealed that the most prominent bird monger was a fellow named Mustafa.

With only a few clicks and links I managed to locate the phone number of a fellow at the bird market by the same name. I reached for my cell.

Amazingly, Mustafa answered the phone. Piecing together his broken English, I learned that in 1999 he had helped Saddam acquire an African grey parrot that had been under study by animal communication experts at Baghdad University. The bird had astounded researchers with a large working vocabulary, counting skills and memory. His vocabulary was over 1500 words in English and Arabic. Mustafa was unaware of the bird's fate after the American invasion.

The next morning I explained this to the gathered members of *The Offshore* herd. Alex suddenly landed on the sill, which surprised me because he had been scarce since Marianne had changed shifts.

"So the way I've got it figured, Saddam had no time and was forced to leave Alex behind when the 3rd Armored and First Marine divisions blew in to Baghdad."

"But why so silent after 2003?" asked Darrell.

"He probably knew who he was dealing with in Haney, Harmsworth and friends," declared Tony: "That'll turn you silent if Saddam hadn't already scared you shitless."

"Or he didn't feel comfortable in his new home."

I turned. It was Marianne.

"I had to drop by and get my check. I want to hear the rest of this."

I filled her in on what I had learned from all my sources about Alex's history.

"I knew from the first minute we met that he was no ordinary parrot," declared Marianne.

Alex let out a squawk and then declared, "Let's have another piece of pie."

"So Alex picks up the tune from Harmsworth. I just wonder if there's more to it than that. It didn't sound to me that Harmsworth was even around the bird that much."

I reached for my cell and dialed up Vincent. He answered right away.

"Just thinking about your recent insight about animals—Barney the talking-dog and all that. Harmsworth said something interesting that might relate. Says his pop used to sing a special tune when the pig money came in. Maybe you could ask around and see if anyone in the White House sang that tune."

"Back in twenty minutes if I get lucky."

Exactly twenty minutes later I was summoned by my genius lawyer, author of the polemic New York Times best-seller and *j'accuse*, and general thorn in the side of all Republicans.

"Do you want the performance or the banal, prosaic news

report?"

"I'll take the performance."

James Carville: "What do you mean, have I heard that term? My wife blurted it out all the time in the days when she was working in the Bush II White House."

Vincent: "In describing the conversations going on there?"

James Carville: "No, in expressing her satisfaction in the bedroom. We were pretty fair jack rabbits back then."

Vincent: "So it meant that..."

James Carville: "Everything was just great and we should repeat all the good work—"another piece of pie...with coffee"—that was the pillow talk."

Vincent: "So what does this have to do with anything?"

James Carville: "I finally got her to tell me where she got the ditty—she said that everyone in the White House was using it to mean that something terrific had happened—good news, political *manna* from the sky—like when they found Saddam in that hole in Tikrit. Or like when they got those pictures of John Kerry sailboarding and looking like a spoiled snot. That's what really swiftboated the poor SOB, and Rove and friends actually broke out pie for everyone. And then they all sang the tune like the Mormon Tabernacle doing Hallelujah."

Vincent: "Are you and Mary still getting along these days? It's pretty damn amazing that two people at opposite ends of the spectrum can keep a marriage going."

James Carville: "It's been a little rocky of late. Arguing a lot over all this illegal wiretap and PERP business. One piece of pie every two weeks and lucky to get that."

Chapter 20
Mixing Paper and Glass

With Vincent's help making connections to the right people in Washington, I soon verified that both after the escape of Osama bin Laden and the capture of Saddam Hussein, George W. Bush had been heard to sing "Let's have another piece of pie."

I followed this up with phone calls and learned that Haney and members of the inner circle had used the phrase in conjunction with the outing of Valerie Plame. I now figured I had enough substance for an article and wrote the following:

Torture and Invasion
Boys Just Want to Have Fun
by Pankaz Panday

The expression "Let's have another piece of pie" seems to have been the preferred toast for Bush insiders and was sung with intoxicated glee at every glowing news item or positive turn of political events in the War on Terror.

George W. Bush himself spouted forth when Judith Miller published an article in the New York Times before the invasion stating that Saddam had WMD; Haney after special forces found Saddam Hussein hiding in a hole in Tikrit, and BD Harmsworth after Osama bin Laden escaped Tora Bora. The ultimate celebration, complete with pie for everyone and a group sing-along, came after John Kerry was pictured by the media sail-boarding and looking like a spoiled rich boy.

Karl Rove was reported to have ordered the pie and performed in duet with Don Haney.

...The childhood ditty came from BD Harmsworth, the notorious author of shock and awe, who picked it up from his own father, a Cairo, Illinois butcher who proclaimed it gleefully in celebrating the "harvest" of each fatted hog that assured that next month's rent was covered.

I made no mention of the fact that the thread to all revelations led back to Saddam's parrot, the distinguished Einstein of a bird whom everyone thought was retarded and mute. I knew that it would make the story even more interesting, but instinct told me that it was always a bad idea to reveal a source before a story completely played out. I wasn't sure that this one had.

Chapter 21
Conversing with Mephisto

I didn't expect any further communication with BD Harmsworth, so I was surprised by the arrival of an email inviting me to another interview and discussion in Vegas during the upcoming weekend. I didn't recall even giving him my email address.

There was coincidence in this. I had actually been thinking about going to Vegas with Marianne and the herd on this particular weekend. Marianne first suggested it before Hansa took a turn for the worse. Darrell was going to be there competing in a national impersonation contest called the Reel Awards, and she wanted us to be there supporting him. He was going to be impersonating Nixon—his best act.

Marianne had cancelled because of another problem with the elephants, but Darrell, Tony and Roger had booked a room in flea-bag motel for Friday and Saturday Nights.

The Friday appointment would fit perfectly. I confirmed it and passed word to the group that I would meet them at the *MGM Grand* early Friday evening. We would take a stab at the slots, tune up Darrell, and then head for the flea-bag.

When I arrived at the Hegelian Arms on Friday evening, I was shocked into near-heart attack to discover Don Haney on Harmsworth's living room couch, cradling a snifter of brandy and gazing at me with a crooked smile. I had never seen him before in person. It was like a cartoon coming to life.

Harmsworth delivered a sobering defib: "Mr. Haney found your recent articles interesting and asked if he could join us. I figured you wouldn't mind."

"You've got this shock and awe business perfected," I replied, trying to compose. I mumbled something to the effect that I had wondered about Harmsworth's relationship with the Vice President.

But Mr. Haney interjected, "You are a clever writer. I always enjoy forceful writing, even if it's psychedelic fantasy."

"Like what?" I answered a little timidly, impressed that he could insult me with such confident, seemingly objective calm.

"Like a celebration over the escape of Osama Bin Laden, or some delight taken in defeating those who opposed enhanced interrogation."

I was irritated enough by this to rebound: "Enhanced interrogation... You're still sticking to that?"

He only chuckled, showing no sign of offense or being caught off-balance.

For most of the next 45 minutes he responded to points raised in my articles, correcting "my simplistic misunderstandings." Mostly I took mental notes, including notes on the perfect conviction in every word, and a faint incredulity that I or anyone else would see his actions as anything less than high-minded.

As I listened, I pondered what I found so disquieting. It wasn't that he didn't smile or laugh. And he certainly was civil. Unlike Harmsworth, his vocabulary was also down to earth.

The chill lay in something else. He seemed so disembodied, words coming from head and brain that bypassed his heart or whatever the current apparatus was. He seemed like the sort of person who just wouldn't be very convincing in telling you he grieved for your lost son or for your pet that got tangled in his barbed-wire fence.

The words were there but drained of pathos and empathy. More than this, he didn't seem to show any vulnerability, as if all that governed him was a calculus of loss versus gain bleached of all sentiment.

At least Harmsworth lovingly fondled Franny and Zooey.

It was also pretty obvious that he didn't much care what anyone at my level thought about him. If he had any peers or appraisers whose opinion mattered, they were people who were a lot more powerful than anyone who would ever answer my phone calls. And yet he was here, at least for the moment wasting his time with me.

Finally my curiosity got the better of me. "Let me ask you— does it bother you that you aren't able to travel out of the country for fear that you'll be nabbed for war crimes?"

"I've traveled enough to exotic places." His gaze was most direct and relaxed.

My eyes fell on his pudgy hands. I noticed that he was wearing garish, gold and diamond cufflinks. I looked closer—they were inscribed with the same shield as Harmsworth's ring.

"What about those?" I asked motioning toward them. At first he didn't seem to realize what I was talking about.

"Oh, the cufflinks. Quite nice, don't you think?"

"Look expensive."

"Darn things need to be adjusted. I have to be careful or I'll lose one."

"What's that shield about?"

He showed no change in manner but I noticed that I had

gained the attention of Harmsworth.

"Never really thought about that," he replied casually. "I do have a question for you. I understand that you have some kind of relationship with this Red Bill fellow."

"A valued source."

"Is he your source for suggesting that I got my heart by violating medical protocol?"

"I don't think I actually suggested that, did I?"

"No, but your recited statistics came from somewhere. Correct me if I'm wrong, but you don't seem mathematical—at least based on your education. On the other hand, this Red Bill seems quite proficient in statistics and probability."

He clearly thought that he had cornered me and convinced me that I was out of my league.

"I'll take my information from whatever credible vertebrate I can get it."

"I understand that this Red Bill was somewhat of a whiz kid in card tricks and illusion."

BD nodded, "Until he headed to the sidelines and was eclipsed by a Russian."

"I don't know if he was eclipsed," I added. "I've done some background checking on this since I last spoke to Mr. Harmsworth. Is this something you are interested in as well, Mr. Haney?"

He shrugged. "Somewhat. BD brought this magic business to my attention in Aspen. We watched the Russian perform a trick called the *Stalin*?"

"Actually it was the *FDR*," corrected BD with a chuckle. "No one has performed the Stalin successfully. Callison came closest 30 years ago with the *Half-Stalin*."

"Sounds like someone, the CIA or KGB, would be interested in. Why didn't you hire him?"

"Who's to say that I didn't?" He grinned and Harmsworth laughed.

Mr. Haney rose to his feet and declared, "I have another engagement, but I thought that given your interest in legerdemain, you might want to see this impressive act." With that he handed me tickets to the show and a room reservation at *The Mirage*.

He didn't wait for me to accept or thank him: "It's been a delight," he declared, offering his hand.

No twinkle or genuine smile suggested delight, but he ejaculated an audible puff-with-hiss that suggested that he had fully satisfied his reason for meeting with me. On the other hand, the hiss might have come from Franny and Zooey in the back room.

Jim Currie

Chapter 22
Hack by Another Name

On the V-2 down to the lobby of the Hegelian, an inner voice erupted, "What that hell was all that about? Why would someone like Haney want to talk to someone like me? Why care about anything a reporter for an online radical rag had to say about him?

All that I could come up with was that he thought he could get me to reveal something about Red Bill that would put him out of commission.

A few minutes later I was out on the sidewalk about to dial for a cab to the Mirage when a Green Top cab pulled up alongside me. Through an open window the Pakistani hack declared in undulating diction, "I was told to pick up a fare named Panday—already paid for—some guy named Harmsworth took care of it."

"Well, in that case, I think I will." As I settled into the back seat, it occurred to me that this might have been a bad idea. People like Haney and Harmsworth gave people free cab rides and those cabs took people to abandoned warehouses or to private airstrips where planes were waiting to take off to black sites in Poland. Then it occurred that I had never heard of Green Top Cabs. Geez. *What the hell was I going to do now? The car was traveling too fast to bail out.*

The cabbie had begun whistling a show tune and seemed to be headed toward the airport. I even recognized one of the tunes—something from Marat/Sade. Suddenly he broke into "Let's have another cup of coffee." I caught a glimpse of him through the rear-view mirror—he was grinning. Damn—it was Red Bill incognito.

"I was in the neighborhood and figured I would play witness just in case you vanished off the face of the earth. You met with Mephisto?"

I shot him a look of surprise, "How did you know?"

"Signs pointed in that direction."

I reconstructed most of the dialogue for him as he navigated a circuitous route toward the *Strip*. "It was strange. He seemed to have read most of my articles and seemed curious about my opinions on everything from animal rights to terrorism and magic acts. Except for the arrogance, it could have been conversation with a stranger in a San Francisco cafe.

"Haney never shoots the breeze with anyone. You must have struck a nerve—maybe with the story about his heart replacement."

"I'll tell you one thing—I'm glad to be out of that deep freeze. It gave me shivers."

"We're headed to the *MGM*?"

"Where did you get that?"

"Members of the herd filled me in."

Halfway there I declared, "How about the true and unexpurgated story of Wily Coyote—American Underground Radical?"

"Abridged shuttle version," he declared.

"No family?"

"Sister and cousins but haven't talked to them in years. No enmity or anything like that. Just solving problems on a different level."

"What do you mean?"

"They're family folks. Everything revolves around family—getting kids educated and self-sufficient, paying off the mortgage, making sure the paycheck comes in every month and the IRA is fully funded. "

"That isn't for you?"

"Never had much interest in the Grid and its restriction."

"Where did this begin for you?"

"As long as I can remember I loved the idea of traveling light. As a kid, I loved stories of Jeremiah Johnson and the frontier trappers who lived by their wits among bears and cougars. Loved what I read about Marco Polo and Lawrence of Arabia. Most toys held no interest, unless there was mental challenge. I guess I did have a Mr. Wizard Chemistry Set. Of course, there were card tricks. I loved sleight of hand."

"Same affliction as Harmsworth—except for this jag to change the world. Where did that come from?"

"I'm a Vietnam-era babe. It was formative for me in the exact opposite way that snakes and evangelists informed our buddy BD. I couldn't get over the slaughter and the lying that made it possible. Couldn't get over Tricky Dick. Did you ever read Kierkegaard, Kohlberg and Frankl when you were in college—better yet, the Bhagavad Gita?"

"Sure, but don't remember much."

"So much of it was about taking the right stand when faced with moral dilemma. Unlike so many of my classmates at Stanford who just flirted with moral philosophy and went on to business and banking, I took it seriously. When the recruiters from Merrill Lynch and Monsanto arrived, I wasn't going to whore myself out and sign up for the kind of life that required constant rationalization. I'm quite sure I would have gone postal if I did what my classmates did. Fortunately, I discovered that I could survive *en marge*."

"So the cause is setting things straight—delivering the reeling blow to Monsanto and Union Carbide and the people you view as craven exploiters?"

"This might surprise you coming from a Marxist, but I do believe there is a God in small things."

"God and Marx—how do you pull that off?"

"Marx missed a lot—never looked beyond the material world."

"Wow. Never would have thought of you as a man of God."

"Well, I don't exactly picture a guy in a flowing beard speaking Aramaic, parting seas and smiting heathen. I think the first time I saw God was when I first understood Fermat's Theorem and Euler's Law. That's some pretty cosmic juju—elegant and beautiful. Then I began to see a lot of wondrous improbability that was being exploited for money and personal power."

"People make choices in a democracy. Why isn't the democratic process good enough for you?"

"If everyone had the same rights and influence, if there really was a free market, there would be no need for people like me stirring things up."

"You're a stirrer, not a destroyer?"

"I don't think I've ever caused anyone any direct physical harm—mostly made people uncomfortable over 'wanton' property destruction—have jammed up more than a few polluters and earth destroyers."

"So the goal here is a John Lennon world and replace the haves with the have-nots?"

"Hardly. I know how corruption and decay work in both business and government. I don't glamorize poor people or workers. Power corrupts and impels even more concentration of wealth and power. That's what Marx got right but didn't take far enough."

"Here's one of my curiosities: how do you keep these missions going? "Money's got to be a problem."

"Not really."

"Word has it that you once beat the casinos."

"I crushed them at a time when they were naïve and stupid about card counting and how someone with a good memory could hurt them."

"And nowadays?"

"That should probably remain confidential. Let's just say there are still opportunities."

"You worry that your adversaries are getting smarter?"

"No doubt about that," he laughed. "Nowadays Bill Ayers and Eldridge Cleaver better know crypto tools and some of the math behind them or they're dead meat. And by the way…if you're going to stay the course on your reporting, you should assume that all cell calls are being monitored by Haney, Harmsworth and friends in the NSA."

I nodded.

"Harmsworth seems to think that the Russian can pull off the *Stalin*. He and Haney gave me tickets to see it. Go figure."

"Generous guy," Bill chuckled, falling silent.

"You realize that luck and numbers eventually run out?"

"Yeah, and it might be sooner rather than later. This PERP

business is very worrisome, especially when combined with NSA wiretap and massive computer power."

He pulled up to the curb a few blocks from the *MGM.* "Too many cameras on the concourse. I'll be letting you out here."

"One request from me: protect Marianne. Don't let her get sucked into all this."

"I don't have any control over her. She's got a mind and conscience of her own. She makes her own choices with open eyes."

"Just make sure she is never sacrificed for some greater good. That would make me very angry."

"Promise. I love her like the daughter I never had."

Chapter 23

Stalin Meets Red Bill

The herd-minus-Marianne arrived on schedule at the *MGM* and jumped at the idea of abandoning the *Fleas-Are-Us* for *The Mirage* suite. Upon learning that room service was covered, we ran up a tab of liquor and room service reminiscent of Genghis Khan sacking the Asian steppes. In mid-evening we left a message on Marianne's answering machine with bird imitations and Nixon spouts that was either going to lighten her spirits or provoke a call to the Vegas Crisis Clinic.

I thought Darrell's growing inebriation might undermine his Saturday impersonation of Tricky Dick, but it seemed to liquefy boundaries between real and imagined. His face turned plastic as he morphed spontaneously from Nixon to Reagan, and then back to Nixon with whistle-stop-imitations of Henry Kissinger and Chairman Mao.

His voice box joined the jowl jiggling with deadpan that would have confused Pat and Tricia. "There were no tapes....let me assure you...Dean, you tell them. Where's Hunt and Liddy? Trust me when I say I am not a crook." And then we took the craziness to the main floor of *The Mirage* where we fed chips to the one-armed bandits like Saddam dosing Alex with Doritos.

That's all it took to light up his bird brain—suddenly he was Alex the Parrot: "Squawk. No tapes," followed by Arabic bird observations enough like Saddam that security guards were giving us all the evil eye. Somehow we avoided handcuffs.

The next day, at blood-alcohol level that had to approximate Chevron with Techroline, Darrell copped "best Presidential impersonator."

I remained within flailing grasp of sobriety, just because I was curious about the upcoming Sunday magic act, and my instincts were telling me that I needed to pay attention to it as a story opportunity.

By mid-Sunday morning when everyone else was dealing with hangovers, I was filling with disquietude. Red Bill was right—people like Haney didn't just shoot the breeze with people like me. He obviously had an animus toward Red Bill and was out to snare him. This had to be what the free-tickets and the interview were really about—and all of this business about the Russian surpassing Red Bill's old magic act.

Did he really think that Bill cared about this and was going to take the bait?

Our tickets from Haney got us a prime-viewing table at *The Mirage* near the stage where Korblov was going to perform his masterful card trick. Darrell, still "in character" with full makeup, arrived late. I was pretty sure he had stopped to liquor up in one of the bars, except that he wasn't very talkative.

Already the warm-up was in progress—a Cher impersonator who had worked out an act with "John Belushi" at the Reel Awards.

Right away I could see that poorly-disguised security guards were watching all the exits. What was more striking was that the room was over-full with celebrity impersonators or liquored-up wannabees, a good many of them wearing celebrity masks that had been on sale in the casinos.

Everywhere were Nixons, Reagans, Kardashians and Rube Pauls. An adjacent table was populated by an entire family of Kardashians. Behind that was an obnoxious Donald Trump bloviating "hugely" to two blonde bombshells in drag. To make matters worse for the agents, the room was only lit with blinding stage lights, a dazzling chandelier, and a huge rotating glitter ball radiating glare like an exploding super nova.

The agents were clearly struggling to figure out who was a performer from the competitions and who might be a serious suspect.

I thought I spotted a prime candidate just as Korblov was introduced to generous applause—a fellow in a Reagan mask about the same size as Red Bill. He was standing not far from the main men's room—standing alone, watching intently and from his non-slouch, probably sober. He had a drink in his hand but he wasn't sipping.

On stage Korblov's hands were being tracked by the overhead camera as he raced through several cuts of an over-large card deck which initiated the hardest part of the Stalin. To his obvious irritation, the crowd was raucous and not paying much attention. His brow furled slightly at the distraction from the sloppy Kim Kardashian in drag at the nearby table, but he proceeded to the "faros" that defined the difficulty of the act that no one had ever successfully performed in public. Behind him a 20-foot screen showed his lithe fingers prestidigitating at a speed that would have envied the Artful Dodger.

Suddenly out of the blue he stopped dead in his tracks and

blurted out, "Someone's sabotaged my deck." At first people seemed to think this was part of the act. At that moment I watched as the fellow I thought was Red Bill step toward the men's room door. He broke the silence in the room with a sneeze and then a cackle that sounded like a mocking raven.

"There he is—the bastard who did it," cried out Korblov. But Red Bill was already in the men's room. Several guards rushed to the door but for some reason couldn't push their way through. All the while, Korblov was screaming and pointing his finger. Finally, the agents broke through the door and emerged with the Ronald Reagan in handcuffs.

They removed his mask, but to their great chagrin it wasn't Red Bill, only a celebrity who was quick-witted enough to take advantage of the spotlight and declare, "I'm sorry but I...I really don't think I traded guns for hostages. Nancy, Nancy—please help me."

The story appeared in *The Barb* on Tuesday morning:

Radical Escapes Sting at Vegas Fete
"Stalin" Trick Botched Again
by Pankaz Panday

It all began with a methodical plan by federal agents and private security guards to lure and net the celebrated, elusive radical, William "Red Bill" Callison, whom they believed would appear at *The Mirage* in Vegas to watch a Russian cardsharp, Igor Korblov, perform the famous *Stalin* card trick. This was the difficult card trick that had foiled card-sharpery and magic acts for 38 years. The only one who had come close to mastering it was William

Callison, the notorious radical believed to have masterminded the Berkeley pieing last month.

The crowd was in a raucous Jim Beam-mood as the trick began. It was Sunday Happy Hour. It was Not-So-Happy Hour for federal agents.

The room was full of competitors and wanna-bees from the just-concluded *Reel Awards Impersonation Competition* at the *MGM Grand*. Every headliner from the *National Enquirer* had incarnated in cartoon form and most of them seemed to be staggering from inebriation.

...It all went horribly wrong—not just for Korblov when he botched the *Stalin,* but when he himself fingered the wrong saboteur which triggered pandemonium and a comic bust.

...Meanwhile Callison slipped away unnoticed, as he has so many times before. Some say he was the gay Kim Kardashian with the bulbous caboose, or maybe the Rube Paul with slits on stilts. It could have been the Donald Trump with fast hands pawing the two 'hohs' in drag. Or just maybe he was the Richard Nixon at the front table who couldn't jiggle his jowls and just might have traded places with one who could.

Jim Currie

Chapter 24
Swimming Elephants

When I arrived at *The Offshore* in mid-week, I was delighted to learn that Hansa had improved and Marianne was back on the morning shift. Best of all, she was upbeat and glad to see me. She joyfully explained that Hansa's temperature had receded as a result of an experimental therapy for the normally resistant bacteria that had been infecting elephants at so many North American zoos.

I started to fill her in on the Vegas adventure, but she said she already knew about it and breakfast was on her.

That night I decided I would give her *The Book of Elephant*. I was sure Dinesh would have approved.

I presented it to her the following morning when she was on her break. She was taken aback by it, her mouth frozen in the awed position.

"Really? But this is your family heritage."

"You guys are my family now."

Her fingers caressed the pages like those of a Tibetan lama handling a lost sutra. She came to the passages on elephant intelligence and play.

Astounding Intelligence
    As formidable as the unique physical features of an elephant is its great intelligence, innate and acquired. Elephants are intuitive and sensitive to

changing weather; they are skilled in pattern recognition, reading friend from foe, and appraising hazards. A wise man will pay attention to the migrations of elephants across a landscape and their mindful behavior to follow a straight or circuitous path when confronted by natural impediments and threats.

An elephant knows instantly how to swim and ford powerful and wide rivers. Elephant and water are a marriage dating back to antiquity. Playfulness and intelligence seem to go hand in hand.

There is no joy in life that surpasses that of baby elephants playing with one another in a summer rain or at a mud hole on a hot day. They are so happy they turn and run into one another with unbounded exuberance.

Her eyes fell on my father's picture of an elephant swimming. It was captioned: An elephant can swim for up to six hours straight. She uses her trunk as a snorkel and paddles proficiently with her great legs and feet.

"Oh, my goodness, look at this! I only saw elephants swimming once and I'll never forget it."

For nearly a minute she simply stared at the picture with a dilated smile and then burst forth, "Oh, yes, yes, I would very much like to complete your father's sacred mission on behalf of elephants. We will marry your father's dream with my own of having a sanctuary for abused circus and zoo elephants."

This was the first time she had revealed anything very personal to me, and I listened intently.

"A sanctuary here in California?"

"Yes, it will be spacious, wooded and maybe even have a

lake where the elies can swim."

I nodded.

"A place where elephants could just be themselves, not forced to do tricks, to parade in sequined costumes and make all the 3-year-olds with cotton candy squeal with delight. And it would be educational too—where we could teach people about their amazing history, their amazing awareness."

"Wonderful." I replied. I didn't verbalize my thought, but she must have read it—*You better have a major bankroll.*

"I have a little savings," she added, "and with a little more I should be able to make a down-payment on some land, perhaps in Marin County."

Tony and Roger chimed in that they wanted to help in whatever way they could.

"This might require more than spare change from Tony's pigeon act."

"There's good money in pigeon racing...Maybe I can make a big score...maybe it should be a sanctuary for all kinds of animals," declared Tony.

"Yeah, pigeons need a refuge and parrots, too," declared Darrell wryly.

"Especially the pigeons," declared Roger. "Completely misunderstood and treated like dirt which explains why they poop on everything."

"You don't get it, my friend. They're noble creatures if you take time to understand them."

I left them to argue it out and to nominate other feral critters to be liberated to Marianne's refuge for wayward and abused elephants.

Jim Currie

Part 2 - A Convergence of Tributaries

Under the hot lamp of Marianne's interrogating gaze, it would be hard to deny that the tragedy of Deli and the Tin Can affected me in more ways than I had been willing to admit. I really hadn't done a very good job of leaving it behind.

As a kid, post-*tin can*, I hadn't realized the full epiphany, but was getting there quickly: that the human floodplain was a more perilous environment than imagined, and most human inhabitants were governed by dangerous blindspots, myself included.

Putting this in bird-terms—surprise and shocking events are hardly ever the result of "Black Swans" flying—completely unpredictable fly-ins that change everything in your life. It's just that inattentive observers, and more than a few victims, fall into a comfortable mindset, ignoring the accumulating signs that a dark bird is on the wing.

No doubt that leaks out in most of my stories and fixes my stories-in-progress.

Ivan's haplessness bothered me. He couldn't seem to "win for losing" and was obviously under a very dark cloud. Were there signs that he should have picked up on that his roof might collapse? Had he not been paying attention to cracks in the ceiling? And how did he miss the recent tremors on the San Andreas Fault, ubiquitous in the last month, that almost all San Franciscans pay attention to?

I wondered as well about my own jeopardy. What gave me the most pause was that I was now on the radar of some as powerful as Don Haney and for what? A not very threatening story about neo-Yippie theatrics? Even the theory that the Bushies wanted a piece of Red Bill didn't quite make it. He just didn't seem that important.

The more cynical view authored by my days in India was that people like Haney didn't really get motivated unless an issue was about serious money, a threat to their core interests, or coverup. So then what was tectonic enough to fit?

The one rumble that might be relevant, besides the passage of the new Patriot Act itself, was that in recent months more and more stories were popping about "environmental terrorism" abroad—about threats or even sabotage at oil rigs and chemical plants abroad. Most were poorly sourced with suspicious authorship—as suspect as the stories that Saddam possessed WMD or was shredding babies.

Environmentalists had always been high up on the FBI's *Most Wanted List,* not just because of what they tried to protect, but the larger threat they seemed to represent in attacking, Big Oil, Big Chemical, coal mining and the big banks.

In this light, it made more than a little sense that people like Haney and Harmsworth would be interested in dimming the lights of Red Bill and painting his environmental friends as domestic *jihadi*, as intent on attacking business as stopping torture or protecting some abused or threatened animal.

Of course, people like Haney and Harmsworth knew better than to do the dirty work themselves—always better to work within well-crafted laws that would enable a crackdown.

It wasn't lost on me that if this occurred, Marianne could soon be in the middle of it. I was especially worried about one environmental protest—the planned confrontation of a circus train in Santa Rosa. Marianne had told me that elephants were going to be on that train and her group was going to be in Santa Rosa when the train arrived. I couldn't dissuade her from protesting, She was just too much of her own person for that. What I could do was make sure that I was there if she got in harm's way.

Jim Currie

Chapter 25
Circus Train to Nowheresville

My original plan was to arrive early at the fairgrounds, connecting with Marianne for a cup of coffee a few hours before the arrival of the train. That was scuttled when I awakened at 6 AM and learned that a massive fish kill had occurred in the Sacramento River following a break in an important hydraulic barrier. A story being reported by Fox suggested that "anarcho- environmentalists" had sabotaged the barrier and were intent in crippling the entire California Aqueduct.

It took me a few hours to get to the bottom of it—nonsense; no terrorist threat and the problem was due to an electrical failure. I was halfway out the door for Santa Rosa when another reporter hailed me down: "You've got a very agitated caller on line one."

"Can you take it for me?"

"He says he won't talk to anyone but you."

I made my way back to my desk, thinking *this better not take long.*

Right away I could tell that the caller was nervous: "Is this a secure line?"

"No line is secure these days."

"But you're Pankaz Panday?"

"What have you got? I'm in a hurry."

"You need to know that some agents are working undercover

among the elephant protesters. Pretty sure it's going to play out in that anarchist action at Santa Rosa. Don't know exactly how."

"Who's this? I could use some detail."

The caller was gone.

I checked my watch. I would have to floor it to get to Santa Rosa by 3 PM when the demonstration was supposed to start.

As I raced toward Santa Rosa in the gutless *Barb* van, I decided that my caller probably wasn't credible. I had never received a good crime tip from an anonymous caller and this one was vague. What bothered me most, however, was that he called the Santa Rosa protest an anarchist action.

If the caller was right and the police viewed it as such, Marianne, Julian and friends could be walking into serious trouble.

When I arrived at the Santa Rosa Fairgrounds, I discovered about 60 activists chanting with signs. Some looked familiar; some didn't. More than a few were carrying scarves, as if prepared for a tear gas attack. Bad sign.

The media was out in full force, including a large contingent from Fox News. The coverage was way out of proportion for the usual circus protest.

"Stop the circus; save the elephants," came the collective chant.

Over a bullhorn, one of the demonstrators began reciting the number of circus elephants that had died in recent years—one in Oklahoma City, another in Mobile, another in Tallahassee. All had been abused. I was pretty sure this had come from Marianne.

I quickly learned that the main strategy of the protest was to make sure the demonstration crested when the elephants entered the "backstretch" behind the Santa Rosa Racetrack where they would be domiciled in enlarged horse stalls. For the moment, a half-dozen gray-haired private cops were preventing the demonstrators from entering the gated area.

Counter-demonstrators from a group called *Save Our Circuses* were also gathered at the gate. They were more regimented and quick to follow the orders of what looked like a supervisor, suggesting the circus had paid for their services.

I found Tony and Roger carrying protest signs and wearing t-shirts showing an elephant that looked like one from the *Book of Elephant*. Marianne was a few feet away in the same uniform, trying to be heard as she conversed with Julie Jensen. Actually it was more like "argued". Marianne was adamant that the demonstration was spiraling out of control and needed to be shut down.

I had never seen her like this. She was even pointing her finger at Julie who looked bewildered but trying to hold her ground.

"I don't want elephants to get caught in the middle of this or there will be bloodshed and chaos that you can't imagine."

"I told everyone to cool it," answered Julie Johnson, "but there are new people here—the ones with the scarves. I don't even know most of them."

"Exactly," exclaimed Marianne. "They're goading the cops. They want a bust."

I quickly squeezed off a dozen photographs of the most militant protestors darting back and forth from the demonstration line to confront the fairgrounds security guards. Some of the militants were now wearing Guy Fawkes masks, the head gear of anarchists. The aging guards looked nervous and intimidated. The guy I was focused on was fingering a tazer.

I knew that if he used it, all hell would break loose.

Then I noticed that another two circus trucks had arrived in the parking lot outside the backstretch gate. At first I thought they might be carrying the elephants, but the back doors opened and out poured a dozen or so cops. Right away I could see that they were much younger and more fit than those facing the demonstrators.

Something else was different: they all wore *Bilgewater Security* patches on their shoulders. This was the private contractor that had gained so much notoriety in Iraq and Afghanistan for black ops and what went on at Al Jazar Prison. What were they doing here? Immediately I thought of what Red Bill had said in Vegas about an escalation against protesters. This had all the feel of a pre-planned bust.

I approached Marianne and again eavesdropped on the verbal fight between Julie and her. Julie was intent on sticking to the plan to keep the protest going until the elephants arrived—"After that we disperse."

"No way, " answered Marianne adamantly. "You don't know when that will be. You don't even know whether the elies will be arriving by train or truck."

"It will be by train," answered Julie. "The circus train."

"How do you know that?" challenged Marianne.

"I was told."

"Told by whom?"

She didn't answer. The silence was broken by a faint train whistle. "I think that might be the circus train," declared Julie. She checked her watch. Roger, who had been eavesdropping, interjected—"That's got to be it."

The whistle sounded again and I was pretty sure it was coming from the southeast. But there was something alarming about that whistle—it was sounding in staccato bursts—sounding a warning. At once I was in the grip of a discharge from childhood that will forever be associated with imperiled trains on the Indus floodplain in danger of colliding or running off the rails and killing all aboard.

It sounded again, and I filled with inchoate dread.

"Something's not right," I declared. "I know train sounds."

Julie overheard us. "I wonder if it's Willy."

"What do you mean, Willy?" asked Marianne, this time at higher descant.

"He said we should stop the train."

"What—stop the train?" Marianne was livid.

Julie bit her lip, then meekly replied, "I'm pretty sure I talked him out of it."

I raced for the van with my two cameras swinging from my neck. Roger read my attention and climbed inside the van when it was already moving. We were soon turning onto the highway and pointing in the direction of a frenetic train whistle.

Three miles up the road and to the east, we caught sight of a diesel plume. Now I could see the train: strangely, it seemed to be headed toward Napa rather than for the fairgrounds. I removed my glasses for a better view. It was an impressive sight—a classic re-stored Challenger locomotive, gleaming in the wine country sun, complete with cow-catcher, and pulling three gilded Pullman coaches, several box cars, a fancy club car and a caboose.

As I drew closer to the locomotive, I noticed something else: above the cow-catcher was a larger banner in bold-faced print that read "No Circus Animals. End the Abuse." A black anarchist flag was flying from a tender. I spotted another sign draped across the back of the freight car: "FREE THE CIRCUS ELEPHANTS."

"Jeez, they've hijacked the train," I declared.

Roger shook his head.

The highway diverged from the grade and for several minutes I was disoriented, not sure which road to take. I could hear the cry of sirens from several different directions.

Finally, I caught a view of a locomotive plume in the distance and floored the gas pedal. The speedometer needle was now hovering at 75. In my rear-view mirror a police car suddenly appeared with flashing lights and I was sure we were going to be stopped, but it raced by me at over 90 MPH. I had just breathed a sigh of relief when a helicopter streaked overhead just above tree elevation.

"Did you see that?" declared Roger. "No markings."

Though I tried to focus on the road, surges of dread welled up from deep inside. This was all too familiar.

Suddenly I was age 17; it was July 1991, and I was clinging to a railing onboard the *Faizabad-Lucknow Mail* packed full all the way to Lucknow.

Chapter 26
Halfway to Lucknow

In the days after my mom and sister began working at *Lucknow Textile and Clothing,* I would rise early every morning, make them lunch, fix them breakfast and walk them to the village train station on the Lucknow-Faizabad train line to catch *The Mail.* The rest of my day was about school and homework.

In late June of my junior year of high school, five years after my father died, my hard work bore fruit. With a recommendation from a teacher I was awarded a special scholarship for promising young teenage writers at Lucknow University. It was a 6-week, weekend class at the school of journalism. My sister and mother were so proud of me.

To my delight I was now able to accompany my sister and mother on their Saturday commute to Lucknow. Our stops were only five stations apart.

In mid-August on a hazy and hot morning with hints of the Himalaya in the background, the three of us waited at the village station for the arrival of the *Faizabad-Lucknow Mail.* With a full fifteen cars, the train eased into the station and promptly emptied a hoard of passengers onto the platform. Another immediately surged on-board.

I let my sister and mom go first, but got separated from them in the cattle-rush. The car instantly filled and I was left behind on the platform realizing that I needed to find another car fast or I would miss the train.

As the train started to move, I raced down the platform in the direction of the locomotive. At the last moment I found an empty stair-step on the carriage two coaches down from the locomotive. I didn't mind. I had traveled like this before and actually found it a relief from the oppressive heat, body odor and jostling inside. You just had to make sure that you held on tightly when the train turned, tilted, hit bad stretches of track, or braked. I knew where most of the worst spots were.

About six kilometers down the line and halfway to Lucknow, the train slowed as we navigated a bend in the Gompti River. A band of pasture lay on our right side, the side I was on. I knew that this was an unusual stretch for the train to slow.

The Mail was barely moving now and issued a shrill complaint and then another. I craned my neck and could see the reason—cows on the tracks. The engineer clearly didn't want to run them down, sacred as they were to so many devout Hindus, so he simply whistled and waited.

Now the train was completely stopped.

I turned and caught sight of another train approaching us rapidly from the rear, also westbound. I was sure it was the *Jamalapur-Delhi Express* that usually followed us all the way to Lucknow.

She was a flyer with powerful engines. Incredibly, she didn't seem to be slowing down. Suddenly she seemed to realize that *The Mail* was stopped and screamed out wildly.

The engineer of *The Mail* instantly popped his head back inside the locomotive and we started to move, slowly at first, then slightly faster. He wasted no more cries on the cows who immediately scattered and looked back with an expression of hurt feelings.

Still, I could see that the distance between trains was shrinking rapidly. Now we were at 10 km/hr but the distance was only 300 hundred meters. Now we were at 20 km/hr and the distance was a mere 150.

The trains collided with explosive force. I was immediately thrown free and landed in the pasture, bloodied and dizzy. The locomotive of the *Express* collapsed the cars of our train like the compressed bellows of an accordion.

From my position on the grass, I watched the horror unfold in slow motion. The cars had derailed in twisted, collapsed segments and were tumbling toward the river under the force of gravity. I gathered myself to spot my mom's car which was third in a segment of four.

The two cars ahead of hers, both on fire, groaned and slid into the Gompti, in the process issuing forth a death halo of smoke and steam from the extinguished heat and flames.

In a spinning daze I tried to stop the slide: "No, No," I pleaded as the car holding Amita and Arundhati hit the water and slowly started to submerge.

Now it was almost completely submerged. I willed myself toward the bank of the river not sure what to do. Somehow I had to help them.

I threw myself into the river, not even considering the fact that I was no more than a chaotic flailer when it came to swimming.

The chill of the water against my face clarified my resolve: I could paddle to the train and free them. I just needed to breathe and stay calm.

Suddenly, I felt a heavy hand on my shoulder and then an irresistible downward pull. I turned slightly and was at once face-to-face with a body attached to a nearly severed head.

Though I knew this was a corpse, I couldn't disentangle myself from him. His full weight was on me and it seemed that the more I tried to wrest myself from him, the more clinging was his grasp. Finally, I pushed myself free and his anguished desperate eyes vanished in the murky brown water.

Now I was completely out of breath and it took all that I had left just to paddle back to shore. Perhaps a minute later I decided to try again, plunging into the river and this time trying to navigate a more careful path through the debris and bodies to the car which was perhaps 50 feet away.

As soon as I got to it, I took a deep drag of air and submerged, trying to reach a carriage door. A latch turned but perhaps because of pressure, I couldn't open the door. Once again out of air, I surfaced and somehow found a hand-hold above the waterline to re-gather myself.

I dove again, this time trying to find an open window, my eyes meeting those of one after another woeful, miserable soul pressed against the unbroken window. I could now see that the car was half full of water but the collision had sundered and crushed the poor trapped bodies inside, most of them distorted and twisted.

No sign of Amita or Arundhati. I couldn't give up. And then I saw Arundhati lying sideways half-covered with rubble. Her eyes were open but she wasn't moving. She was looking right at me with no sign of desperation.

I beat hard against the window. "Arundhati, Arundhati," I

cried out silently. But I could only make a nick in the thick glass. Out of air, I resurfaced and paddled back to shore where I caught my breath and then found a sharp rock to break the window. I then dove back into the river and paddled back to the car that cradled the perishing lives of my precious mother and sister.

Three times I dove and three times banged as hard as I could against the window with the rock. All to no avail; I couldn't break it. I was too fucking weak.

Finally, I realized I was spent, and like a beaten animal, half-floated, half-paddled back to shore, gasping for air all the way. On land I coughed and coughed, expelling water from my lungs in violent spasms. And then doubled over, still gasping for breath, I told myself that I would make one more try. I would gather my strength and this time I would break through. Instead I slumped to the ground and began to cry inconsolably. Seconds later I gave in to exhaustion and fell motionless onto the grass of the grade.

I awakened to the scream of ambulances and the frenzied, aspirated thumping of an Indian Army helicopter almost directly overhead.

Jim Currie

Chapter 27
Deranged Druggies on Wheels

Just outside of Yountville, Roger and I spotted the train in the distance, then lost track of it as it circled around a bend. Another helicopter raced in pursuit of the train like a raptor after wounded prey. I could hear an ambulance approaching rapidly, then a second one. I pulled to the shoulder as they raced by at break-neck speed.

We followed them down a barely paved access road and were soon enveloped by three unmarked sedans that took to the weeds to pass us. We followed them to an abrupt, dirt-skidding stop at the right-of-way where the train was stopped and cops were already cordoning off a crime perimeter in yellow ribbon.

I pulled the van to the edge of the right-of-way, just outside the perimeter, and reached for my cameras. An ambulance inside the perimeter immediately caught my eye. Medics were loading a large human from the train onto a gurney. Based on the strain of the EMT's in lifting the gurney, I was sure this was Willy, The Jolly Green Giant. I couldn't get a face shot before the back door of the ambulance slammed. The ambulance began rolling down the dirt road.

"Not exactly hurrying, are they?" declared Roger.

"Bad sign," I added.

While I was squeezing off several more pictures, two large bulls arrived and demanded ID. I flashed my press credentials.

"No press beyond this point. Homeland Security issue," he answered gruffly.

"Homeland Security?"

"Are you hard of hearing, my friend?"

"We just want to take a few more pictures."

"You ain't going beyond my perimeter or you're going to jail. And right now you're 50 feet over the line."

I decided to avoid the gruff bull and headed to the other end of the perimeter that wasn't closely guarded. I slipped inside the tape and managed to engage the driver of a second ambulance.

"I'm with *The Barb*." I flashed my press credentials.

"Anyone else hurt?"

"Not with us—just the DOA"

"Any ID on him?"

"Someone named Davis. Police called him Giant."

"What got him?"

"Rifle shot, I'd guess. Only got a quick look at him," he shrugged.

"Where are they taking him?"

"Santa Rosa Memorial."

Other reporters descended on the scene and began barraging the local police and FBI with questions. An FBI spokesman claimed that radicals had taken over the train at gunpoint, the "threat to public safety had been neutralized," and details would be released later. He added that the train appeared to be carrying drums of flammable chemicals but these were now under control.

When it became clear that the FBI was playing it close to the vest, I approached the Santa Rosa sheriff who had been one of the first at the crime scene. He was more willing to talk.

"Early this morning we got reports from credible sources that radicals would be trying to hijack the train and might be releasing wild tigers and elephants at a shopping center outside of NAPA."

"What? I declared in disbelief. "What sources? The circus? The FBI?"

He turned mum, apparently realizing that he might have said something he might have to substantiate and couldn't.

I decided to see if I could get an eye-witness report and noticed several circus people behind the caboose spouting among themselves. I asked what had happened and a fellow who said he was high-wire acrobat, declared, "This fat boy and his deranged terrorist buddies climbed on-board just outside of Santa Rosa." His accent was eastern European—Croatian, perhaps.

"How many?" I asked.

"Two or three—crazy-fuck druggies," he declared.

"You said deranged terrorists—how did you get that impression?"

"When they forced their way on the train, they were acting crazy. "They pushed their way to the locomotive."

"So how did they get control of the train? Did they have guns?"

His explanation spiraled into incoherence about who pushed and threatened whom, and for a second I imagined that this might have been close to the original report out of the Balkans in 1914 how Archduke Ferdinand had been assassinated. But this muddle and the historical antecedents were easily surpassed by the explanation of how Willy was killed and what did him in. The FBI wouldn't say; the acrobat claimed he had been brought down by FBI agents on the train; and a shapely female gymnast, who could have easily been mistaken for Nadia Comăneci in her prime, said she saw a rifle flash from an overhead helicopter.

My story complete with speculation was picked up by AP and included photos of ambulances, the police, the smoking train and the helicopters. I also included a thumbnail on Willy Davis, listing his involvement in past environmental protests.

I only realized later that it was a bloodless, emotionless account that just as easily could have been filed by a medical examiner and the county sheriff. I guess this was the only way I could prevent the two trains, one headed to Napa and the other to Lucknow, from coupling and again dragging me back into the shallows of the Gompti River.

Chapter 28
Dimemoral and the Devil in Small Things

In the days that followed I was occupied with reporting the story and seemed two steps ahead or two steps behind Marianne. Finally, we crossed paths at a market off Broadway. She seemed low and dispirited and almost a different person from the assertive and vocal activist at Santa Rosa. Was it because of Willy's death or was something else wrong?

I asked if I could walk her home and she nodded wearily. As soon as we were outside, Alex landed on her shoulder but she barely acknowledged him.

"Homeland Security questioned me," she declared.

"This morning?"

She nodded.

"They were convinced I had some relationship with Willy. I said there was no relationship." She sighed heavily, "I only talked to him a couple of times and only briefly. He was at most of the elephant protection meetings…You mind if we stop for a second?"

"No, not at all."

"I just need to catch my breath."

Before I could ask if she was feeling ill, she declared, "From what Julie said, Willy was just planning to attach the banners, drive the train a few miles and jump off. Maybe he got in too deep or just couldn't stop the train."

"*Bilgewater* guards claim he and others took over the train at gunpoint."

She shook her head. "I don't believe it. You know there's a whole lot here that doesn't jibe."

"What do you mean?"

"What happened to the other hijackers?

"I hate to admit it, but I didn't think of this. I never saw anyone in cuffs at the crime scene and no other arrests were mentioned later."

She nodded. "Exactly. One person doesn't just take over a train and there should have been others arrested."

I agreed.

"I think it was a big set-up. The circus knew and so did *Bilgewater*. It was all provoked and orchestrated. And why didn't I figure it out? I knew Julie wasn't listening to me—that all of those new people were getting to her. I should have been more emphatic."

"I wouldn't beat myself up. You can't control everything and everyone. Trains get moving and one person can't stop them."

Her lips were pursed.

"What I wonder about is why the FBI or anyone else would go to such lengths to nail one person. It's not as if he was a killer."

She pondered the thought and I verbalized: "Unless it was about making a statement."

She nodded, then heaved another whale-like sigh that morphed to a cough, then another. "What kind of country has this become? The constant hate from right-wing radio and cable TV; people like Willy getting gunned down; kidnappings that are probably a big charade; the NSA sifting everyone's email; fake news about *jihadis* and anarchists everywhere. It reminds me of the days after 911—'cept worse."

"You hear the claim that radicals were threatening to blow up the California Aqueduct?"

"Yeah," she answered, "and that comes after the fish kill that people should really be upset over. The irrigators won't be happy until they've taken every ounce of water out of the river. Everything is upside down and backwards. Everyone is caught up in fear."

She stopped again and glum turned to abject. "What are people and animals supposed to do when they have no place to go and no way to survive? I work full time at minimum wage. I would be flapping around in a shallow puddle if I didn't have some savings to cover the monthly deficit. But it was all supposed to go to the elephants." She exhaled deeply. "I guess I shouldn't complain. Tony, Roger and Darrell make less than I do."

We came to her apartment, and after the key was in the lock, I thought she might actually collapse from fatigue. This had to be the toll of stress and pressure she put on herself to control the demonstration at Santa Rosa. For too long she had taken on the burdens of others, taking care of the Gigi and Hansa, propping up Julie and the elephant protectors, holding down her job and supporting Roger, Tony, Darrell and me. No one could do that endlessly.

"How about I cook a meal for you, help clean up your apartment—whatever you want?"

She offered only a meek resistance. "You've got important stories to work on."

"Nah, nothing that can't wait." I picked her up and carried her to the couch. She nodded off and awakened when I arrived with quickly prepared stir-fried vegetables. She gobbled them down.

For a few minutes we didn't say a word. The only noise was Alex on the sill reminding Marianne that he was a pretty bird and tossing in a word or two of Arabic.

"I should take a hot shower," declared Marianne. "You know I still have elephant pee in my hair from the zoo?"

"'I was pretty sure it wasn't Calvin Klein."

She brushed the sticky hair out of her eyes. "I don't know the last time I actually just turned on the steam and scrubbed myself down to the roots."

"You take a long hot shower and afterwards I'll give you a massage."

She nodded. A few minutes later the vapors escaped the bathroom and she followed them obediently to the rug in front of the couch where I had laid out a long beach towel for her plus a pillow on which she could rest her head.

I helped her dry her short hair with another towel and couldn't take my eyes off her soft skin and tight athletic body. No makeup whatsoever. No apparent awareness of natural beauty. Only the rarest of 30-year-old models wouldn't have envied her. Hard to believe she was really 35 years old.

She rolled to her side and shot me an appreciative smile that quickly eclipsed to weary repose. She made no real attempt at modesty as I kneaded her shoulder blades and worked my way down her back. She heaved a heavy sigh as I smoothed out a knot, and then when I came to her hips she turned and kissed me.

"Why don't you sleep with me?" she declared, rubbing her lips across mine. I don't think I would be a good lover tonight, but it would be nice to sleep in your arms."

"Perfect," I answered.

Sighs and exhalation passed between us like winds over a tropical sea. I could hear her pulse in sync with my own as fins and reflective scales flashed against one another; then in unison we spiraled downward to deeper pools. Before long she surrendered to sleep and I was soon to follow.

A violent scream roiled the air and then came a blow to my chest.

"You can't do this," came the cry followed by another blow, this time to my cheek.

"Geez, what's wrong," I answered groggily.

Marianne took another swipe that grazed my face. Then she screamed again, "Why are you hurting them?" Her fist crashed against the wall and she started to flail again, but this time I grabbed her wrist before impact.

"Easy, easy, you're having a bad nightmare. Easy."

It took her several seconds for her to compose. I held her tight.

"You okay?"

"Yeah, yeah. Sorry."

"No, sorry. It was just a nightmare."

For a second I thought of Deli's nightmares.

"I shouldn't have had you over," she declared.

"No, no. It was just a bad dream. Don't worry about it." *Except that I wondered if this was an isolated nightmare.*

"I was suppose to take my *Dimemoral,* but I was so tired, I forgot."

"*Dimemoral?*"

175

She seemed to be weighing whether she should continue. "It's nothing, just a med to make me sleep better."

"How about it if I boil us some tea?" I answered.

She nodded. "Good idea. I'll take care of it."

As she heated the water I took a quick glance at a bottle near her bed. It was the med she had mentioned—*Dimemoral*. I had never heard of it before.

We shared a pot of chamomile and I waited for her to tell me about her dream, but she said it was nothing worth talking about —"ridiculous jumble."

"About what?"

"Nonsense...a burglar rifling through my apartment. Nonsense."

"I swear to you I didn't touch your jewelry."

She half-smiled. "I hope I can sleep now. You know, this might seem terrible of me, but it would be better if you left me alone. I'm so unused to having anyone else in my bed. I promise you it has nothing to do with you. And I so appreciate everything you've done. I just really need to be alone."

"So you can box with the wall without gloves?"

"It's just bizzaro eruption—nonsense from the far side of the moon."

As she spoke I couldn't help but notice the knuckles on her right hand were thickened and calloused. Maybe this wasn't such a rare occurrence.

I could feel her withdrawing. I wasn't sure how to bring her back. "Listen, I understand nightmare. Looking for a good train disaster? I've got one in Technicolor."

"I just forgot to take my medicine."

She didn't seem willing to budge.

"I'll do anything you want, sweet one," I replied.

I slipped into my coat. She approached and kissed me with exaggerated appreciation and then I retreated to the door.

I was two minutes onto the fog-bound San Francisco street when I reached for my smart phone and Googled *Dimemoral*: "Strong, serotonin uptake inhibitor, used to suppress schizophrenic episodes, myoclonia and extreme anxiety." I clicked through to several more links that suggested it was frequently prescribed to help those suffering from PTSD and the traumas of war, rape and loss of newborns.

Jim Currie

Chapter 29
The Big Boot

The next day I received word at *The Barb* that Vincent wanted to meet with me at *The Offshore*. No specifics were given but I was pretty sure it was about the results of his sleuthing regarding PERP and maybe the shooting of Willy.

He cut an impressive sight with long hair and a silvery coif. He was even wearing a cape. "Very nice but I have one question—do all you guys defending Snowden, Assange and Roman Polanski go to makeup together or is this genetic selection at work?"

"It selects alcoholically," he declared, billowing his cape in the manner of Bela Lugosi. "Bottle of scotch a day turns the coif gray."

He seated himself at my booth and reached for his glasses.

"First thing to report is that Ivan is missing. I think the poor bastard has been detained under PERP. I've already filed in district court for a review of *habeas corpus,* but my source in the AG's office is telling me that because of PERP, it will probably fail."

"What does that mean?"

"It means that all we talked about before is coming to pass. If you've been elected or selected to the Order of Terror, all you have to do is breathe bad garlic on someone important, and you can be detained. Worse still, law enforcement is suddenly given a pass if they decide to open up with a shotgun when your tail light goes out."

"Come again?"

"Normally, under the 4th Amendment a reasonableness standard governs how much force can be used to apprehend and arrest a suspect for every potential or probable crime. Because the threat standard would be lowered for anyone on a Class-A list, a lot more force would be considered reasonable."

"You think this explains what happened to Giant?"

"This and the fact that he presented an opportunity to impart a lesson to radicals."

He went on to explain that review of *habeas corpus* depended heavily on the circuit in which a request for review was made. At present, four of twelve circuits were currently presided over by judges whose fidelities lay with folks named Franco, Genghis, and Il Duce.

I worked all day tracking down leads and legal history to fill out the article and submitted it to Betty by email around noon the next day.

Bochinsky Gets Big Boot from Perp
In Suspension of *Habeas Corporus*
by Pankaz Panday

The new Private Enterprise Security Act (PERP) is now being used, in combination with a host of anti-terrorism laws and Presidential war powers, to suspend *habeas corpus* and effectively detain, incarcerate and "vanish" American citizens who happen to land on the "Class-A" terrorist list. To make the list you do not have to be a fugitive felon or even a person under indictment. A judge presiding over a secret court who happens to be in a foul mood can simply decide you are a "threat".

The Berkeley pie maker and practitioner of political Dada, Ivan Bochinsky, who baked the pies that were used in the banana cream attack on James Mee and David Badminton, was apparently listed. This virtually guaranteed a very bad day for the hapless Bochinsky.

On Tuesday, he was visited at his business establishment, *Pope Pie Us III* on Telegraph Avenue, and spirited away by federal agents in a black sedan to an unknown location. After four days, no charges had yet been filed. Bochinsky's last recorded public words uttered to lawyer Vincent Berlioti by cellphone before loss of transmission were as follows: "Man, I'm getting the boot again, and this time it's the big one."

He appears to have been referring to a purgatory of indefinite detainment without legal counsel and any assured review of habeas corpus. It might even be worse.

Only four times in the history of the United States has there been a suspension of *habeas corpus,* the civil right of judicial review dating back to the *Magna Carta.* The first occurred during the Civil War, invoked by Abraham Lincoln following a rebellion in Baltimore. The three others occurred during Reconstruction, in the Philippines after the Spanish-American War; and in Hawaii during World War II, after the bombing of Pearl Harbor. Each was formal and explicit, in contrast to the current shadow suspension.

On September 14, 2011, Congress set in

motion the first of a series of acts that provided a legal pretext for the latest nullification. Then Congress authorized the President to exercise all necessary and appropriate force against "persons, organizations and states responsible for 9/11."

At first this was largely restricted to non-Americans outside the United States, but embedded in the act was an implication that "persons" could include Americans, even Americans inside the United States.

A major leap forward in the decommissioning seems to have occurred in 2004 when Yaser Hamdi, an American citizen, was captured in Afghanistan in 2001 and turned over to U.S. military authorities. Eventually he was incarcerated at Guantanamo. The U.S. Government claimed a right to secretly hold and interrogate Hamdi without benefit of attorney, without notice or formal public arraignment. Essentially the argument pivoted on the notion that Hamdi had forfeited his right of habeas corpus and American citizenship.

The case of Jose Padilla might be even more relevant to the plight of Bochinsky. In 2002, Padilla, an American citizen, was nabbed at O'Hare Airport and accused of planning to detonate a dirty bomb in the United States. Claiming executive power, the President authorized a detention by the military that lasted 42 months.

Charges were eventually dropped, but not before a three-judge panel of the US Fourth Circuit, Court of Appeal, ruled that the detention was legal and Constitutional. Eventually Padilla was charged with lesser crimes in what has sometimes been described as a legal game of "bait and switch."

Since then, judges in the fourth, sixth and

eighth circuits have shown even more willingness to suspend civil rights during times of declared crisis, war or "imperiled national safety."

The new PERP law fortifies the bad news for defenders of *habeas corpus*, defining "imperiled national safety" as a "threat condition" in which important national assets, including designated members of industry or the military as well as strategic corporations are "prevented from commerce and essential activities, or placed in bodily danger."

Jim Currie

Chapter 30
White Feather and Nimba

Only Marianne could have stirred any interest from me in signing up for Tony's upcoming pigeon-training mission to Marin County. When I learned she would be coming, I didn't hesitate. I had seen very little of her since the nightmare, one week earlier. I had called and left messages that I was concerned about her, but she hadn't replied.

Besides exercising Tony's pigeons, we would be checking out property for the elephant sanctuary that Tony had gotten a tip on from a pigeon racer. Conveyance would be provided by Tony's recently refurbished Pigeon Mobile.

I was notified of its arrival by several "Ah-Oogas" from the street below my apartment.

An impressive sight it was: a 1950's Ford flatbed truck with a pigeon coop covered with a mural showing oversized pigeons in caricatured close-up. They were overflying a WWI battlefield compleat with siege guns and trenches. The cab was extra large with a backseat, easily providing room for all and our rucksacks.

Tony was on the sidewalk when I arrived, dressed in a fitted army coat with brass buttons, a commander's cap and pleated riding gloves to impress on us the fact he was a hands-on pigeon master.

"Sweet ride you got here, " I declared. I could see Marianne in the cab. She looked good.

"It comes from a British design—WWI in fact. Everyone had their own mobiles—the French, the Brits, the Belgians. That was the heyday for pigeons. They were used all across the Western Front. The programs survived into Korea where I got involved with the Signal Corps."

By the cooing coming from the roost, at least ten pigeons were on-board. Tony quickly explained that they were "homers" needing exercise. He would be releasing them at designated spots and with a little luck they would return to the home roost on the roof of his building in San Francisco.

"Is your star on board?" I declared opening the door.

"Rosy," he answered. "But this jaunt is just to stretch her wings. She could do 300 miles on her back."

"She's going to win the world championship," declared Marianne who was clearly in higher spirits. Her eyes were bright, and she was wearing form-fitting coveralls.

"And when she does, Marianne will have her elephant sanctuary—assuming we bet our brains out on her. Speaking of money—got any jingle for gas? This baby drinks like a sailor on liberty."

"How much do we need?" I answered.

"How much you got? Three hundred? We can stick *The Barb* for it, right?"

"Maybe we should be putting the bling-stealers back into training," I answered.

Tony shot me a look to clam up. Clearly Marianne didn't know about this.

Her eyes were elsewhere—focused on something out the

window. It was Alex:

"Sweet one," declared Marianne as he landed on the roof. He rode the Pigeon Mobile all the way to the Golden Gate and then turned back.

"That bird loves you," I declared.

Marianne pretended to blush. "Aw shucks." She smiled brightly and I was glad to see some of her vitality had returned.

Near Mount Tam we gassed up, then diverted toward Petaluma. A few miles outside of town Tony pulled to the side of the road and released two pigeons he described as sprinters. They both circled twice to get their bearings and shot for San Francisco. I had to admit they had afterburners. I managed to catch two good shots with my telephoto lens.

"Just curious but why would the Army want to use pigeons when they had radios?"

Tony chuckled. "Radios get captured and malfunction. Pigeon-mail always gets through—98 percent, anyway."

"Tell him about what you did," declared Marianne.

"Learned the art form with the 279th Fighting Pigeoneers under the guidance of the legendary Colonel Clifford Poutre." He doffed his cap.

"Our birds could do magic—fly at night and return to mobile coops—perfect for intelligence drops too. They saved a lot of boys on the beach at Inchon." He was gleaming.

"I told you Tony was a celebrity," added Marianne.

After two more releases we passed Santa Rosa and worked our way into the coastal range following scribbled directions to get to the property that supposedly was a candidate for the elephant sanctuary. We passed into Mendocino County and somewhere between Boonville and the ocean turned onto a dirt road in a mixed conifer and cottonwood forest. The road dead-ended next to a "no-trespassing" sign.

I focused on the sign as the Pigeon Mobile burped, sputtered and came to a stop.

A note on the bottom said "Mortal threat! Stay out."

"Sounds pretty serious," I declared. "You sure we've got the right spot? I don't see any *For Sale* sign."

"This is it," Tony declared confidently. "It ain't listed."

"Man's got a compass in his head, just like his birds, " declared Marianne.

"You folks plow ahead. I need to take care of Rosy and the others. I'll catch up."

"Now this is the trouble I'm having with my friends—lots of enthusiasm until the mortal threat arises."

"Ah, you'll be okay. The guy you're looking for is Rae-Ron."

Marianne didn't seem at all worried about the sign, grabbing her rucksack, bouncing down an overgrown footpath edged in willow, wild rose and Douglas fir. We had traveled about 100 yards when we came upon another sign that read, "Extreme Danger: Wild Animals."

"Not what I wanted to see," I declared.

"Don't worry," she answered. "Tony knows this Rae-Ron, and I'm pretty sure he knows we're coming."

"You sure?"

She bounded past me. I was surprised by her energy. She must have made a full recovery from the flu and fatigue that had laid her so low.

We passed a boulder pile along the bank of the stream and

soon began gaining elevation. Suddenly she froze in front of me. I caught up with her.

"What's going on?" I whispered.

"Listen."

"I don't hear a thing."

"Exactly. All the birds have stopped chirping. It's way too quiet."

"What are we talking about here—a black bear?" My heart was starting to pound. I removed my glasses.

"I doubt it. Black bears are pretty afraid of humans."

"What's that mean? What could be worse than a bear? A cougar?"

Suddenly, I knew. In the thicket ahead of us came a deep rumble that almost everyone from Bengal north recognizes instinctively as the harbinger of instant death—a Bengal tiger on the prowl. There he was, his eyes peering out at us from a willow thicket maybe 100 feet ahead. He was poised in the strike position.

"Run, Marianne—run for the rocks."

I turned down the path, running helter-skelter toward the boulder pile. I knew we only had a few seconds.

A roar broke the silence and I knew the tiger was on the move.

Now I could see the rocks. Yes, they could provide cover. I turned back toward Marianne: she was perhaps 20 yards behind me. To my horror she turned to face the oncoming tiger.

"Jeezus."

"Rrrr—arh!" came another cry—but now I realized it was too high-pitched to be coming from the tiger. It was from Marianne. Was she nuts?

The tiger was bearing down on her quickly. She sounded again, and to my utter amazement, the tiger stopped in his tracks just in front of her. And then the two of them just stared at each other, both of them motionless. The tiger clearly seemed surprised by this overly brave human.

Just when I thought the tiger would leap and break her like a twig, a human voice bellowed out from afar, "Nimba. Enough."

It was a powerful looking man in camouflage, perhaps 50 years old. It was hard to tell. He was toting a long rifle with a large scope.

"Nimba. Here, girl."

The tiger retreated, turned and rushed to his side.

"I gather you are the friends of Tony. Relax. Nimba is just a playful cub. She won't attack unless I allow it."

"Playful?" I was shaking like a leaf.

"You wouldn't have even seen her if she were serious."

I didn't doubt it.

"My name is Rae-Ron or *Byda* if you are partial to Arabic. Quite brave of you to come here. I don't get too many visitors."

"Visitors, or visitors who survive? I'm Pankaz and this is Marianne."

"Tony already filled me in."

He focused on Marianne and smiled. "You seem to have a way with tigers—smart enough to know that it would be futile to run."

"I've spent time with them."

"I would have guessed that. Circus?"

"Yeah, in a previous life."

"You never told me that," I replied.

"Need to know. You didn't."

"We have another friend back at the trailhead," said Marianne. "Tony—I guess you already know him. The tiger might give him a heart attack."

"Yeah, he doesn't trust Nimba even though she's just a kitten. You follow her back to the cabin and I'll fetch Tony. Home Nimba," he declared.

Nimba gracefully pivoted and leaped off down the path.

"You better get going. You'll lose her if you aren't nimble."

Rae-Ron vanished down the path in the other direction, and we hurried to keep up with nimble Nimba. Well, Marianne hurried. I was a bit more cautious, not convinced that this tiger could be trusted.

My curiosity got the better of me: "Why exactly did you stop and face the tiger?"

"I knew it was our only chance. Also, I realized she was a babe. Young tigers are different than fully-grown ones. Almost impossible to stop the large ones."

Jim Currie

Chapter 31

Pigeoneers at NORAD

Ten minutes later we arrived at a cabin that was really more of a bunker built into a small hill. I had a pretty good idea why. From the air it would be very hard to spot, maybe even hard to spot by infra-red satellite. Rae-Ron was clearly living underground in more ways than one.

The cabin door was open. Nimba raced inside and settled near a fireplace to jaw on a pterodactyl-sized bone.

Marianne took a seat in a rocker a few feet from Nimba and began talking to her while I surveyed the insides of the cabin.

"Quite a bone there, girl."

I let them discuss the bone and surveyed the cabin. It was austere but well designed. It included a sleeping loft, a compact kitchen, an adjoining study and small bathroom. It was wired for electricity, which I assumed was coming from some on-site source.

I took a few steps toward the study and peered inside. It was filled with impressive electronic gear—several different high-resolution screens and computers.

I was still inspecting the equipment when I heard Nimba rumble and bound out the front door playfully. Rae-Ron had arrived in the clearing with Tony. Tony was carrying two birdcages. I watched the sight through an open window. Tony caught view of the tiger and turned away, in the process losing his balance.

With cat-like quickness Rae-Ron grabbed Tony's arm, preventing the fall and steadying the cages. But now the tiger was airborne and landing on Rae-Ron's chest, knocking him over. With the tiger licking his face, Rae-Ron broke into a laugh.

Tony shook his head ruefully.

"She knows you're not food," smiled Rae-Ron. "She may even realize the pigeons aren't food."

"*Not* food, girl," Rae-Ron chastised with a faint grin.

"Sure thing," declared Tony.

Tony thrust one cage toward Rae-Ron. "This one's from RB and the other is mine."

It suddenly dawned on me what was going on. "This is a pigeon exchange."

Tony rolled his eyes.

"You know about this?" I asked turning to Marianne.

"I knew about the pigeon network but not the tiger."

"I need to give Pankaz and Marianne the tour," declared Rae-Ron.

Inside the cabin Nimba returned to her bone and Rae-Ron showed me his electronics.

"Looks like NORAD here," I declared.

"Gets the job done," replied Rae-Ron. "Most of the electronics for the phased array are below ground. Gadgetry to keep the drones at bay," he grinned.

"I guess you knew we were coming."

He chuckled. "Message flew in this morning with a carrier and after that I picked you up outside of Petaluma."

I noticed a rack of rifles on the wall. No hunting rifles these—several mounted with high-power scopes. On the back wall I noticed several old photographs of Gulf War vintage. I approached and gave them a closer look.

One of them showed what looked like Rae-Ron as a younger man, posing with some buddies next to a dead Iraqi tank. Another photo showed him cradling a rifle and proudly displaying some kind of medal.

Now a faint memory flew back to me, about a decorated Gulf War marksman who wasn't exactly adjusting to civilian life and had turned survivalist. Could this be the guy? What was his name? Something very distinctive.

Rysht Byda—that was it. The Iraqi's had given him that, supposedly because he left a white feather on his dead targets.

Bingo. There it was in one of the photos sticking out of a unit baseball cap.

We detoured to Rae-Ron's pigeon coup located outside a back door. Tony was already there inspecting and feeding the pigeons.

For ten minutes they talked training, including diet, practice flights and even favored music. Rae-Ron had a pigeon who preferred Sinatra; Tony's were serenaded with R and B. Rae-Ron wanted to know about Rosie's development and Tony beamed, "She's a world beater—getting stronger every day. I can't wait until the molt."

I left them alone to discuss pigeon conformation and molting and returned to the front room, discovering that Marianne had now become Nimba's second best friend. She had planted herself at Marianne's feet and was purring. Marianne was stroking her.

Rae-Ron and Tony appeared, and Tony took one look at the tiger and retreated to the kitchen.

Rae-Ron seemed amused that Nimba had bonded so quickly

with Marianne.

"I guess this fits with what I heard from Red Bill. Apparently she whispers to tigers as well."

"So you know Red Bill?"

"Actually he's the one who connected me to Tony and his pigeons. Met Bill playing cards in Vegas. He was the best—no one even close."

"And he knew you were a sniper in Kuwait? How could that work out?"

"It turns out we shared an interest in math."

"Math?"

"Yeah, figured out proofs together, working on corollaries and thinking up applications. Before long we found that our equations were matching up on lots of things."

"Like what?"

"Leadership, corruption, real freedom."

"The guy's a Marxist."

"I don't hold that against him. We still argue but manage to find lots of common ground."

Rae-Ron whistled for Nimba to follow him and announced, "Time for dinner….This will take the edge off her."

"I'm all for that," Tony declared from the kitchen where he was soothing his nerves with a beer.

Returning from the feeding, Rae-Ron set to work on fixing us a meal. Twenty minutes later he announced "Soup's on." Nimba appeared and now seemed sleepy.

We seated ourselves at a small table in front of a steaming plate of Thai stir-fry. Rae-Ron inhaled and exhaled deeply, closed his eyes and murmured some sort of mantra I thought might be Tibetan. His eyes opened and he poured us all wine.

"Let us all learn to travel on soft paws and leave shallow footprints," he declared.

"In praise of all such creatures that enrich our lives," declared Marianne.

"Pretty tasty," declared Tony after his first bite.

"Fresh spices are the key," added Rae-Ron. He ran through the ingredients which included several chilies and gingers I had never heard of. Both Tony and Marianne seemed to know something about this—even knew where you could get the ingredients in Chinatown.

"I used to have a Thai girl who cooked up a storm and after awhile I started to figure out what she was up to. Anything with ginger and chili peppers was her specialty."

"And now you've got a devoted tiger instead of a girl friend," declared Tony surveying Nimba who was now slumbering.

Rae-Ron smiled, "More predictable," he answered, "And better hunting companion."

The cat was snoring, but her ears seemed perked to the conversation.

"If you don't mind me asking, where did you get her?" asked Marianne.

"Her momma died at one of those animal parks, and I didn't think it made much sense for her to be living alone. I knew she was going to be sold to a zoo. I couldn't let that happen."

Marianne nodded.

"So you liberated her?" I asked.

"I guess you could say that."

"I know a couple of elephants that need liberation," answered

Marianne. "Are you interested?"

"Like I told Tony, tigers and elies don't mix but some of my neighbors might be interested in selling land—pot growers who figure to get out before they're busted."

"What would they take?" asked Marianne. "The elies will need 20 acres. We might not have much left if we have to pay off the zoo."

"We'll get the money," answered Tony.

"I'll inquire and get back to you."

He turned toward me. "Red Bill thought I might be able to help you get to the bottom of what happened at Santa Rosa."

Tony nodded. Now I realized that this was another reason for the trip.

"You're so devious," I declared shaking my head.

Tony grinned. "I would have told you but I was afraid of bugs," he answered.

"I've already got some ideas about the killing," declared Rae-Ron. "Can you pin-point where the shooting took place?"

"You got a map?"

"Maps I got." He handed me one within arm's reach.

I circled where the train was stopped.

"Got any pictures of the body?"

"No, but I talked to the medics and they told me he died from a single bullet."

"Do you know where he was hit?"

"The medics at the hospital said between the eyes. They said it was a rifle shot—high-powered."

"Your article said there were *Bilgewater* guys at the fair-grounds?"

"Yup."

"I'll just tell you this. If this poor kid was killed the way I think he was, a lot of people should be nervous. Still, I don't want to jump to conclusions. Once every thirty years I'm wrong," he laughed.

"Fair enough," I answered. "You might also take note of the fact that in the last 48 hours, more people have been disappearing."

I already know about this. "I could see it coming a long time ago. It's one of the reasons for all of this." He gestured toward the back room and the connections to the dish.

We finished the meal and agreed to stay in touch. "I guess you know how to reach me."

"Coo, coo, coo," declared Tony.

Rae-Ron retrieved five medium-range homers from his coop, placed them in a large box cage, and handed it to Tony.

"Take especially good care of Rosy," declared Tony. "Let her go in a couple of days. If you want, you can give her a taste of brew. She likes that when she's listening to BB King."

Jim Currie

Chapter 32
Heartful Caretaking

After we returned to the city, I immersed myself in work, surfacing several days later to learn from Tony that Hansa had taken a turn for the worse. Marianne was back at the zoo full- time, taking vacation days.

At the zoo I found Marianne reflexively shuttling back and forth between the intensive care room and the barn, alternately comforting Gigi and hovering over Hansa and the vet, trying to be of some use. Apparently the experimental immune system drug had quit working and the zoo vet, a fellow named Davidson, was at a loss trying to knock out the infection.

Dr. Shipp remained in the background allowing Marianne to be present, knowing that the elephants trusted her. Finally, he suggested she should go home and get some rest, but she wasn't about to do that when she thought the elephants needed her. She had now been up 28 straight hours and had hardly eaten.

I managed to pull her away for a quick meal at a restaurant next to the zoo, but she only picked at her food, absorbed in wondering what more she might do to help.

"There's a really good vet in Santa Monica who might have some ideas about the infection."

"I thought Davidson was one of the best elephant docs around."

"Right now nothing is working. Someone's got to do something fast."

"I think you have to leave this in the hands of the vets."

She didn't seem to hear me, or maybe she just didn't agree.

"Why don't you give me your key, and I'll make a speed-run to your apartment. I can bring you what you need and you can stay here."

"I think her name begins with an "A"—Anderson or Andreison or something like that. Maybe it was San Diego she was from—where the zoo is. I'm getting all my cities confused these days. I think I wrote myself a note on this when I was at that conference."

"That conference, which conference?"

"At the Denver conference—a week ago."

"That's when we saw Rae-Ron and Nimba."

"Whatever." She looked very puzzled and seemed to be gazing past me.

"Just give me your key and tell me what you want. Your key, Marianne."

She fumbled through a pocket absently and handed me a pen and a slip of paper."

"No, your key sweetheart."

She produced her key, and I laid enough money on the table to cover the meal plus a generous tip.

"Anything in particular in terms of clothes or meds?"

"Who could I call? I need my address book."

"I'll get your address book. Anything else? Drugs and toiletries?"

She didn't answer.

"I'll just pick up everything you might need and meet you back at the elephant barn…Are you all right?"

"Everything's fine. I'll meet you in a few hours after you go to my apartment. You'll probably need my key."

"You already gave it to me, sweet one." I kissed her on the forehead and raced for my car. I had never seen her like this. In this unraveled state she couldn't be of much help to any two-footed or four footed being.

At her apartment I quickly filled a back pack with clothes from a dresser along with toiletries and a couple of prescription bottles from her bathroom cabinet. The *Dimemoral* was there along with two other prescriptions from the same doctor.

When I arrived at the zoo and made my way to the elephant barn, a terrible series of wild and erratic distress calls pierced the heavy San Francisco fog. It morphed to a deep rumble that was dark with horror. Instantly I knew that baby Hansa was dead and Gigi was beside herself.

As I approached, I could see that Marianne, Dr. Davidson and two staff members had carried baby Hansa's lifeless body out to the yard so that Gigi and Sari could be with her. The sight was heartbreaking. Gigi kept trying to lift the baby to her feet, and with every failure screamed with agony. For a flickering moment I pictured myself flailing underwater at the glass window of the *Lucknow Mail* with my bare hands. Sari was doing her best to help but seemed to realize that Hansa was gone.

My eyes fell on Marianne. Her full attention was focused on Hansa and Gigi. She first tried singing but it did no good, and Marianne herself seemed equally distraught. In the background, Dr. Shipp was talking somberly with Dr. Davidson. As I approached, I heard them discussing the need for a necropsy to see if they could figure out why the drug had failed. Marianne seemed oblivious to this.

I decided not to distract her by asking what had happened or to tell her what I had brought from her apartment. I just took the pack to the caretaker's room and left it in the open locker where her jacket was hanging. On my way out, my eyes made contact with Dr. Davidson and then Dr. Shipp. They both shook their heads despairingly. Shipp seemed to anticipate my question. "We'll wait a bit on the necropsy. Marianne says Gigi and Sari need to be with Hansa to deal with their grief."

For 24 hours, Gigi refused to leave the dead baby, continually nuzzling the body with her trunk and emitting eerie, woeful rumbles. Marianne remained nearby, comforting Gigi in ways I didn't understand—words and touch together with knowing looks that I suppose females of all species understand much better than any male. At night, she remained at the zoo rather than returning to her apartment.

From Tony I learned that after the third day of vigil, Dr. Davidson conducted the necropsy and determined that the actual cause of death was a leakage of the herpes virus from the intestinal tract into the bloodstream.

Because of Marianne's insistence, Hansa was buried in the yard so that Gigi and Sari could be near her. There the three of them remained for most of a week, Marianne imploring the elephants to eat, occasionally offering a banana or another favored fruit, just being with them and meeting their own sorrowful eyes with sympathy and caring touch.

I knew that Marianne had to be running out of clean clothes

and decided to visit her apartment again to prepare another CARE package.

After gathering what I thought she might need, I sat at her kitchen table and noticed all the subtle touches that expressed Marianne's personality. An incense burner lay on a small altar of sorts across from her bed. On the table a bejeweled Indian elephant bore a votive candle on his back next to a serene Buddha. I drew closer for an inspection. The candle was well-burned. Behind the elephant was an animal-husbandry badge. Next to that was a regal painting of an elephant matriarch and her family.

I was quite sure that this was the famous African elephant, Echo, that so many TV specials had featured. Behind Echo and her family was a card with an artistic rendering of a joyous African elephant and her baby. I inspected it more closely: it was from the Kruger Elephant Reserve in South Africa. Inside was a picture of Marianne and a friend next to an adorable baby elephant whose trunk was wrapped around Marianne's leg. It said the following:

"There is always a baby elephant out there needing our help and asking for a chance to teach us to love again—trunks of love from Jody (and your adoring Kibo)."

Clearly this was someone who knew Marianne very well. Perhaps she was the one who would know if there was something in Marianne's past that explained that nightmare on our night together.

Nearby on a small fold-down desk I discovered *The Book of Elephant.* Marianne had clearly been working diligently on it before the crisis. She had removed the binder and placed each chapter in a separate stack. Next to each were her own notes and planned additions.

Ironically perhaps, she had devoted special attention to the chapter on memory and elephant grief. I was sure my father would have appreciated this.

Blessing and Curse:
Burden of Memory for Elephants
(Excerpts from *Book of Elephant,* Chapter 10
with additions by Marianne Moresby italicized

An elephant's great memory is a blessing as well as curse. Because of its huge brain and keen senses of smell, hearing and touch, an elephant can identify and imprint threats from a distant past and recall who was friendly, who was generous, and who was kind.

Memory is used to find food and water in times of drought and hardship, and even to decide who to cooperate with in solving problems of the herd and family.

An elephant's trunk and sensitive feet play an important role in constantly picking up sensations, vibration and textures. An elephant can carefully hover its sensitive and massive feet inches above a beloved dog or downed companion, allowing it to make contact with or lick the elephant. There will be no danger to the friend.

An elephant can recognize the distinctive smell of up to 20 different individual elephants by their urine. Its fantastic trunk is made up of hundreds of small tactile muscles that scan the subtleties of form, granularity and smoothness to record a textural snapshot.

But these same sensitivities can make for great pain and hurt. An elephant will be repelled and run from bees and remember the pain they inflicted on her ears, her feet or around her eyes. She will know where this occurred and steer clear of it in her future visits and migrations. An elephant is equally wary of places where she has encountered snakes that might bite her sensitive feet or those of her babies and friends.

Elephants are among the most social of species and prone to despair and depression if isolated and unable to commune, communicate, play and socialize with other elephants. Young elephants will not forget being torn from the parents and supportive members of the herd, being forced into isolation and confinement. For an elephant, this kind of abuse is a living form of death which may go underground for years but then suddenly be visited on her captors just when they think she has been tamed and cowed to be docile and obedient.

Remembering the trauma of childhood, elephants have also been known to lash out many years later at poachers or killers of their parents. An old saying among wise men is that it is never smart to make an enemy of an elephant, especially an alpha elephant who other elephants take counsel in to decide who is friend or foe.

An elephant will not forget betrayal, abuse or abandonment.

An elephant's grief over the loss of a loved one, particularly a baby elephant or beloved leader, is profound and deep. When an elephant dies, its family engage in intense mourning and burial rituals, conducting week-long vigils over the body, carefully covering it with earth, brush and limbs, often revisiting the bones for years afterward. At the grave, they will caress the bones with their trunks, often taking turns rubbing along the teeth of a skull's lower jaw, the way living elephants do in greeting.

Elephants have been known to mourn the loss of human friends and protectors, sometimes traveling great distances to stand in vigil at the place where the loved one has died.

A story from generations ago tells of a great Brahmin descended from Gautama who defended elephants of several herds over many years, protecting them from those who overworked them in the forests, who broke up families, who sold babies barely weaned. When the great man died, elephants passed the word of his demise across the land using their long-distance rumbles. Soon thereafter, wild elephants began streaming to his burial site single-file in long lines that stretched across the landscape in many directions. The gathering of elephants was quiet and reverent and lasted for nearly a week as the elephants showed little interest in food. Finally, perhaps on a signal from a wise leader, they turned and returned home on silent feet in the same gentle and mindful manner by which they had come.

I made sure that I left no footprints in Marianne's apartment when I headed for the zoo with my CARE package. I hoped to talk to Marianne, but when I arrived, I could see that she was busy with the elephants. I left the package with a staff member and returned to my car.

Chapter 33
Salvation Army Airlines

I wanted to remain in San Francisco for the end of the vigil but five days after Hansa's death I received word from Tony, apparently communicated to him by pigeon from Red Bill, that a fellow fitting Ivan's description had been picked up by emergency medical technicians in a dump outside of Jackson, Mississippi.

I called the hospital and the local papers in Jackson and was able to confirm that it was Ivan. He had suffered serious head injuries and was now recuperating in an extended care facility. I knew there was a story here. Betty agreed, advancing the grand total of $300 to take care of all my expenses including airfare to Jackson and back.

I reviewed the red-eye possibilities and judiciously selected Salvation Army Airlines. The itinerary included flights on a fleet of abused 727's and wind-up Beechcrafts shuttling to and from airports in the rural South. The seats of these molting birds didn't recline; the snacks glorified WWII K-rations; and the stewardesses were unmarried, undated, life-time members of Weight Watchers. They were friendly, cheery and flirtatious to a fault, which I suspected was part of a plot to keep me from noticing the late-stage COPD of the engines glued to the wings with stale Elmer's.

Midway to my terminus at Stonewall Jackson State Airport on a 5000-hour layover in Dallas, serendipity struck in the form of a notice for a book reading. Daphne Drakenfeld, head of the Kruger Elephant Reserve in South Africa was making a presentation at a Dallas bookstore for her memoir *My Life Among the Elephants of South Africa*. Timing and location were perfect—the reading was only an hour away.

Bad bus connections and disorientation delayed me. I reached the bookstore just after Daphne had finished her talk and was signing books. When my turn came to talk to her I introduced myself as a reporter on elephants for *The Barb*, interested in reviewing her book.

"Terrific," she answered, handing me a press release.

"I have more than a professional interest in what you do," I declared. "I grew up around elephants and my father was a mahout in India. I'm also a very good friend of one of the people who worked for you—Marianne Moresby."

"My gosh, you know Marianne? She was always one of my favorites, and the elies adored her. How is she doing? How is her health?"

"She's doing fine. Why do you ask?"

She seemed to draw back slightly. "We didn't want to lose her, but she felt she needed to go to the States. I just assumed it had something to do with health or family."

"Maybe you talk about this in your book, but were there any terrible tragedies at the reserve?"

"Yes, I talk about the many babies we lost. It's so sad and heartbreaking. The young ones are especially vulnerable, as I am sure you know."

"Yes, very much so. Were there any terrible traumas that involved Marianne or her friend Jody? Wasn't there also a baby named Kibo?"

"Darling Kibo is doing fine. She is one of our great success stories, thanks to both Marianne and Jody. She just came back on her own to visit us after being returned to her herd. In fact, I believe I have a picture of her that perhaps you might want to pass on to Marianne or Jody."

She handed me a precious picture of Kibo at the gate of the reserve with her trunk extended toward Daphne.

"Jody's not at the reserve, either?"

"No, she's gone back to school to get a PhD in zoology. I believe she's at LSU. We're hoping she'll come back to us when she's finished her dissertation."

I thanked her profusely and headed back to the airport, along the way playing with possibilities for a return re-route that might take me to Baton Rouge.

After a two-wheeled mother-of-God landing on the weeds at Andrew Jackson Airport, I found my way to a nearby bus stop and domiciled at a cheapo trucker-hotel just inside the Jackson city limits. The next morning I arrived at Ivan's care facility.

The nurse led me in, explaining that Ivan was under heavy doses of codeine but could probably use a "bit of cheer." I got the feeling I was going to be his first guest.

I would have been hard-pressed to recognize the fellow in the bed with bruised face, bandaged nose, and crop of face-stubble as Ivan Bochinsky. From half-destroyed dark glasses, he was staring blankly at a relic television set showing a rerun of the *Dukes of Hazard.*

"Is this red-neck hell or my imagination?" he muttered to the nurse with slobber on his lips. Then he met my eyes: "My God, I know you."

I thrust my hand toward him, and he gratefully offered me a resolute grip that approximated pasta el dente. The poor son of a bitch had seen better days.

"I came to find out what happened to you."

He shook his head woefully. "They dumped me in a goddam landfill as if I were a gutted catfish. What kind of people dump a human being in a landfill?"

"It looks like they did more than that."

"I only remember part of it. I'm sure I was drugged. After I got picked up, there was this young snot telling me that I could trust him and that no matter what he would make sure that I got a chance to repent and embrace Jesus as my savior—one of those immaculate shitheads they groom at Bob Jones University." Ivan wiped his mouth. "I can't stop drooling. Then some heavy comes in and starts telling me that I might as well spill my guts because my life is over."

"Any identification shown to you?"

"I demanded it and they just laughed at me. They said a new confessor was in town."

"Did they mention anything like PERP or what they were arresting you for?"

"They said I was an enemy combatant, and that meant they could do whatever they wanted and no one would ever hear about it."

Ivan rattled off a choice description of his interrogators that I had to use in my copy. "...Then, Tom Cruise says he'll tell my grandkids that I was truly sorry for all the terrible things I did."

"What things?" I answered. "Ain't done anything except exercise my pecker too little."

"The little one said I was a pervert, and the big one said it was time to tune me up."

"You don't remember getting hit?"

"I remember this terrifying needle in the side of my neck and then everything getting woozy. I remember going through the security entrance of a military base and then another hypo."

"I wonder if they gave you something so that you wouldn't remember."

"Bingo."

"Do you remember the dumping?"

"Sort of. Remember the big 'muthah saying, let's get rid of this godless Communist filth...remember him pouring alcohol on me—thought it might be gasoline."

"I started crying, and I soiled my pants. Maybe that's what saved me. He dropped me on a pile of hospital waste. It was probably radioactive. And there I lay for however long it was."

"And then the police found you?"

"No—the black dump scroungers. I remember this big black guy in coveralls and his lady friend. They're the ones that saved me. Picked me up in his big Black arms and carried me down the road and called the police; after that came the medics."

"People need to hear about this."

"If anyone cares," he answered woefully. "If anyone believes it."

"They will. I'll make sure of it. You got family coming?"

"My grandson's on the way."

I started to turn toward the door, and I heard him whisper back at me.

"Pankaz," he declared drooling again.

"Yes."

"You're a good and decent person."

"You too, Ivan."

I placed a call to Vincent who was shocked by the story, and said that he would make sure to contact Ivan's grandson and send some money to help Ivan get back to Berkeley. He would also send money to test for any drugs still left in Ivan's system that might erase memory.

In two different Podunk airports, while waiting for connecting flights via Salvation Army Airlines to Baton Rouge I submitted the following special for *The Barb*.

Guantanamo Comes to America
Ivan Bochinsky Tortured and Dumped
by Pankaz Panday

Ivan Bochinsky, the Berkeley maker of specialty pies who was recently picked up and detained without warrant under the Private Enterprise Protection Act (PERP), was found earlier this week in a mound of syringes, old scrubs and rubber gloves in a radioactive dump in Jackson, Mississippi. He was in serious condition after treatment normally reserved for inmates of Guantanamo, Abu Ghraib and the Black Hole of Calcutta.

His vacation trip, unadvertised in Conde Nast and Gulag Quarterly, began with a spirited pickup three weeks ago by two men on Telegraph Avenue. He described one as a "sawed-off religious smiler with a cross and a buzz-cut," and the other as a "Chetnik with a toothache." They both claimed to be acting under authority of the Private Enterprise Protection Act (PERP) but no credentials were presented.

Over the course of nearly two weeks, Bochinsky reclined comfortably in car trunks, black vans and body sacks, traveling to an array of secret retreats probably recognizable to Edgar Allen Poe, Joseph Conrad and Alexander Solzhenitsyn.

The abuse began when Ivan demanded to know the reason for his arrest, to which one fellow replied that he might as well embrace Jesus Christ as his savior along with a full confession of terrorist associations. Intemperately flouted by Mr. Bochinsky who saluted with his middle finger, this was followed by a hypo to the side of his neck.

For several weeks Bochinsky was grilled with questions unlikely to appear in the TV quiz show, Jeopardy. Categories included, *What Are You hiding? What Jihadists Are You Talking To? Why Are You Visiting These Terror-Porno Websites?*

"Enhanced interrogation" followed—leaving telltale signs: a broken nose, a fractured right orbital, deep contusions to his skull, electrical burn marks on his scrotum, and a mysterious pneumonia that has been observed among past recipients of waterboarding.

Bochinsky's return to American civil society came five days ago when he was discovered up to his neck in hospital waste by two indigent scroungers in a Jackson, Mississippi landfill. He had been doused with Rot Gut Red to make it appear that he was drunk.

Blood samples and a tox-screen have been ordered to determine whether Bochinsky was given a drug to induce amnesia. Federal authorities from both the FBI and Homeland Security have refused comment.

Chapter 34
Jody Reveals All As She Knows It

Jody was working away in a graduate study room at LSU when I found her after a phone call to the Department of Zoology. She wore Tina Fey dark rims, giving her a studious look, was warm and gregarious and glad to meet any friend of Marianne, whom she said she hadn't talked to for nearly a year.

I gave her a quick run-down on the recent flurry of elephant activism in San Francisco, as well as the death of baby Hansa. When I came to the way Hansa had died and Marianne's vigil over the baby's grave, she held her breath.

"I hope this doesn't scar her any further."

"What do you mean?" I replied.

"I don't know if I should tell you this," she answered with hesitation. "You are very close, right?"

I nodded.

"Marianne took the loss of the baby elephants very personally."

"Yes, I've seen that."

"At Kruger, we knew that the young orphans might do well at first but their immune systems were very weak. They needed their mothers and their mother's milk. Just when you thought they were getting strong enough and able to make it, something would happen."

I could tell that she was feeling me out to see if I was revelation-worthy.

"Marianne would go into these terrible tailspins when an orphan died. She was as bad as the momma elephants themselves when they lost newborns. The worst part was the way she would blame herself for not doing enough. Even Lady Daphne had to talk to her about this, telling her that such grief didn't do any of the other orphans any good. They needed someone strong to help them get through their own trauma. I even got into an argument with her about this."

I nodded. "Yes, she takes every loss to heart."

"Sometimes I think people are born with too much empathy. That's what I told her and that's what made her mad."

"Nothing more than that?"

Again she hesitated and inspected me closely.

"I won't say a word if you don't want me to. I just need to know."

"Okay, but this is only for you. When we first became roommates at the sanctuary we shared a room in the bunkhouse. At night Marianne would have these terrible nightmares and sometimes wake up crying."

"I know about this," I answered.

"I begged her to tell me what was wrong and finally she did. She told me about how she first started working in South Africa circuses with the cats and the elephants. She loved all the animals."

"Yes."

"Well, she said the wrong thing about the horrible bull hooks they were using to control the elephants, and they fired her. She couldn't get work right away and finally landed a job at *Wild World* outside of Sarasota.

"*Wild World* put her in charge of all their elephants, mommas and babies included, and at first it worked out pretty well, but then the park started losing money and decided to supplement income by breeding elephants." She stopped abruptly, surveying my reaction.

"I'm following you."

"Well, they started separating the babies from the mothers at too early an age and selling them to zoos and circuses. The elies realized what was going on and started to go crazy. Marianne did her best to stop this, but these people were pretty craven."

"So this is what scarred her—and created the nightmares?"

"Sort of..."

"Just trust me, please."

"Okay, I'll tell you the rest if you promise not to tell anyone. It was one incident in particular. She never gave me the full story, but what she said was that there was this one momma elephant, named Winkie, who was pretty skitterish because her first baby was ripped from her at age one. So Winkie gave birth to this second baby two years later. It was premature so she had it in a forested area of the wildlife park when no one but the other elies was around. The next day she brought the baby back to the barn where Marianne showered it with love and affection.

"Unbeknownst to anyone including Marianne, Winkie had given birth to another—a twin—but left it in the forest with the female nannies.

"But Marianne realized that something wasn't right. Winkie just didn't have enough milk for the baby in the barn and this was because every day when she was allowed to go out on the range.

she would sneak off into the woods and suckle the hidden baby until it had had enough.

"One day, Marianne figured out what might explain the lack of milk and trailed Winkie into the woods where she was joyfully nursing her favored baby."

My heart was beating wildly; I was breathless.

"Apparently Marianne assured Winkie that if she brought the baby back to the barn, she would make sure it was never taken away from her. Winkie resisted, trying to protect her baby, not fully trusting Marianne. Finally she relented and followed Marianne back to the barn with her baby."

Jody stopped as she could see that I was shaking my head with recognition of the way the drama played out.

"Yes," declared Jody. "The first baby was sold early and then *Wild World* took the second one and put it up for sale as well. Marianne protested, but it didn't do any good. According to Marianne, Winkie went crazy after that and would never let Marianne touch her ...Two years to the day after the twins were born, August 1, Winkie was put down as a violent elephant, and it broke Marianne's heart. This was the wound that she revealed to me on the night that she woke up crying at the Kruger Reserve."

The tears streamed from my eyes.

Jody kissed me on the cheek, and I told her I had to go. I cried my way all the way to the Baton Rouge airport. I cried for the baby elephants; I cried for Winkie; I cried for Marianne and I cried for the promises I had made to Amita and Arundhati that I would come back for them.

Chapter 35
Prize-Winning Journalism

When I arrived back in the Bay Area, I learned that Marianne had called in sick. I had no idea whether she was actually ill or just too distraught to work. I called her at her apartment but she didn't answer and her voicemail had been shut off. I checked with Tony, Roger and Darrell, and they all said that they too had called and weren't able to get reach her.

What I worried about most was that she might be recriminating over what had happened, blaming herself for letting the elephants down, perhaps repeating the self-indictment over Winkie and the twins.

As each day passed without hearing from her, I thought that she might be dropping into a sinkhole that was too deep to climb out of.

I remembered how relatives had tried to get me to talk in the aftermath of the *Lucknow Mail Disaster*. I had no interest. My only soul mate was an imagined other for whom I composed pages of detail about every bloody and horrific train accident from Calcutta to Bangalore, complete with detail about the stupid, lazy, incompetent people responsible for them from mindless cowherds to superstitious Hindu engineers to idiotic train schedulers who should have known better than to stack train after train on overworked, poorly maintained tracks that crossed pasture land populated by cows that were bound to find their way onto the tracks.

The indictments were all between the lines and buried in the statistics, but they were there for my attentive friend. I reserved a special animus for those who ushered their loved ones onto broken-down, overcrowded trains that collided with other derelicts and ended up killing everyone onboard.

I didn't deserve to be the one who lived. My sister was much smarter, more caring with a bigger spirit. I never would have made the sacrifice she had for me, at least willingly. I would have begrudged her for every second I spent in that dehumanizing sweat shop, and the future she had stolen from me.

If you read closely, you might even catch my contempt for unkept promises. I spoke of diverted money allocated to track repair, missing steel and equipment that traced to the black market, and secure fences never built to keep cows off the tracks. What I didn't divulge were the vacuous promises that still whispered back to me.

Yeah, I had returned dutifully to the half-submerged train to make my pathetic, ridiculous attempt to break the glass with weak fists and failing breath. So weak, I couldn't even shatter it with a sharp rock. And then I had paddled back to shore where I simply laid down and gave up. I gave up. I couldn't imagine Arundhati or Amita ever giving up.

Derailment and Disaster: Horrors of the Indian Railway System—this was the title of the essay I submitted that summer for my class paper. My teacher raved over it. It won best journalistic essay and was then forwarded for consideration to the national review board endowed by a rich Brahmin. I won the competition and with it a scholarship upon acceptance to the University of California,

Berkeley.

No one was more surprised than I that Berkeley admitted me. No one penetrated how that essay had come about and the kind of person who had authored it.

Nine months later when I flew out of Calcutta to London and then onward to the US, I knew that I would never return to India. If possible I would disremember all the horrors of the cursed Vedic floodplain and its sentinel elephants. It was the only way I figured I could survive without my beloved sister and mother.

So I knew first-hand the ravages of grief and the importance of dealing with nightmare in whatever manner possible, free from the assumptions and judgments of others. I knew also the impotence and complications of self-administered nectars to induce amnesia.

Jim Currie

Chapter 36
Grim Reaper at 400 Yards

I wanted to do another elephant story about the plight of captive elephants if only to buoy Marianne's spirits, and was mulling over the possibilities on a walk down Broadway when I spotted Tony. He approached and stumbled on the sidewalk in front of me. I helped him up, in the process realizing that he had slipped something inside my jacket pocket. We exchanged pleasantries and a few minutes later I was reading the note he had left: Ralph Cramden, his star middle-distance homer, had just arrived from the Tiger Ranch. Rae-Ron wanted me to meet him at a pub in Petaluma. The rendezvous was scheduled for the following Tuesday at noon. I was to bring throwaway clothes and shoes, and make sure I wasn't bugged.

The next Tuesday when I arrived at the pub, a waitress appeared and after studying me closely declared, "The restroom is down the hall."

There in one of the stalls I found a package of clothes and put them on. At the bottom of the package was a note that I should exit the back door and "meet RR at Peggy's Diner." It was a few hundred yards away.

Rae-Ron was occupying a booth at the back of the diner when I came through the door. While finishing off a piece of banana cream pie, he asked to look at my cameras. It only took him a few seconds to declare them bug-free.

"Just follow me," he declared, waving to the owner, Peggy, a silver haired octogenarian who blew him a kiss. He led me toward another back door. We were soon on our way by Land Rover to the outskirts of Santa Rosa, not far from where Willy's train ride had ended.

After parking the car in a grove of trees a few miles outside of town, we made our way by foot to a sage-covered hill approximately 400 yards north of the rail line. "This is it," he declared, "This is where Willy Davis was taken out by a world-class sniper with a Grim Reaper."

"How do you know this?"

"I found tracks, or I should say attempts to cover tracks. I'll show them to you."

He pointed to a smooth patch of ground that showed no evidence of tracks. I shot him a questioning glance.

"That's part of the clue," he declared. "You can see how smooth it is—different from normal weathering. The person who was here traveled on tiger paws."

"Okay, so you've got some subtle indications that someone was here, but how do you conclude that it was a sniper?"

"Not a sniper, a very special sniper." He moved to his right and pointed with his right arm toward the rail line as if it were a high-powered rifle. "This is where the shots took place from a tripod that cradled the Reaper."

"What's all this reaper business?"

"The .338 Grim Reaper Rifle is the weapon of choice of the several fellows I know in the US who could make this shot other than yours truly. There's more to it. I made some additional inquires with some people who saw the wounds, and everything fits with a .338 fired from this distance. Among other things, this is the only point that satisfies elevation criteria. From here he would also minimize wind-drift and glare.

"From this far away?"

"You've also got to understand the mentality of an ace—he would pride himself in making a difficult distance-shot."

"Okay, so maybe an egotistical sniper did kill Willy, but snipers are hired or ordered to put someone's lights out. Why would a boss go to all this trouble? If you could provoke Willy to hijack a train, you could certainly have three FBI agents or Bilgewater guys cuff him the second he got on the train."

"Sure," gleamed Rae-Ron. "But then you don't deliver *the white feather* if you get my drift."

"So you think there was a message in this?"

He smiled. "Shock and awe."

It did make sense and it did fit with the entire concept of shock and awe down to the visual of a runaway circus train driven by an anarchist who had to be stopped at any price.

"Okay, I'm starting to buy it, but as good as this sniper might have been, he still had to be very lucky to get a good shot. What are the chances that someone like Willy on board that train is going to be exposing himself at the right time?"

"That's good. He wouldn't be exposing himself unless there was a wrangler—someone making sure he showed himself at the right time. "

"So an agent-provocateur would have to be on the train? And all of this was carefully scripted."

"Exactly."

I decided to take some photos of the hill as well as the view toward the train line. When I was done, Rae-Ron said we had one last stop to make. We legged our way to the train line over a field of black sage, chaparral and buckbush. Along the right-of-way we came to two discarded wooden wine crates.

"Take a look."

I inspected them. "Looks like three bullet holes."

"Exactly." He reached inside his pocket and produced three relatively undamaged bullets. "These were his practice shots to calibrate the one that counted."

I nodded and reached for my camera.

When I finished, I popped the most critical question: "Who did it?"

"I've got two candidates—assuming that we can rule out a Russian and a Frenchman who are in the Middle East."

"My pen is poised."

"I need to make some inquiries, but I should be able to nail it down."

My article for *The Barb* didn't include the names. Vincent also helped me work through legal details.

Sniper Executes Green Giant
Link to New Police Powers
by Pankaz Panday

It was confirmed today from authoritative sources that Willy Davis, "The Jolly Green Giant" and elephant rescuer who hijacked a train from the Santa Rosa Fairgrounds on July 8, was killed by an elite marksman using a high powered .338 Grim Reaper rifle. The shot occurred at a distance of 400 yards just outside of Santa Rosa by a sniper of unknown affiliation lying in wait.

The available forensic evidence confirms that this was a shot that was planned even before the train was hijacked, thus suggesting that authorities or perhaps a private contractor either knew the hijacking was going to occur, or even instigated it with provocateurs. According to expert riflemen, only a limited number of marksman world-wide possess the skill to make the shot. Besides that, a "wrangler" would have been required to insure that Willy was exposed to the sniper at exactly the right moment.

State and Federal law officials, including chief counsels for the FBI and the US Office of Homeland Security, refused to answer questions as to whether they were investigating the possibility that the killing was authorized or enabled under the Private Enterprise Protection Act.

Davis was a known fugitive on the FBI's Most Wanted List and the Class-A Terrorist List, which includes all of the former.

It has been asserted by critics that the new law stands *habeas corpus* on its head and permits almost indiscriminate use of deadly force to protect people claimed to be "National Security Assets." Officials of the ACLU have decried the law as the most obscene insult yet to the 4th Amendment to the US Constitution.

Chapter 37
Chinatown

To my amazement, the story was picked up by *The Los Angeles Times* and then the *Guardian* in the UK. I even got a call from *Frontline* staff who seemed interested in a special if I possessed any unreported information.

I didn't share with them the disquietude that had nagged me since filing my story: I couldn't quite figure out the *Bilgewater*-Homeland Security connection.

I had never been much of a believer in conspiracy theories. They always seemed to violate Occam's Razor—the idea that the best solution in science or news reporting was the simplest one that explained the facts. I had no doubt about the malevolence of people like Harmsworth and Haney, but they were no longer in power, at least official power. Rae-Ron's theory about what happened at Santa Rosa would seem to require at least knowledge or complicity by some number of people working for Homeland Security or the FBI. Even if they left the dirty work to *Bilgewater*, they had to know what was going on.

Just two days after my story broke in the *Guardian*, I was making my way to *The Offshore* in hopes of seeing Marianne when I turned the corner toward Truman Jefferson's newsstand. Suddenly I was face to face with BD Harmsworth, smiling and offering me *The Sacramento Bee*.

"Looks like *The Bee* picked up your story."

"What do you know?"

"Care to have breakfast on me?"

"If it's a public place and out of the line of sniper fire."

"I know a place just down from your watering hole."

This was clearly mentioned to make me wonder what else he might have learned about my private life.

It only took a minute of chit-chat at the cafe before he declared, "You seem to be getting a lot of national attention with your stories."

"Funny how that works. I can never predict it."

"People love conspiracies, especially assassination stories. It simplifies the world for them so that they don't have to think seriously about messy problems."

"Now that seems a little fatuous coming from a master of deception. We both know that all kinds of people are tipping over these days who happen to say and do the wrong things. Some even land in garbage dumps covered with radioactive hospital waste."

"Yeah, poor Ivan had a bad day and so did Willy. Times aren't friendly to radicals."

"Yeah, but I'm wondering who the radicals really are. I also don't get how *Bilgewater* is connected to Homeland Security. Can you help me with this? Looks a lot like Iraq come-home-to-America."

"Can you help me understand a bit more about this Red Bill and his friends? What 'authoritative sources' did you rely on for your article? Must have been someone familiar with high-powered rifles and snipers, right?"

For a second we both simply smiled at each other.

"Ever see the movie Chinatown, Pankaz?"

"Sure, all about California water and the Sacramento floodplain."

"No, it was about Chinatown, a micro habitat where different rules apply. People vanish; people get deported for small discrepancies in their naturalization papers, people who are vulnerable become prey."

"Are you threatening me?"

"Of course not. Frankly, I like you. You're smart and we've got some things in common. I've learned a lot about you. I daresay you've dealt with a lot of nightmare and quite admirably, maybe better than I have."

"'I appreciate the concern. I hope you found someone to take care of your snakes."

"They can go several days without becoming dangerous." He smiled.

That afternoon, I took my curiosity about *Bilgewater* to the UC Business Library where I found a missing piece of the puzzle—a holding company with majority ownership of *Dingaling Brothers* including directors who sat on the *Bilgewater* board. Members also included two of the names from the Bush Administration War Council. Secondary tendrils extended to think-tanks and political action committees. The incest here rivaled that of Noah Cross, the John Huston character in Chinatown.

What troubled me most was that I wasn't sure how many people cared that Ivan had been kidnapped or worse-yet, arrested without benefit of *habeas corpus*. Add to this, the fact that Willy had been provoked into the hijacking and then assassinated. And now here was Harmsworth, the architect of shock and awe, coming to North Beach, arrogantly giving notice that there was no territory out of bounds. The reptiles were now out in public, sun bathing as they digested, and not at all worried that someone might put them back in a cage.

Chapter 38
Negotiating for Elephants

I shrugged off the intimidation attempt by Harmsworth, made a few notes about the corporate-government incest and checked my voicemail to see if Marianne might have left me a message. No, nothing. I was soon back at work on my story for Marianne about the plight of captive elephants.

Jody had mentioned that elephant breeding was big business, but how much could a private breeder make on a baby elephant? I was shocked by what I soon learned: zoos and circuses would pay $50,000 or more for a healthy baby, causing zoos, sanctuaries and breeding facilities to spend large amounts of money on artificial insemination, endlessly trying to impregnate the fertile females despite awareness that they could be carriers of the virus.

The infant mortality rate for elephants in zoos was over 40 percent, nearly triple the rate for elephants in the wild. The herpes virus that had killed baby Hansa could lie dormant and undetected for years and was transmissible to babies through childbirth. Because a lot of the females were shipped back and forth to breeding facilities, a large proportion of the 400 some elephants in the United States could easily be infected. It was clear that many breeders would go to extraordinary lengths to impregnate the females.

This was no simple and benign procedure. A poor Seattle elephant named Chai had been artificially inseminated 112 times, despite losing two babies to the virus. Finally, the zoo decided to give her a break.

Maybe most disgusting was the fact that babies born in the elephant mills were commonly jerked away from their mothers at age-one to meet the market demand. This struck me as especially heartless and I could see why Marianne would be so disturbed by it. In the wild, mothers and their female babies stayed together for life. Even males, which the zoos had little use for, maintained a lasting psychological link to mothers and nannies.

After calling a number of zoo breeders and the American Zoological Association, I managed to trace at least three of the baby deaths to *Wild World,* the park where Marianne had worked before leaving for the Kruger Reserve.

The Barb published my story in two parts. It included touching photographs of several of the babies that had died of the virus and an elaborate "forensic tree" that showed which babies in which zoos and circuses were related to which mothers. It also documented the age of nearly half the babies that were taken away prematurely from their mothers.

The story was picked up by papers all across the country. It provoked a follow-up by all the TV channels in the Bay Area and prompted a series of editorials calling for zoos to release their elephants to sanctuaries that would take better care of them.

Best of all, it prompted a hand-written letter from Marianne that arrived in a beautiful envelope on which she had drawn a picture of baby Hansa: "You did good for all of us, Pankaz. Love from Marianne and all your elephant friends."

It warmed my heart, though I guess I hoped for more. It

brought to mind passages from the *Book of Elephant* how elephants might be separated by great distance but stayed in touch with family through low-frequency rumbles. Yes, I could accept that. She knew how to reach me.

I left that letter on my kitchen table for a week and never let a cup of coffee or ice cream get near it.

Soon after the story broke, Vincent called and suggested that now was the time to meet with the zoo. He had already talked to Marianne and she had told him that for negotiation purposes she had over $30,000 in life savings that she would be glad to write him a check for or put it in some kind of trust to free Gigi and Sari.

She preferred not to come to any meetings with Dr. Shipp, but to devote her attention to helping Gigi who had recently turned listless and was again refusing to eat. She trusted Vincent implicitly.

Two days later Vincent and I met with Shipp in his office. As usual, Vincent cut a dashing image with his long gray hair and theatrical bearing, complete with cape. We exchanged pleasantries and Vincent stared directly at Shipp and declared, "Sir, we both realize you've got a problem on your hands. You've got sick elephants, mounting costs, members of your board who obviously aren't happy about the publicity you've been getting, and the prospect that your adversaries are going to ratchet up the pressure."

"I'm not sure who you've been talking to on our board, but I think you will find that nothing has changed. I think you need to come to the point. I've got pressing issues to attend to."

"The point is that you need to look at practicalities."

"What do you mean?"

"How much are they bringing in to the zoo versus their costs.

What's your bottom line?"

"I might be making a mistake here, but I don't think you've been elected to our finance committee."

"All I'm suggesting is that there is clearly an agreeable number that would bail you out of a very uncomfortable PR problem that is only going to get worse."

Shipp seemed to be thinking about it.

"Let's say you approach your board and tell them that you've got a buy-out offer of $75,000 for your elephants."

"Are you nuts? Do you know what they cost us and how much we've spent on them?"

"These are sunk costs. How much do you net on them? It's got to be a declining amount, given how sick they've been."

"There would be any number of zoos willing to offer a cool half million for Sari and Gigi. Healthy, child-bearing females are a valuable commodity."

"Assuming that they are healthy, which I wonder about based upon what Pankaz had turned up about the virus being ubiquitous and able to lie dormant, you would still have a PR problem on your hands. How many nasty letters has the zoo received in the last 48 hours?"

"Seventy-five thousand dollars is ridiculous."

"You know where to reach me if you have a counter-offer. My clients will give you five days to consider and reply. After that you can expect that the temporary moratorium on demonstrations will be lifted, to wit, a website assault that will look like Normandy on D-Day. I have a firm conviction that it might change the entire equation. Keep in mind that it's important to sell when you can get a decent price. Prices do go down and bubbles burst."

"I think you know the way to the door," replied Shipp.

Out in the parking lot my reservations erupted. "I don't think he's buying it."

"On the contrary, my read is that he's shifted and the only issue is the dollar amount. He knows that the zoo is in a precarious position, and they want out."

"Not for seventy-five thousand dollars—and by the way, where did you come up with that?"

"We needed a working number."

"Our working number is Marianne's life savings—thirty thousand dollars, which is not right to touch anyway, given her current state. Plus, this ignores what would be needed for land, feeding and taking care of the elephants."

"The idea is to first establish a cognitive commitment to sell. Once this is realized, we're in the game. If nothing else, I can begin making calls to see who wants to be a hero. I know a few folks with money who care about animals."

I detoured to the Elephant House to see how Marianne was doing in her nursing efforts with Gigi. Marianne didn't see me as I came through the door and was talking to Gigi who was prostrate on what amounted to a very large futon.

"Listen beloved one, we're in the same boat here," declared Marianne. "Sometimes, it seems impossible to go on. Sometimes the suffering is overwhelming, but know that you are loved. Sari loves you; Tony, Roger, Pankaz and I love you. I'm sure Hansa loves you as well."

Marianne stroked Gigi's great gray head and then her trunk, and I could see a faint response in her tired grief-stricken eyes. Then came a low rumble. Gigi was listening.

"I promised you that I would get you out of here and that is what will happen, even if it takes all the energy I have left. But you will need to help. You will need to get up. Even if you don't really want to, you must do this for Sari. She too deserves a chance for a better life."

Gigi rolled her trunk toward Marianne and touched her cheek.

"Sweetness. There are a lot people who are planning to help. In fact, I want you to know that you will be taken care of. The money has been set aside and will make sure one way or another that you will be able to run free. I want you to imagine yourself on forested acreage with Sari.

"There will be trees you can rub up against to scratch an itch and a lake where you can swim—swim to your hearts delight. Picture it, my love. Picture the nice mud hole where you and Sari can toss mud pies at one another and fill the air with dust.

"It will be oh so beautiful and spacious, maybe there will be a river that you can wade into, then fill your trunk with water to bring rain just like Airavata. No worries sweetie—your chance to be an elephant, trunk play with Sari and other elephants, much snorting—go running off and bump into each other; send your rumbles out across the hill and then listen to see what comes back. Maybe the spirit of Echo is out there; maybe Kibo…maybe Winkie and the babies."

I made just enough noise so that Marianne might think I had just come through the door.

"I think I can get her up," declared Marianne, obviously surprised. "I'm worried more about her eating."

I could see that she wanted to give Gigi her undivided attention, so I said I would talk to her later.

Jim Currie

Chapter 39
Swans of Srinagar

As I made my back to my car, I puzzled over Marianne's wistful whispering to Gigi.

I had heard this kind of gossamer intonation before but couldn't quite place it. I paged back to the way my father spoke to Deli—no it wasn't like that. And then I realized that it lay in a deeper stratum, pool and sanctum of childhood—in those precious moments years before, when Amita gathered Arundhati and me around her to send us off to safe and protected dreamland.

As early as age 4 or 5 she would read to us the poems of Tagore and Rumi, passages from the *Ramayana*, the *Lotus Sutra* and the *Upanishads*, and particularly what was said about Srinagar. They filled us with wonder and enchantment as we followed her like fledged cygnets in a v-shaped flock headed for this distant Shangri-La. We held fast to the sweet vapors of her every in-breath and dramatic exhalation, certain to arrive on a plateau beyond fear and worry.

Despite the harshness of her life, especially after my father's death, Amita never lost her whimsical imagination.

In the days that she worked overtime at *Lucknow Textile and Clothing*, she would come through the door dead-tired. About all she had energy for was to clean herself up, eat the meal I had prepared for her and ready herself for bed.

She would try to spend her last few waking moments with those poems and stories that were now dog-eared and painted with fingerprints—ours as well as hers.

More often than not, she would fall asleep with those open pages shining at her smiling face. More than a few times I would pick the book up off her breasts and she would open her heavy eyes and say to me, "Tell me about Srinagar and the swans, Pankaz."

So I, the dutiful son, would tell it back to her, doing my best to impart the mystique she had conveyed to Arundhati and me so many times before.

"According to the pandit, Kalhan's Rajatarangini, the Valley of Kashmir used to be an expansive lake called Satisar. The great sage Kashyapa prayed for a long time to Maheshwara to provide him dry land out of this lake. His prayer was accepted, and Lord Vishnu taking the form of a unicorn pierced the mountain range at a place called Varehmula, and a lush land and garden formed that would forever be sacred and represent awakening, peace of spirit, and higher knowledge."

Then I would reach for the lacey words of scholars and poets to describe the virginal waters that since antiquity had flowed to the valley out of the Himalayan glaciers. "They would start their journey in the fringes of the sun-blistered snow fields and pass to the beckoning streams, each drop adding to a gathering life-force, whimsically dancing as much as flowing; underground as above.

"A gathering would occur at Dal Lake, blossoming the pink lotuses of rebirth, followed by an outfall to the Jehlum River, whose own marshy aprons would be perfumed by wildflowers."

"Tell me about the swans," she would beg like a young girl

holding fast to a belief in winged sorcery and soluble spirits passing over the Hindu Kush and the rooftop of the world.

And so I would continue on, following obligation and devotion to this eternal child, who in giving me life had taught me to travel into the gray realms of greater dream and fantasy.

But there was more of her own enchanted brushwork here than my own, a texture and tint from night study of birds that flocked on the far side of the moon and then constellated in the heavens.

"In the marshlands of Dal Lake, the pure waters would find the Hamsa Swans awaiting their gift. These were swans from Lake Manasarovar on the Tibetan Plateau, that carried Brahman and Sarasvati. They were only visible to those who had achieved *The Third Awakening* as described in the *Shiva Sutras*.

"Touched by the spirit of Brahman, they had escaped the cycle of life and death. They were free from s*amsara,* flew effortlessly and hovered weightlessly on the calm serene waters of the lake. Though they lived on water, their feathers were never wetted, nor were they soiled by the *maya* of the physical world.

"Over time the great sages came to understand that the swans represented the oneness of human and the divine, and the name of the swans themselves, the inhalation and exhalation of oneness: the in-breath, ham; the out-breath, sa, and thus the breath of life."

And my mother with blissful sighs would shutter her barely open eyes, giving herself up to sleep and the downy embrace of the Hamsa Swans at Srinagar.

Jim Currie

Part 3 - Coming Home

Chapter 40
A Tall Glass of Lemonade

A few days after my visit to the zoo, I learned from Tony by phone that Gigi had risen to her feet. I was sure that Marianne was relieved and elated, and I looked forward to seeing her the following Monday at the diner.

I arrived only to discover that she had departed early in the AM for a trip to the East Coast. Tony had given her a ride to the airport, and she had handed him a package to give to me.

I had no idea what this could be about, unless she had confused my birthday. And yet the box was unwrapped, so perhaps it was information passed on from Red Bill or Rae-Ron. I popped the top and came to the following note:

> Dear Pankaz,
>
> I'm deeply honored that you would trust me to complete *The Book of Elephant*, but at the moment it is beyond me and I need to focus on matters of energy and health. So I'm returning it to you with appreciation.
>
> Love, Marianne

My heart sank. It was the one thing we shared that I never thought she would give up on. Why would she do this? Had I done something that had offended her? I couldn't imagine what. I read the note again. "Energy and health?"

If she were as traumatized as I thought by Hansa's death, then wouldn't having the book salve her wounds and maybe energize her rather than sap her strength?

There was one other oddity here—why go on a trip now, just a few days after Gigi was on her feet? Wouldn't she be worried about a setback?

I shook my head and showed Tony the note. He seemed baffled as well.

"When you took Marianne to the airport did she say anything else about the package?"

"Nope."

"Did she say the purpose of the trip or where she was going?"

"She was pretty quiet but said she had family to visit in Florida. I gave her the same ride last year at this time. Yeah, late July."

"I didn't think she had family, especially in this country. Jody didn't mention anyone."

Tony shrugged.

"Do you know where exactly she was going?"

"No, but she said something about a direct flight on United. I think it was a 5 AM departure."

I puzzled over the contradictions all the way to Berkeley. When I arrived at *The Barb* , I checked the departures and found a non-stop to Sarasota at 5:02 AM. This had to be it. And then all of a sudden it hit me that Sarasota was the location of *Wild World.*

When was it that Winkie died? I was pretty sure she said

August 1.

Today was July 28, so it would fit that Marianne were returning on a pilgrimage to nuzzle old bones.

In only took a few minutes to book a flight. My editor, Betty,
agreed to pay for it when I promised to do a story on the nature
park and a follow-up on elephant training. The plan was to spend
several days at *Wild World*, and then go to Venice, the location of
the *Dingaling Circus* elephant training facility, 50 miles away.

I managed to schedule an interview at *Wild World* on July 31
at noon. I arrived a few hours early to survey the grounds and
sleuth for signs of Marianne. The temperature was well over 100
degrees F. and the humidity was close to 80 percent. Even the children at the nature park seemed less interested in the wild animals
than cooling themselves with snow cones. The animals were le-
thargic and smart enough to find shade.

I had brought along a head shot of Marianne from one of my
stories, just in case I needed to jog someone's memory. I soon
found a couple of people who recognized her, but no one seemed
to have seen her for many years. It had now been five years since
she had worked at the park.

In early afternoon, I interviewed the female assistant director
on the pretext that *The Barb* was doing a domestic-travel special
with a focus on nature parks. She offered me a packet of promo-
tional literature which I replied to with friendly and dim-witted
awe at the fine education service *Wild World* was performing on
behalf of children everywhere.

When I was sure that my syrupy empty-headedness was fully
imparted, I mentioned that I had heard that the park had experienced the rare occurrence of a mother elephant bearing twins. "Can

you tell me about this?"

The woman recited some of the same details related by Jody but with critical differences: "Yes, the second baby was found in the woods, but wasn't well from the beginning and this was one of the reasons we kept it."

"Kept it? For how long?"

"About 18 months, as I recall, and then it died."

"From the herpes virus?"

"No, a genetic problem with its heart, I believe."

"And the first one—the one that was given up—went to the circus?"

"Yes."

"It died as well?"

"No. Last I heard it was on the circuit and doing well."

"Are you sure about all this?"

"Quite sure, but I would be willing to double-check my records."

I thanked her and gave her my card with phone number and email address. As I left I asked if I could use her name in trying to set up an interview with the staff at *Dingaling*.

"If you like, I could call them for you?"

"That would be wonderful," I answered.

"Tell you what, I'll call them after my next meeting and get back to you."

I headed across the street to a pub called *Fergie's* to await the phone call and seek refuge from the heat and cool myself with a tall cold drink.

A waitress there brought me an icy lemonade, as I puzzled over the discrepancies in Marianne's story. According to Jody,

Marianne said that both babies had died but this was now in doubt. This could have been a simple mistake, or a slight exaggeration, but because it was all verifiable I didn't think I was being fed a lie by *Wild World*: they had to know that I would be checking the facts.

It made me realize that I might have been too quick to presume—out of my affection for Marianne—that Jody got the true story from Marianne.

The one thing that I had learned from my 16 years as a journalist is that original accounts are seldom the truth when something horrific happens. Emotions always distort and Marianne was waist deep in the Gompti River on this one.

It was equally clear that getting at the truth of what really happened at *Wild World* was the only way those nightmares were going to dissolve. It might even determine whether Marianne and I were going to have any future together.

My cellphone rang and it was a receptionist at *Wild World*. She said that she had heard from *Dingaling* and had arranged an interview for me at 4:30 PM, if I could make it. I said I could and thanked her.

I still had a few hours before I needed to depart, so I ordered another drink. A few feet away from me was one of the women I had previously talked to about Marianne. She was perhaps 35 years old, Hispanic and wore an engaging smile.

"Can I buy you something to drink?"

She shook her head.

"You sure? Pretty hot out to be turning down a cold drink."

"Well, okay," she replied.

As she drew down the drink, she asked if I was a reporter.

"How did you guess that?"

"The questions and pictures you were taking—pictures of elephants and not the happy ones."

"Not bad," I declared. "You said you sort of remember Marianne?"

"Yes. She loved the elephants."

"Sure you haven't seen her?"

She didn't answer.

"I'm a friend of hers and elephants."

She studied me closely.

I reached out and offered her my hand.

"I'm Pankaz. To be honest, I'm more than a friend. She's family and I'm worried about her."

She broke into a broad smile. "I'm Rosalie. I always loved Marianne."

I smiled. "Me too. I'm not sure but I think she might have come here out of overwhelming grief. I would like to find her and help."

She took a draw on her lemonade. "I haven't seen her, but I know she is here somewhere. She comes every year at this time—for 5 years now."

"What do you mean?"

"She comes to see Winkie and her baby."

"What do you mean 'comes to see'?"

"She comes to the grave, and she usually spends the nights there."

"Where would this grave be?"

"On the grounds."

"You mean out on the *Wild World* acreage?"

She nodded. "The grave is back in the forest."

"Could you draw me a map?"

She nodded.

Her map showed the location of Winkie's grave not too far from the northeast fence-line.

"Be very careful if you try to go to the grave," added Rosalie. "It could be pretty dangerous, especially at night if you don't have much experience with leopards."

"Leopards?"

"The elephants used to be there, but the areas were switched a few years back."

Her look suggested I would have to be pretty crazy to hazard it.

"But Marianne's there, right?"

"Yes, but Marianne is half-animal herself."

"How would I get in?"

"You would need some help."

"I would pay someone to help me get inside."

"I think I know someone."

Jim Currie

Chapter 41
Likrot and Training with Bananas

I arrived at the *Dingaling* headquarters, armed with my portable video camera and notepad, and waited in the lobby on the second floor for my appointment. On the walls I studied several photographs of the site showing piecemeal expansion over 100 years, including the addition of rail lines for a circus train, as well various buildings for the animals. An elephant facility was apparently behind the headquarters building which actually filled a gap in a long fence-line with a main security entrance.

A few minutes later the suit-clad receptionist, wearing a snappy D-emblazoned crest on her breast, announced that a Mr. Likrot in Public Relations was ready to see me. She ushered me down a hallway past a stairwell toward Likrot's corner office.

There Likrot, a fellow half my age, dressed in an expensive *Dingaling* blazer, introduced himself. His pearly whites were too big for his mouth and belonged on a mega-church evangelist. I could tell right away that he wasn't going to be divulging anything of any value. I mentioned that I was looking for confirmation that Winkie's first baby was alive and well, and he said he had already checked on this. He added that at the moment she was on tour outside of Chicago.

I was tempted to ask if she was at the Cairo, Illinois Fairgrounds warming up Ebenezer Jehosavat and his snakes, but thought better of it and asked if he could give me any information on the training of baby elephants. He was quick to reply that the circus used "approved and standard techniques."

I asked if he could explain them as they related to circus tricks and he launched into a well practiced spiel that elephants were natural performers and the circus only drew out this propensity for the enjoyment of children and families. As he spoke, I cast my eyes out the window in the direction of the elephant barn.

Several juveniles were passing in and out under close control of staff. I noticed one of the staff split off and head in the direction of the administrative office, presumably to a first-floor entrance. Likrot slowed down and I declared, "Any chance I could visit your facility or observe the training?"

"That might be difficult to arrange," he replied. "This is a busy time of year for us."

"Well, you have my number. Why don't you let me know if you could set up an observation. I'll be around for a few days."

He shook my hand and ushered me out into the hallway. When he turned back toward his office, I reversed directions and continued down the hallway until I came to a stairwell.

On the first floor I found a door to the yard labeled "Authorized Personnel Only" with a security keypad attached. I thought I had been foiled, but heard someone approaching from down the hallway. Immediately I ducked underneath the stairs in the stairwell. The fellow entered a security code on the pad and cast open the door. I caught it just before the latch clicked and held it until I was sure the fellow wasn't looking back.

A few minutes later I reached the elephant barn. I passed inside unnoticed and watched two workers—trainers or their assistants—leading a baby elephant to another room. I raised my camera and took four quick shots of it, then followed the procession.

Over perhaps ten minutes I watched six staff members place a squealing, fearful baby elephant into a stress position, apparently trying to get her to lie on her stomach. Her front legs were bound and pulled forward as her lower legs were pulled back by ropes. Meanwhile, her trunk was held up by another rope suspended from a beam. Another trainer hovered over the baby with a bunch of bananas as putative reward.

I shot video with audio continuously for nearly two minutes, and then I heard voices behind me. It was time to go. I ducked inside a covering doorway, let two workmen pass, and fell into a brisk walk, retracing my path to the administrative office.

At my hotel room two hours later, I inspected my video carefully. I had never taken shots like this. They really needed neither caption nor story. The most sickening frames showed the trainers chiding the baby to hold up her trunk.

Her alarmed squeals were almost too hard to take. I couldn't help but think of the torture pictures shown by Red Bill at Boalt Hall. The main difference was lack of bananas.

It wasn't lost on me that I was holding footage that the circus and probably *Bridgewater* would be highly motivated to intercept and destroy. There were big-money implications in this and I needed to be very careful who knew about it or saw it before printing or posting on *The Barb* website.

Jim Currie

Chapter 42
No Way Loco

I had just downloaded the best stills to my laptop and sent them off to my editor encrypted as a precaution when my phone trumpeted. It was a male with an Hispanic accent: "My name is Marcos. Rosalie said you need to get into the yard. I think I can help you."

"Yes," I answered.

"It will be fifty dollars."

"No problem."

"You meet me exactly one-point-five kilometers down the north fence line from the main entrance at ten thirty at night. *Comprende?*"

"Yes."

"Can you lead me to the grave?"

He chuckled. "No way, Loco. You on your own."

My hotel was located across from a suburban shopping center which I realized I needed to visit before the rendezvous. There I found a sporting goods and hardware store and picked up a flashlight and heavy gloves that I figured might come in handy if I needed to be dealing with barbed wire.

My greater need was a firearm, preferably a canon that could take down a T-Rex, but it was too late to deal with this. I considered best available alternatives—various hunting knives, a torch, flares. They all had liabilities. I didn't want to be detected by security, and I was quite sure that at the distance a knife would do me any good, a man-eater would probably already have my head in his jaws.

Then my eyes fell on a barrel of used golf clubs. I scrounged through it and found a 5-iron that felt right. I was under no illusion that it would really save me in death-fight with a leopard, but it might give the leopard pause.

When I arrived at kilometer one-point-five with golf club in hand, a fellow about five feet seven inches with a slightly amused smirk was waiting.

"You playing night golf, Loco?"

"Yeah, I thought I would get a round in before sunrise. You Marcos?"

He nodded.

"Want to caddy for me?"

"On groundhog day, Loco."

He removed brush and branches from a freshly dug hole at the base of the chain-link fence. I could see right away that this was no ordinary hole, but one crafted by someone with much experience in border crossings at night. The excavated dirt was well camouflaged and distributed so that it wouldn't immediately draw attention.

I was tempted to ask him for his own back story that probably included dramas along the Rio Grande with coyotes, Federales and crazed American militia, but decided I needed to stick with the program.

"Any local course knowledge you want to pass on?"

"Keep your head up. The leopards will be in the trees. If

somehow you make it back, put the dirt back in the hole and cover it with brush. I leave the shovel for you in the bushes. No need for the man-eaters to feast on the good people of Sarasota."

I handed him $80 and he smiled, dropping it into his pocket and tossing the shovel into a tuft of brambles. I fell to my back with head forward and slithered through the hole like a sidewinder.

As I made my way inside the yard, it occurred to me how the story of my demise might be reported—"Reporter Dead Golfing in Wild Animal Park."

It would be one of those stories that would cause a TV anchorman to shake his head and murmur, "There's got to be alcohol involved in this."

I made my way toward the X marked on my map, my ears attuned to distant rumbles from night dwellers of the African Savannah. It occurred to me that everything had changed since the fall of the sun. Now those with night vision commanded all the advantages over the vision-impaired, slow-footed, upright ones with opposable thumbs and uselessly large brain.

I was no master of wildland survival but did know a few things from *The Book of Elephant*. A herd was always aware of the wind and how it could betray the location of its vulnerable babies. Elephants constantly searched the breeze and the audio spectrum to pick up signs of stalkers.

At present, the wind was out of the west so the dangers I should be most alert to were apt to be coming from the east. I was sure I was at the spot marked on the map, but there was no sign of a grave.

I began to recriminate. I should have been more definite in asking for a location—how many feet from the fence or from other landmarks? I had no idea the landscape would be this expansive and so heavily treed.

I knew also that the longer I remained where I was, the more likely that my scent would be picked up some kind of feline. I decided to imagine a grave site that Marianne might have picked for Winkie. I didn't think it would be out in the open—probably in the shade of a tree. Elephants were always looking for shade and mud holes and Marianne would be mindful of that.

I scanned to the north and made out a small hill in a willow copse a few hundred yards away. I headed in that direction across open terrain, gripping my 5-iron more tightly.

I had just raised it to my shoulder when I was startled by a flapping sound from behind me. It was some kind of night bird, perhaps a hawk or owl. It vanished as quickly as it came but my spiked heartbeat refused to fall.

When I arrived at the copse, I spotted a large rock and next to it a built-up mound that could easily be an elephant's grave. I drew closer and spotted a marker. I shined my flashlight on it. "Dearest Winkie," it read. Next to it was a flat tableau, a devotional altar of sorts with offerings of polished stones, several robust carrots and votive candle holders with exhausted candles. I noticed that one of them was still smoking.

Now I realized that Marianne was near. She had surely detected a human or animal presence and retreated into the darkness. She might even be watching me. Suddenly a growl sounded from one of the overhead trees and terror overcame me.

I turned toward the sound and shouted wildly, "You bastard.." I swung madly but apparently the leopard was still in the branches. "You want some of this?"

"Pankaz?" came the voice from the tree.

"Marianne?"

She dropped from the tree. "What are you doing here?"

I was too adrenalized to weigh my response, "I was worried about you."

"How did you know I was here?" she answered almost tonelessly.

Now I realized that I needed to measure what I said.

"Well, I was doing this article on the park—you know for *The Barb*—and ran across a girl who said she had seen you."

"Really?"

"Yeah, *The Barb* wanted a follow-up because of my last spread."

She fell silent.

"I don't think I believe you."

"What do you mean?" Now I could see her face more clearly. It looked even thinner; her eyes drawn; hair bedraggled. She looked exhausted.

"You followed me."

"No, really, I'm doing this article."

She shook her head, clearly holding fast to her conviction that I was lying.

"I think you need to leave." She fell into a sickly cough and then a paroxysm. "You need to leave me alone."

"Okay, look—it's partially true. I was worried about you, and I decided I could write this story on *Wild World*."

She shook her head dismissively.

Now I realized I had almost nothing to lose and my only hope was confrontation.

"You and I have been dancing around the truth for a long time. You don't reveal anything to people who care about you."

Her lips pursed. I had upset her but instead of provoking candor, I had only brought down another steel door.

"Yes, I know the story of the twins. I got it from Jody and from all the other clues you left. But I'll tell you now that I think it's convenient distortion."

"I don't know what you are talking about."

"You can't get the story straight—which baby got sick when, and who died and who was responsible. It's all too cut and dried."

Her brow furled with anger. "You went behind my back."

"You pretend that every word you say, every solemn promise you make, is taken to heart and determines everything. That seems awfully arrogant and self-centered. Selfish, in fact."

"Oh screw you."

"Now we're getting at it aren't we?" I halved the distance between us and was now inches from her. "You didn't betray Winkie. Your grief-stricken pilgrimages here are based on wallowing. You did your best, but it just wasn't good enough. It happens. I've got news for you—none of us are gods or avatars with miraculous powers to save and protect. It's just the way it is, and you can't change it."

She lashed out and hit me in the face, but the blow was so feeble I barely flinched. She struck again and it was even weaker. Something wasn't right here.

And then she began back-peddling irresolutely, coughing uncontrollably and fell. It wasn't the fall of someone tripping, but someone succumbing to weakness. In the process her pockets emptied of several bottles. She reached for them but with the dissolute grasp of someone overboard and about to be taken by breaking waves.

I picked them up for her, one at a time, and she seemed to recover slightly. She brought herself to her feet and ran a free hand through her tangled hair.

"What are these?"

"*Dimemoral* and prion medicine."

"What do you mean, 'prion medicine'?"

She looked up at me with dilated woeful eyes. "I've got this problem."

"What kind of problem?"

"Encephalitis."

"Encephalitis?"

"I take this medicine, but it's really strong. I looked at one of the bottles—*Quinacrine.*

"How long has this been going on?"

"No one seems to know, 'cept it's gotten worse."

And now I realized exactly what was going on. This was an illness that no one survived—Creutzfeldt-Jakob and related to mad-cow disease. I didn't know all the symptoms, but I was pretty sure they involved delusions and distortions and probably also explained the use of *Dimemoral.*

"Let me help you." I gathered her in my arms. She practically collapsed.

"I didn't want to hurt you, Pankaz. You mean so much to me. I just couldn't bear any more responsibility in my sad, stupid little life. All I ever wanted was to protect elephants."

"We're going to get you out of here, and we're going to find some help."

I carried her to the fence and managed to help her through the hole to the other side.

From there I carried her to my rental car and then to my hotel room. Along the way, she vomited three times. She was feverish and ached everywhere. I begged her to let me take her to the emergency room, but she said she had been through this several times before and had all the medicine that they would give her. At a loss, I pleaded with her to let me call the doctor listed on her meds. Finally, perhaps out of exhaustion, she consented.

I left a message on the doctor's emergency voice mail at 2 AM San Francisco time. Ten minutes later he called back. As expected, he wanted me to take her to the hospital. He spoke to Marianne briefly, and she handed the phone back to me. She didn't want to go; she wouldn't go.

I explained this to the doctor and he answered with an explanation of her disease. Yes, it was Creutzfeldt-Jakob. He added that he could understand her reluctance to go to the ER.

We seemed to be at an impasse, but when it became clear that she was going to end the call, he conceded that there was a good chance that her current problems were mostly side-effects from the *Quinacrine* and not illness symptoms: "There's also some chance that you'll feel better in a couple of days—assuming you've reduced the dosage." The call ended with no resolution.

A few minutes later, I told her I didn't know what to do but would honor her wishes.

"I'm not going to spend a cent more on hospitals," she said. "Everything has got to go to the elephants."

I wasn't going to argue with her. She had a right to make this decision, and I was going to stand by her, no matter how this played out.

For three days she remained in my hotel room while I tried to meet her every need, helping her to the bathroom, cleaning up after her, bringing her cold compresses for her fever. On the fourth day her temperature broke, and on the fifth we caught a plane home.

Jim Currie

Chapter 43
Selling Crazy Somewhere Else

The pictures from the circus and my accompanying article on the breeding and training facilities caused outrage that reverberated to the offices of congressmen and senators. The full video of the baby elephant abuse was posted on *The Barb's* website and the traffic immediately knocked out the server. Three million hits were recorded in the first 48 hours.

In the midst of this, the zoo, which had previously let Vincent's offer lapse, called back and countered with an offer of $125,000. Vincent declined, stating that the climate had changed and he was now offering $60,000 which would be going down shortly.

The next day, Vincent rang me up at *The Barb*: "The zoo called back again and said it would agree to seventy thousand dollars, but there is one glitch: the breeding rights to both Sari and Gigi are owned by a private company—*Trunks to Go*. The zoo has an option to buy them back, but at one hundred fifty thousand dollars."

"You kidding? They didn't say a word about this."

"I know. In any case, the key player here is *Trunks to Go*. We could play out the same angles with them as we have with the zoo."

"I know all about these people," I answered. "They're not so easily influenced by gate receipts and bad PR. They work behind the scenes."

Later that day I discussed the issue at *The Offshore* with the herd minus Marianne. Once again she was ill and had called in sick. Alex was on the sill only feet away, watching us closely. I explained the latest development in negotiations, and they upwelled with anger.

Tony spouted first: "So no matter what, we're probably looking at fifty to seventy-five K for the zoo and another one hundred K to *Trunk Fuck?*"

"But what about Vincent—didn't you say he had friends in Hollywood?"

"The phone hasn't been ringing off the hook," I replied. "This isn't to say that it won't."

"There are bound to be more exposés now that the pictures are up on the web," declared Darrell. "I think time works in our favor."

"Not exactly," I answered glumly.

"What do you mean?" answered Roger.

"Marianne," answered Tony. "She's sick isn't she?"

"Yup," I answered.

"Bad?" replied Tony.

"Very bad."

"We're family here," declared Darrell.

"It's supposedly a terminal illness that progresses very fast— Creutzfeldt-Jakob, it's called—a brain disease." They seemed to know about it.

"How much time does she have?" asked Darrell.

"It could be a few months; maybe a year. No one knows."

"Maybe it's time we step up," declared Tony. "I'm an old man. As far as I'm concerned I've only got two things left when it comes to unfinished business. One's about a little pigeon cup and the other is Marianne. If we're out of options maybe this is worth taking a high flyer on—for me it is."

Across from me Darrell was nodding. "What am I holding out for? There's no corporate recruiter or Vegas impresario ringing my phone off the hook."

Declared Roger, "Hey, I'm a gay, Black, washed-up football player with no other family—next stop for me could be the dump with Ivan."

Darrell seemed to metamorphose. Suddenly, he was Jack Nicholson, "No more of us from this wanna-hump-hump diner are ending up in the dump. The muvafuchs can go sell crazy some-place else. We're all stocked up here."

From the sill, Alex suddenly spouted: "Wanna-hump-hump-diner. Awk!"

"That's what I'm talking about!" answered Darrell.

"So you're in, too?" asked Tony.

"Jeezus, man, what do you think?"

"I think we all need to take a little walk," I declared, pressing my hushing index finger to my lips. Everyone got it.

I rose from the booth and was about to head for the door when Alex across from us blurted out, "Wide stance. Prevent de-fense."

I turned to Roger and laughed, "Are you teaching the bird, football?"

"Hey man, don't look at me. He must have caught a glimpse of the Niners on the big screen."

"Wide stance. Prevent defense, awk!"

"They ought to hire him as a coach."

We were soon on the hoof toward Telegraph Hill with Alex overhead. As soon as it was clear that no one was trailing us and we could talk openly, Tony declared, "I know we can park the elies at the Tiger Ranch temporarily. Rae-Ron already mentioned it. I think we need to get back to him before we get too carried away."

Everyone nodded.

"I can launch a pigeon on this right away and see what comes back," he added.

"Before we firm anything up, I need to visit with Vincent," I replied. "I'm thinking of one last hail-Mary to *Trunk Fuck*."

From a call later in the day I learned that Vincent had made direct contact to *Trunks to Go*. Unfortunately they refused to cede contract rights for anything less than $100,000. We were out of options.

Chapter 44
Rae-Ron and the Night Visitors

On September 25, a dense marine fog rolled in over the western part of the city, obscuring a timid quarter-moon. City sounds were tamped and muted, everything merged in a universal whoosh—the in-and-out breath of winds disturbing the urban reach of the human floodplain. No fire alarms or cries of ambulances pierced the night but instead muffled complaints that quickly dissolved into the background hum.

I wondered what those with flapping ears and rumble-sensitive feet might be taking in on a night like this. What seemed alien and unnatural to those born to the Serengeti, Tsavo or the foothills of the Himalaya? How much had they acclimated in this paved over, overpopulated human habitat? Would those sensors, attuned after so many centuries to the presence of tigers and the dangers of those upright bipeds, be able to pick up the footfall of friendly humans at the edge of their known world?

I arrived just outside of a maintenance gate on the west side of the zoo according to the plan laid down by Rae-Ron. His electronically-equipped van was nearby. He was inside the gate, somewhere in the dark preparing a timed overload of the zoo's electrical system that would take down surveillance cameras, create a diversionary alarm and spring a main door to the Elephant House. Best of all, the overload would fire the alarm that vipers had escaped the Reptile House. If it worked, even Harmsworth would have to be impressed.

The most difficult step was getting the elephants to walk a plank into the van. This was Tony's job, who hopefully had inspired enough confidence from Gigi and Sari in caretaking trips to the zoo with Marianne.

Rae-Ron had rated our glorious chances at something less than 40 percent, plus or minus.

Because he figured that the police would immediately be looking for an escape to Marin County, we would first head south for Daly City where Red Bill had apparently helped him rent an old warehouse for "temporary storage of road equipment."

My assignment on Rae-Ron's signal was to break a large padlock on the maintenance gate and swing open the gate for entry to the yard by Tony, Roger and Darrell in the van.

I saw a shadow approaching in the distance and knew it was Rae-Ron. According to plan, I flashed a single burst from a blue light indicating that we were all ready. He replied in kind. This was his confirmation that he had triggered the electronic sequences.

In seconds, the jaws of my heavy-duty bolt cutter were making short shrift of the padlock. It had barely fallen to the ground when Tony and Roger were rolling the van toward the Elephant House.

Roger, Darrell and Tony got out of the cab and lowered the ramp.

"The Reptile House alarm will go off in fifteen minutes. Chop, chop." Tony looked nervous.

"I think I can do it," declared Tony.

"You think?" I replied. "Geez."

A loud click signaled the release of the door lock. Now we were in business. With Roger doing the lifting, we raised the door manually. It was no more than halfway up when I spotted Gigi and Sari who were clearly surprised. Sari emitted a frightened trumpet and backed off. Gigi held her ground, and Tony called out to her.

"We're coming to free you, girl. You understand?"

He slowly moved toward her, and she backed away.

"Oh, geez," I declared. He tried again and this time she seemed to realize he wasn't a threat. But this wasn't good enough. He had to lead or shoo her into the van. *How could this possibly work?*

"He reached out to her with what looked like a denim jump-suit. It was Marianne's jumpsuit. She raised her trunk and seemed to recognize the scent of her beloved caretaker. Still she wasn't moving. All of a sudden Sari gave forth a bright trumpet which I recognized immediately as a happy greeting. I turned and there was Marianne.

She shook her head. "I knew you guys were up to something. Let me handle it."

She approached Gigi and Sari and touched each of their trunks lovingly.

"This it, girls. We're getting the hell out of here. I want you to walk up the gangplank and into the van. Com'mon—just follow me. Nothing to be afraid of."

Just as Gigi took her first step, a cell erupted—it was Darrell's.

"Jesus," declared Rae-Ron. I told you guys no electronic gear of any sort. Let me look at that damn thing." He grabbed it out of Darrell's hand and seconds later declared. "The jig is up boys.

We've been made."

"What do you mean?" replied Darrell plaintively.

"Someone's replaced the *simm* card in your phone. We've got to get out of here fast. "

"Without the elies?" answered Tony.

"No elies. We'd all be dead meat." He raced for his own van, and Tony and Roger ran toward the moving truck.

Marianne didn't budge.

"I can't leave," she answered.

"Yes, you can. It's not over Marianne." I pulled her away and tears streamed down her cheek.

"Don't worry. I swear to you, it isn't over."

Chapter 45

Desperate Measures

Somehow we had escaped. I expected flashing police car lights and sirens, but there were none.

A few days later we learned from Rae-Ron that his electronics suggested that a geosynchronous communication satellite had gone down. Apparently someone had launched a drone, but it didn't arrive at the zoo until we were gone.

Darrell wasn't sure how someone had gotten hold of his cell but did recall that he had misplaced it for a few hours at a San Francisco nightclub.

A puzzle more difficult to figure out was the strange reaction of the zoo in the days that followed—no reaction whatsoever. It was all the more unfathomable because the elephants were left out in the yard when we escaped.

My best theory was that whoever had been tracking us had spoken to Dr. Shipp and the plan was to encourage another escape attempt.

I saw Marianne a week after the failed caper. She had returned to work after switching to a new drug which she claimed had fewer side effects. I wasn't so sure because she looked tipsy and weak. This was no longer the spry athletic waitress who could handle nearly half the tables on her own. I noticed also that her speech had slowed, and she was having trouble picking up her feet.

When I was about to leave, she handed me a message from Tony that had come in from Red Bill:

"This 'wide stance' business might not be about football. Perhaps about some kind of NSA program."

As I pondered the note I could see that she wasn't really interested.

"Do you think you could take me home?" she murmured. "I'm not feeling well."

"Of course," I answered. I let her tell the manager that she had to go home and met her in the back of the cafe to pick up her coat and pack. In the several minutes that elapsed she grew more weary. I helped her into her coat and let her lean on me as I ushered her toward the door. We were barely outside when Alex landed on her shoulder. She barely acknowledged him.

"No hospital, Pankaz."

"No hospital," I answered kissing her on the forehead.

When I got her home to her apartment I helped her undress and put on loose-fitting pajamas. I picked her up and lifted her into her bed. I checked her temperature. It was normal. For the moment, the main problem seemed to be exhaustion. She said she was okay and not to worry about her.

"Call me back when you are up again. If I don't hear from you, I'll call you in eight hours."

"Make it ten," she answered. She smiled and closed her eyes. It only took a few breaths for her to nod off. The smile on her lips reminded me of my mom giving herself up to the Hamsa Swans.

"Downy embrace, sweet one."

That evening Red Bill's thoughts streamed back to me—"Not about football..." Now it clicked that "wide stance" was the excuse and explanation of the Republican senator from Idaho when police arrested him for lewd behavior in a men's room at the Minneapolis-Saint Paul Airport.

Was it possible that someone else in the Bush White House had used that term or applied it to describe someone else's lewd behavior? If so, it wasn't the sort of secret you would ever want revealed—especially if you were someone high in the pecking order trying to protect your reputation.

I decided I needed to discuss this with the herd and let Tony spread the word for a rendezvous the next morning outside the Coit Tower. All were there except Marianne and everyone offered assurances that they had left behind cellphones and checked for tails.

I explained my theory and they all agreed that Alex must have heard this from Bush, Haney or Harmsworth and it probably referred to Haney, Harmsworth or someone at a very high perch who was diddling someone or being diddled in exotic ways that people with family values would consider perverse.

"I've heard gay friends talk about this before," added Roger. "It goes back long before Craig went into his tap dance in stall number three. My guess is that it's at least Harmsworth."

"I agree," declared Darrell. "But I don't think we can rule out Haney, the chief of staff or 'Blossom'. It might even be an oil industry exec."

"In which case this becomes the bargaining chip that gets the elephants out," gleamed Tony.

Everyone nodded, with Roger declaring resolutely, "I think this is a play we have to make."

"No argument, here," answered Darrell. "What else have we got going?"

"Okay, here's what I'm thinking," I replied. "We bait the hook with a story that suggests we've got inside dope from Alex. If the plan works, Wide Stance should be getting back to us right away."

"I like it," replied Tony.

That night I typed away until dawn, finessing every sentence for the perfect facsimile of a lure that would land a derby-winning fish on opening day.

Two days later the following article appeared in *The Barb*, along with pictures of Alex, "Saddam's African grey parrot who was witness to the vices, sexual dalliances and untold perversities within the Bush White House."

Saddam's Parrot Tells All As Witness
Perversion in the White House
by Pankaz Panday

Since 1974, when the White House Tapes and the "Smoking Gun" led to the resignation of Richard Nixon, American Presidents have exercised close control over White House recording devices.

Among those most obsessed with security and unwanted leaks was the administration of George W. Bush. You therefore have to wonder whether President Bush, his VP or any of their chief staffers considered the possibility that one very smart, African grey parrot could be listening and recording confidential conversations that might frenzy grand juries and cause reputations to shatter over perversities and mortal sins.

Alex was his English name but before that Ali when he was a star at Baghdad University's Animal Communication Lab in the 1990's. Here the precocious African grey parrot, first purchased at the Baghdad bird market, began dazzling researchers with an astounding, multi-lingual vocabulary and ability to understand much of what he heard and repeated. Journal articles were written about him with some proud Iraqis even referring to him as the avian counterpart of Einstein and Jean Paul Sartre.

Saddam Hussein took note and around 1999 plucked Alex, aka Ali, from the lab, making him his personal pet. Thereafter the rare bird lived inside the Baghdad Imperial Palace, enjoying luxury and privilege only exceeded by Uday and Qusay.

In 2003, the 3rd Armored Division broke into Baghdad causing Saddam to flee without Alex. And in the aftermath, Alex was presented to President Bush as a spoil of war. He was first viewed with delight and took up residence in the West Wing and the Oval Office. But this wasn't the same bird that had delighted Saddam with both song and recitation. He had turned mute and showed no interest in learning tricks or any of George's Bush's favorite fraternity ditties from days at Yale.

Because of this he was spurned and passed down the line, first to the Vice President, and eventually to BD Harmsworth, Bush and Rumsfeld's architect of Shock and Awe. From Harmsworth—and unbeknownst to Harmsworth—he seemed to have learned the childhood rhyme adopted by most of the insiders in the White House.

"Let's have another cup of coffee" and "Let's have another piece of pie" were frequently uttered by the inner circle in celebration of important political coups, most notably, the capture of Saddam outside of Tikrit, and staff of the Vice President when he escaped prosecution for the outing of Valerie Plame.

What no one seemed to notice, was that despite his silence, Alex was taking in all the song and celebration, the backbiting, discussion of illegal wiretap and torture, and the ongoing chatter about the bizarre sexual eccentricities of those surrounding the President. Apparently there were more than a few and some rivaling Caligula on steroids. Ironically the carnal novelties were being performed by those extolling family values and need to return to good Christian, American virtues.

In late 2007, Alex was no longer viewed as novelty and was sold to a Washington DC pet store. Through a series of commission sales he arrived in San Francisco where he flew the coop in 2009 and joined the Wild Parrots of Telegraph Hill.

Because he was an African grey parrot and not a cherry-headed conures, the dominant species in the Telegraph flock, he went unmated and largely unaccepted, which led him to bond with a group of animal activists. Comfortable now with "birds of a feather," he began a discharge of monumental proportions that is still fulminating and promises a richness of embarrassment and a certain amount of disgust that may well prompt an historical revision of exactly what went on in the Bush White House, including the backlit bathroom stalls.

Based on the latest spout, it appears that sexual antics of at least one high-profile figure may have rivaled the nocturnal frivolities of J. Edgar Hoover.

Details to be provided in upcoming installments. For inquiries about re-publication: PankazP@TheBarb.com

Chapter 46
It Will Be Necessary to Produce the Bird

The next day, I received a phone call at *The Barb* from a fellow identifying himself as Gellman Landes, a representative of a private party with an interest in the stories I was writing. He asked if I would be willing to meet with him about my article and plans to complete the series. I was pretty sure this was the carp-strike I had hoped for.

I agreed. The meeting would take place between us the following evening at a well-known bar in Chinatown.

Any reservations I had about cutting a deal with Landes perished when I learned later that day that Marianne had tried to work but after only 15 minutes had vomited on a customer, clearing out the cafe.

When I arrived at the bar, Gellman came quickly to the point, "My client is interested in purchasing all rights of publication to the series."

"Define rights of publication."

"He would like you to withhold publication of any further stories on this subject, but he realizes you have a significant investment in your work and would need to be compensated for it. Of course, in return you would also have to provide a pledge of nondisclosure of all information you may have gathered."

"Do you have a number for this?"

"My client has a number but there is a second requirement. It will be necessary to produce the bird."

I chuckled, "I don't possess the bird."

"Well, we can safely assume that you know who is in possession of it. The deal requires that you produce the bird as well as withhold the article."

"For what amount? I would need to convey this to those who possess the parrot."

"My client empowers me to offer fifty thousand dollars for the article and two hundred thousand dollars for the parrot. We will need both."

"I can say with some confidence that two hundred thousand won't be enough for either. In fact, I've already been approached by two tabloids willing to offer more than two hundred fifty K for the story along with video of the parrot. There would be no need for a bidding war if you offered four hundred K for both. I'm sure you realize just how valuable the parrot is."

"I can see that you're a businessman. Perhaps three hundred thousand dollars is doable."

"Three-fifty but there would be a few other conditions."

"Like what?"

"Insurance. It's not been lost on us that a lot of people have been vanishing lately and ending up in dumps. Because of this, your client would have to be there to pick up the bird—no one in his place and no one else in the shadows with a Grim Reaper sniper rifle."

"This might work. I'm sure he would want to verify in-person that it's the bird of interest."

"And we would dictate time and place for the exchange.

Also, two hundred fifty should be in diamonds."

"All I can do is pass the word on."

"And I as well." I scribbled out a note for a new phone number that he could reach me at, and said I would need a decision within 48 hours or I would have to reconsider my offers from the tabloids.

"I would strongly recommend against that," he replied. "I'm also pretty confident that we will have some kind of deal. I might even be able to get back to you later in the day."

With that I headed for the door flush with awareness that I had just made myself and my friends targets of someone very powerful and capable of eliminating us when we were no longer useful.

At *The Barb* a few hours later I received word that I had a caller on line one. It was Landes and he confirmed that we had a deal but he would need two days to convert cash to diamonds. I consented, telling him that the rendezvous would be two days later, in the evening in San Francisco. I would leave exact details regarding the rendezvous by phone, two hours before the exchange.

"One last thing," I declared. "Place all the valuables in a birdcage."

"What?"

"You heard me."

We were now making message drops for each other at Truman's newsstand, and he was only too glad to help out. My latest messages called for a meeting at a restaurant in Chinatown. There Tony was quick to report that he had succeeded in "borrowing" a bird stand-in for Alex and that he and Darrell had been giving it a makeover so that it would make for a convincing facsimile of Alex.

"All under control, right Parrot Man?" declared Tony.

"Wide stance," squawked Darrell.

I handed everyone new throwaway cellphones, and we went over our step-by-step plan that called for first contact with Wide Stance by cellphone at the Erewan Restaurant on Nob Hill where Roger had connections with the wait crew. I would be coordinating communication in a small hotel at Sproule Lane and Sacramento that offered a view of the outside of the restaurant as well as Huntington Park across from the restaurant where the actual exchange would occur. Roger would be stationed in the restaurant bar observing the arrival of the mark; Tony would be positioned in the park.

We decided we needed a codename for the mark and agreed it would be Vip for V.I.P.

Tony immediately launched a pigeon to Rae-Ron providing the details of what we were up to, including time, place and stations of each of us. We figured he might have some sage last-minute advice in dealing with the sniper threat.

Eight hours later a return pigeon landed on Tony's deck carrying a note from Rae-Ron that said the following: "Be advised—these people are connected to *Bilgewater* and have no intention of making good on a deal. As soon as they see the bird, their boy will have you all in the cross-hairs. Also, they'll be using sophisticated phone-detection gear and maybe even drones. Look for a mobile command center somewhere near the restaurant."

I had already thought about much of this but didn't know how to eliminate the risk entirely. What I had tried to look for was an exchange location where mature trees would block a clear shot at us and a place that would maximize chances of escape if a sniper didn't erase us.

Jim Currie

Chapter 47
Reckoning

I arrived at my hotel room a few hours before the exchange. At 7:55 PM, ten minutes before rendezvous and just before sunset, I looked through my window blinds and focused on the valet drop-off zone next to the Erewan. Five minutes later a black Lincoln Town Car arrived. The driver gave the valet a bill which must have been extremely large because he allowed the vehicle to double-park on California.

My view was partially blocked, but I could see our man, who could have been anyone of the three possibles, emerge wearing a fedora and overcoat and carrying a hooded birdcage. As near as I could tell, no one was trailing him.

For a split-second he faced toward a van between Taylor and Jones Street. This had to be the mobile command center.

He entered the restaurant, and shortly thereafter I received two rings on one of my cellphones. This was Roger's signal from inside the restaurant that Vip had arrived. I counted to 20 and dialed up the phone that had been hidden underneath the reserved table in the restaurant. It rang three times before a reply came back in a flat, emotionless monotone.

"Yes, where are you?"

I couldn't quite decide who was speaking.

"You are to proceed across the street to the park where we'll get confirmation of the merchandise and make the exchange."

"No exchange without looking at the bird," shot back Vip.

"The bird will be there."

He emerged from the door of the restaurant with the cage and came into full view as he started to cross over to Huntington Park. I focused my high-powered binoculars on him.

"My God, we've hit the mother-lode."

Vip's right hand rose to his right ear, and I knew he was passing on information to people in the van. Suddenly there was a concussive report from up the street that caused Vip to turn his head toward Taylor. I swiveled and trained on the black van that was now smoking. Two men blew through the side-door looking dazed. On the opposite side of the car a fellow leaped over a small stone fence and disappeared on the other side.

Red Bill? It had to be.

Distracted by the commotion, Vip lost track of the traffic on California Street and was almost clipped by a passing car. He lurched away, falling to the pavement, dropping his cage, which disgorged its contents across the pavement. He cursed, inspected what must have been a tear in his slacks, then cursed again. Now he was fumbling in the gutter next to the park, retrieving the bundled cash and picking up diamonds. After retrieving most of the gems he seemed to grow exasperated.

Suddenly he turned erect, as if deciding that no one of his lofty importance should ever be reduced to gutter-diving. He shed some of the disgusting grime on his slacks, then proceeded up a set of steps with the birdcage.

Reaching the park plateau, he scanned for his contact but the only one there was an aging veteran of the Signal Corps sitting on a park bench, cheerfully feeding pigeons and whistling. The conversation could be heard over the old man's open phone line: "Looks like you tore your pants and lost a cuff-link, sir."

Vip said nothing.

"Phone call for you, sir."

Vip seemed surprised. Tony handed him the phone and shooed off a pigeon sitting on his shoulder who shot toward California.

"I've had enough of this," Vip fired back angrily.

"Let the old man inspect the merchandise, then hand him back the phone," I answered.

Vip offered Tony a diamond which he scanned with a jeweler's light and lens.

"Beautiful," Tony answered.

Vip ripped the phone from his hand. "Where's the damn parrot? I want it! Now!"

"On the far side of the fountain over by Sacramento Street," I replied.

As planned, Tony vanished behind a hedge that would protect him from several lines of sight and allow him to escape down Sacramento Street toward Mason.

Vip trudged off in the direction of the park fountain and contemptuously tossed the phone into the pool.

Near the far side of the park—the northwest end—he noticed Darrell with his shrouded birdcage at the base of a fully-fledged elm tree which we were banking on to prevent a clean sniper shot.

Darrell's phone was on when Vip arrived. Now the two of them were only about 50 yards from me. With my binoculars I could see every facial expression. With a free hand, Vip reached to uncover Darrell's cage to view the bird that had caused him so much grief.

Darrell recoiled.

"Let me see the fucking bird," declared Vip.

Now he could make it out, though he didn't have a flashlight to closely inspect the plumage or notice the slight difference in the size of the bird's head. Darrell dropped the shroud.

"Let's have another piece of pie," declared Alex's stand-in. It was a beautiful recitation and as Alex-like as you could get.

Then came the clincher: "Wide stance, cocksucker." With some degree of confidence I would be willing to bet that Darrell's lips were perfectly pursed.

"Gimme that damn cage," exclaimed Vip.

Darrell released it only after he had gained an even firmer grasp on Vip 's cage.

"Good luck, dumbfuchs" declared Vip contemptuously. "You'll need it."

Now came the part I worried about most.

Darrell broke into a jerky sprint toward Sproule Lane, leaving the cover of the elm tree. He reached the base of my hotel and hurriedly attached the cage to the tuna hook that was dangling from the high-test line that led to my window on the 2nd floor.

Feverishly I began reeling it in. This was more difficult than I imagined.

Suddenly it was Bedlam: I was on the floor and blood was pouring from my scalp. Strangely, I felt no pain. Was this the way it was supposed to work—a dizzy sort of evaporation followed by a sense of falling into a great whirlpool and then the darkness of the void? I thought of my mom and sister behind the glass of that passenger car; I thought of the Hamsa Swans carrying them away to Dal Lake .

Then it came to me that I was only in shock. A bullet had shattered my window and hit a light fixture above my head. That's what had brought me down and had caused the bleeding. I reached for a towel to stanch the blood flow and raced for the exit. A minute later I reached Sproule and Clay where Roger was waiting to pick me up and lose all trailers in the alleys of Chinatown.

"Jeezus what happened?" he declared as he floored it down Clay.

"I guess I dodged a bullet."

Unbeknownst to me, the sniper who launched that bullet was 300 yards away in his hotel room, slumped over with a bullet hole in his forehead delivered by another Grim Reaper.

"You look terrible," declared Roger.

"No, I'm okay. I'm just cut."

My cell suddenly rang. It was Tony.

"Vip got into his car with the bird. I can see them right now rolling west on Sacramento Street. Did you get the drop?"

"Nope. The diamonds in the cage landed on the sidewalk."

"Damn. Vip get them?"

"No, I don't think so."

I spent the night in a cheap Chinatown hotel, knowing that my apartment might not be safe. The next day, I couldn't suppress my curiosity about what had been reported and headed for the newsstand. Truman handed me a newspaper with notes inside from Tony and Rae-Ron filling me in on all that I had missed: RB had disabled the van; C. K. Rice, the world-class sniper who had taken out Willy Davis, had been zeroing in on me as I reeled in the birdcage, but he was nailed by a "friendly sharp-shooter" just as he squeezed off his bullet.

When Vip slipped into his stretch Lincoln and began rolling down Sacramento, our friendly White-Feathered sniper took aim on a drone hovering above the scene. Suddenly it lost rudder and spiraled earthward. The driver of the departing Lincoln swerved to miss it, in the process careening off a passing delivery truck and landing on its side. A door flew open and the birdcage rolled onto the street which Tony quickly scooped up.

Shortly thereafter, ambulance sirens sounded and EMT's arrived. Tony wasn't sure who was attended to, but said the EMT's were furiously applying CPR.

Tony's note added the following: "I wish I had been in that car to see the expression on Vip's face when he realized he had the wrong bird."

I checked the paper and could see that the story hadn't yet been reported. The reporters were probably still trying to sort it all out. I headed back to my hovel and laid low for the next twenty-four hours.

Chapter 48
Gifts from Greta and Jo-Jo

Truman had a *Chronicle* and coffee in a styrofoam cup waiting for me the next day when I arrived. "Bad day for the forces of
darkness," he grinned.

I waited until I was back in my hovel to read it. It had to be
confusing to most readers—two unexplained, seemingly uncon-
nected dramas on Nob Hill: a ranking official in the Bush Administration was in critical condition after a car accident on Sacramento Street that involved the crash of a small aircraft. A separate
report on page five noted that $300,000 in jewels and cash were
found on the sidewalk at Sacramento and Sproule Lane, which police believed might be the result of a "drug deal gone bad."

Among other things, no explanations were provided of how a
small airplane could be flying so low over Nob Hill, why the police believed a drug deal was going down, and how the plane hit
but failed to destroy a car that just happened to be chauffeuring a
Bush V.I.P. whose own reasons for being on the hill were unknown.

I was tempted to drop a dime and offer a few anonymous tips
to the *Chronicle* to straighten it all out, but self-preservation dis-
suaded me. Fortunately, a high-profile lawyer known for his best
seller, *The Prosecution of Don Haney for War Crimes* filled the
void, asking the *Chronicle* reporter if the plane in question was ac-

tually a drone.

The next day another article appeared stating that the plane was a U866 restricted use, military drone, operated by *Bilgewater Security Systems*, a major contractor for the Department of Defense.

This, in turn, prompted the California Attorney General to send a formal letter of inquiry to the US Attorney General demanding a full report on the use of military drones in American cities, San Francisco included.

The next turn of the screw came in the form of a letter from a Progressive California Senator to the Secretary of Defense, The President, The Attorney General and the Director of National Intelligence, also cc'd to the New York Times, demanding to know under what authorization a top secret military aircraft was being operated by a private contractor in an American city.

I wasn't sure exactly how all this was going to play out, but I was pretty confident that no one in *Bilgewater*, Homeland Security, the FBI, or their political operatives in Congress wanted to reveal what had really occurred and how it might relate to PERP. I was sure this also explained why no one had reported the death of C.K. Rice, one of the four best marksman in the world, but at least a few steps down the pecking order from a fellow with a white feather in his cap.

For the moment I thought that most of the threat against us was spinning down. It might go away entirely if Vip didn't recover. I couldn't quite suppress my curiosity about this. Through a contact with *The Barb* who knew various docs at San Francisco General Hospital, I learned that Vip's condition was dire—too many vital organs under stress, particularly stress to all his artificial plumbing.

By way of messages through Truman the herd agreed to a night rendezvous at a Grant Avenue, Chinatown diner. The plan was to consider if anything more could still be done to free the elephants.

To my surprise, Marianne was sharing a dim-lit booth with the others when I arrived. Apparently Tony had brought her. She explained that she was no longer working at the cafe—"need to ration." She seemed a little woozy, but she said she was feeling better because of dosage adjustment.

"You guys," she smiled. "I know you're responsible for all this." She dropped a *Chronicle* on the table with a headline that read, "Military Drones Spy on San Franciscans; Renegade Sniper Found Dead on Nob Hill."

"Circus of fools," declared Darrell. "We screwed it up royally."

"FUBAR," exclaimed Roger.

"This is what happens when amateurs get cocky and start believing they are professionals," I added.

"Speak for yourself, ye of little faith," declared Tony with a gleam in his eye.

"Why so smug?" asked Marianne, her watery, unblinking eyes trained on Tony.

"These doughboys have long disparaged my pigeons, but I tell you now they have just provided a deliverance."

"By what—stripping some old lady of her dime-store bling?" declared Darrell with a grin.

With that, Tony reached out with two closed paws and opened them slowly, one at a time. In one palm was a brilliant, gleaming gold cufflink with a very recognizable crest; in the other, four diamonds that had to be worth—well I wasn't exactly sure, but Tony gave the instant appraisal: "One hundred large for the diamonds and 50k for the cuff-link. Don't you ever again say a bad word again about my birds. They've just gotten our elies out of jail."

"You cad!" I exclaimed. Roger buried Tony in a bear hug.

"Thank Greta and Jo-Jo. I didn't find the gems until yesterday morning in the bottom of the pigeon coop."

"So that was what Vip left behind in the gutter," I declared.

Tony grinned ear to ear.

Marianne couldn't believe it: "This is for Gigi and Sari?"

"Yes," declared Tony. "Do you think it's enough?"

I beat Marianne to the punch: "I don't know—but we'll soon find out."

A few days later Tony, Vincent, Marianne and I rendezvoused at Vincent's office for a conference call with *Trunk to Go* and the zoo. Vincent wasted no time in reminding them of all of the bad publicity that was still reverberating and then tendered a combined offer of $150,000—75 K to each of them. They agreed.

After the call ended, Marianne verbalized the obvious: "That only leaves us thirty K. Where do we get the land and feed?"

"Rae-Ron for the land," answered Tony. "He'll do it. He already told me."

"This is only temporary," replied Marianne.

"I think I know how to get the rest," declared Tony with a gleam in his eye.

"Dare I ask?" declared Marianne.

"I think you all know," added Tony, flapping his wings and cooing. "Rosie's ready to take on the competition."

Chapter 49
What is Not Helpful to the Nez Pierce Nation

One week later, Gigi and Sari were unloaded at their new, temporary home at the Tiger Ranch. Nimba watched curiously under Rae-Ron's close restraint.

At first I was worried that she might attack, but Marianne said there was no chance of that: "Tigers, especially young solo tigers, never pick on elephants or creatures larger than themselves. The greater danger is that Gigi and Sari will do in Nimba."

They eyed each other warily, prompting Marianne to chide: "We're all going to get along with each other. There's room for everyone, and I'll be here all the time making sure that everyone is taken care of."

Gigi offered Marianne her trunk and emitted a low rumble that I recognized from *The Book of Elephant*. She wasn't alarmed, just on guard and uncertain about her new surroundings.

We all joyfully joined the considerable effort of taking care of them, setting up a rotating schedule to make sure that at least one person was with them twenty-four hours a day. Usually there were at least two of us. Our first major challenge was to make sure that we had enough water and feed, which required runs to the nearby farm suppliers.

With Rae-Ron taking the lead as master builder, we began erecting a simple pole barn for the elephants and two yurts where

Jim Currie

the human members of the family might stay during caretaking. It was great fun to be pounding nails and sawing lumber together.

I had never seen Marianne so happy and the others as well. So much of it seemed to be coming directly from Gigi and Sari who had changed overnight as a result of their new-found freedom. Suddenly they were cavorting and playing like babies, racing circles outward from the pole barn and back, randomly bumping into trees, trumpeting and then kicking up dust.

"They didn't forget," Marianne declared.

"Forget what?" I answered."

"What it's like to be a free elephant," she replied.

For the moment it seemed that we had stilled the Great Swirling Vortex in all our lives and magically produced a pacific calm free from worry over things we couldn't control. We were all living in the present just like them, attending to the imperatives of bringing down trees, rearranging dirt, and divining underground springs. I couldn't quite remember experiencing such a sense of purpose and well being. Of course, being with Marianne in the realization of her dream also had much to do with it.

She was growing more openly affectionate toward me every day and might suddenly surprise me with her hand in my own or by planting a kiss on my lips. She was affectionate to the others as well, bubbling over with joy at her dream-come-true, thanks to all of us. The gratitude was infectious.

Even Rae-Ron was affected. "I think we might need to get this under control," he laughed. "I'm not sure how becoming this is for a grim reaper."

"Nothing radical," declared Marianne, "Just getting rid of the grim part."

The next day Gigi and Sari found water. At around 8 AM, about two hundred yards from the bunker-house and not far from the yurts, they began trumpeting and acting strange. At first I was a little worried that they might be having it out with Nimba, but she was only watching curiously. Gigi began stamping, and then strangely enough, grabbed a branch from a nearby tree which she proceeded to dig into the ground as if it were a shovel.

Marianne was right behind me.

"I know what this is about," she declared.

A second later it came to me as well, from one of the illustrations in *The Book of Elephant*.

With the elephants trumpeting expectantly, we all set to work digging and within a few minutes our shovels were wet. Rae-Ron speeded up the effort by appearing with his mini backhoe. By the end of the day we had produced a glorious natural pond suitable for dunking and all manner of elephant play.

Rae-Ron was the most surprised by the find. "You know, I paid a douser two thousand dollars to find water on this site and he said it was hopeless. The elephants find it immediately. Amazing."

We decided to name the pond Sarasvati and invited the missing members of our family to the dedication on the weekend that followed. The gathered crew included all the usual suspects, but was augmented by Truman and Vincent.

Most everyone had brought a special delicacy or libation. Truman supplied Golden Delicious apples for the elephants and a salmon to be cooked Nez Pierce-style over an alder fire. I knocked myself out trying to recreate a recipe for *dal* that Amita made for Arundhati and me in childhood.

When we were halfway to an inebriated substitute for Nirvana, Red Bill emerged through the front door with People's Stroganoff—a vodka-fortified recipe he and Peggy had concocted.

"Peggy couldn't be here," he added, "but she sends her feisty love."

"Down with the Czar and up with the Elephants," declared Vincent, already on his lips.

Truman was the only one not drinking, but I had never seen him so emotional. He kept surveying the grounds, the elephants and Sarasvati, as if somehow we had managed to recreate the Great Nez Pierce Homeland. His eyes even seemed to be watering.

"You're going to be a buzz-kill if you don't stanch the tears," declared Big Roger.

"I can't help it," he answered. "This is very good."

After Nimba was fed, and dishes served up, nominations began for the toast. All the fingers were pointed in my direction, but I passed the buck to Truman who was clearly building up for a spout. At first I thought he would decline but he surprised me by declaring, "I will take the talking stick from my drunk Indian brother, Pankaz."

Everyone raised their glasses.

"Bless the animals and bless the earth and let us learn to listen to them."

After a moment of silence he offered up an eerie and haunting chant to "our Good Mother Earth."

"Ho Way Hey Yey, Ho A Way Yah Hey."

Every fake, wannabee Indian spirit in the drunken tribe chimed in—as usual, out of synch and out of tune.

"Jesus Christ!" exclaimed Vincent rolling his eyes. "Let's get it together, folks."

"This would not have helped my people," deadpanned Truman.

Over the course of the evening, small tales and boasts grew to elephantine proportions; gentle aspersions were cast; arrows fired; and rhapsody ran wild. Rae-Ron admitted that he thought we were all insane to try to blackmail Wide Stance and friends, but had arrived at his own conclusion that it was "probably a good day to croak. I really thought Rice was going to nail us all."

Red Bill, who couldn't get enough of his own stroganoff, disagreed, "I didn't view it as hopeless. I figured we had at least a 10 percent chance—as long as we didn't get stupid."

"Touched by the stupid stick," declared Darrell.

"Yes, you can never rule this out," chimed in Truman.

We replayed our own individual versions of the detailed events and what was going through each of our heads at every moment. Tony said that he worried that our stand-in bird would spout and queer the deal.

"You tell me this now?" replied Darrell. "I just assumed he was mute."

"How in God's name did you ever spot Rice?" I asked, turning to Rae-Ron.

"It was deductive," he answered. "There could only be so many perches that would do."

"And then there is the miracle of all miracles," Marianne declared. "Greta and Jo-Jo."

"Yes and no," answered Tony. "The only real break we caught here is that Wide Stance lost his cufflink and dropped the diamonds. There is no way Jo-Jo would have missed them once they were in the gutter."

"I hope they got a juicy reward," replied Marianne.

Tony sparkled, "What do you think? Which brings up the issue of stage two."

"What?" replied the drunken collective.

"Sun City Million. Are we faint hearted or do we reach for the golden ring?"

"What's the investment here?" asked Roger.

"A mere five hundred dollars to enter the Vegas regional which will pay for everything else. After we cop that we're qualified for the 'Million'. This year it's in Hopetown, South Africa."

"I would like to contribute to this mission," declared Truman.

"You don't know a thing about it," answered Darrell.

"I like the idea. I can tell it has great spirit."

We turned the idea upside down and inside out. Marianne wanted assurance that Rosy and the other trainees would not be abused in any way. Tony so promised. Roger asked for a realistic assessment of chances and not a lot of bubble blowing.

All Tony would say was that Rosy was the finest, fastest homer he had ever trained and that he had some tricks up his sleeves that most trainers didn't know about. Darrell, the gambler in the group, suggested that we really had no better options for realizing Marianne's dream and we ought to double-down.

"I intend to win," declared Tony "and this year first prize is $500,000."

Rae-Ron's jaw dropped. "Are you kidding me? Hmmm...I think I know how to enhance our chances." He raised an imaginary reaper to his shoulder. "Pull," he declared, immediately erasing the competition. .

"Would that be okay, Marianne?" I asked with a grin.

Marianne grimaced.

"No need," answered Tony. "She'll dust them like a bunch of broken-winged sparrows."

Jim Currie

Chapter 50
Scripts

In the days that followed, Marianne and I moved to a small two-room apartment in Santa Rosa which I insisted on paying for on the pretext that all of us needed a place to shower and clean up when we got tired of the yurts. She had now given up her San Francisco apartment. I kept mine and was now shuttling back and forth several days a week between Berkeley and Santa Rosa.

To everyone's surprise except Tony, Rosy won the Vegas Regional, destroying the competition, including Gwenny, the bird owned and trained by Rollie the Racer. This brought in $10,000 to the collective proceeds which the group then dedicated one-half of to enter Rosy in the Sun City Million that was now three months away.

In living with Marianne, I soon realized how much she was slipping. Restful sleep was increasingly difficult for her because of myoclonic spasms, headaches, and some combination of nightmares and delusions.

Days were better if she had slept and was free of headaches, but even the good days were less frequent. I could also tell that her attention span had shortened and that she was having more and more trouble remembering what she had said or done only minutes before. Her speech was now slurred and clipped.

From phone discussions with her doctor, I was led to expect

extreme mood swings and even fits of rage, but there were none outside of the nocturnal journeys to hell. I wasn't sure exactly why but thought this might have something to do with a spirit that had come to grips with her own death and a resolution to spread as much love and compassion as possible in her days remaining.

Several weeks after the move, she allowed me to accompany her on a visit to her doctor in San Francisco. First we visited Telegraph Hill and it only took Alex a few minutes to land on Marianne's shoulder. He squawked excitedly and allowed her to pet his fine feathers. Suddenly he flew off to a nearby olive tree, and to my surprise landed next to another African grey. Marianne immediately identified her as a female. We both waved as they flew off together.

At the clinic, the doctor first asked about Marianne's migraines, and she said they had gotten no better. He prescribed a new drug that he thought might help and then ran several tests of her reflexes and cognition. He was pretty poker-faced but couldn't hide what they revealed about her rapid deterioration. When he asked about the pain she was in, I sensed that he now believed her time was very short.

It seemed important to him that I was there writing down what Marianne should be doing for contingencies: "Will Pankaz or family be able to help you decide on a care facility? This shouldn't be left to the last minute."

She only smiled and then surprised both of us by declaring slowly, "Will I be frog..feel the water temp'sure climbing..?"

He paused thoughtfully and replied, "Chances are you won't really know—but others have to take care of you—make decisions for you."

"I see," she said with no show of despair. "How will it...?"

"Pneumonia is the most likely event, but then you should be in a nursing home where the medications will prevent pain and discomfort. There should be no suffering."

"Then every breath...important," she declared.

He studied her curiously, clearly wondering if she was so irrational as to think that she could go through this ordeal without nursing.

"Can you provide morphine...? Nights are biggest problem."

Now he seemed to realize that she was not going to hospitalize herself.

"You realize that last days are very hard to deal with, even in hospice? You'll need help just for pain control."

"I'm here to help," I declared. "I want to follow her wishes."

She handed him a piece of paper that was affixed to her wrist with a rubber band. I hadn't seen it before. All it listed were medications and dosages. You didn't have to be a doctor to realize that these were high dosages, non-label dosages, and the purpose wasn't just to get through a bad night.

He inspected it carefully and read her intent. After a deep sigh he reached for his prescription pad. He then handed her three scripts.

Referring to the first two he declared, "You and Pankaz both realize that this is for pain and sleep. I'm giving you the max. If you exceed these in 24 hrs, breathing and vital functions will be affected. You also don't want to take these two within 24 hours of this one because it dramatically amplifies the effects. I'm going to write this down."

She smiled, placed the scripts in her pocket and replied.

"Bless you."

I looked back at the doctor and read the unspoken words: "I could get in a lot of trouble for this." I was sure he wouldn't have given the scripts to anyone but Marianne, whom he clearly had a great affection for. He didn't want her to suffer when the time came.

As soon as we exited the door of the clinic, Marianne's energy evaporated. She reached up to hold her aching forehead, and then I could see she was growing even shakier. I carried her to the car. Her weary head was tilted against my shoulder all the way back to Santa Rosa.

Chapter 51
Elephant Rumbles from Sri Lanka to Srinagar

I stayed with her for the next several days, helping her through her fatigue and disabling headaches. Thankfully, a new migraine drug had started to work, but she wasn't well enough to leave the apartment and help with the elephants at the ranch.

For the moment I was her stand-in, usually visiting the ranch every morning for at least a few hours before heading to Berkeley to work on my stories. It always made my day to see how well the elephants were doing.

On one such morning, Gigi came running toward me happily and stopped suddenly. For a second I thought she was going to turn me into a tin can. She seemed amused by my reaction, then ran her trunk across my shirt, clearly picking up the scent of Marianne.

"Yes, you're so smart. She hasn't forgotten about you. I'm sure she'll be back soon enough."

Before heading off to work, I learned from Rae-Ron that he had talked to his 80-year old next-door neighbor who was apparently thinking about selling his property. The parcel was 50 acres in size and the asking price would be around $300K.

"We don't have that unless Rosy cops *The Million*, so it's moot," I replied.

"I know," he replied, "But maybe I could convince the owner to give us a six-month option. I don't think it would cost that much—a few thousand, max. In the mean time, maybe Vincent will find some more money."

I agreed that a purchase option probably made sense, but this wasn't a decision for me to make alone—we needed to get concurrence from Tony and the others. Rae-Ron said he had already talked to Tony and Roger, and they were both on-board with the idea.

My immediate concern was our declining bank balance, and where we would be in six months without an infusion of serious cash. Marianne's drug costs were significantly depleting the money we had to feed the elephants and cover their own medical bills. Marianne was clearly worried about this as well. I decided to give this my full attention and the next day met with Vincent at his office to draw up a trust that would protect what Marianne had saved.

I was going over the draft documents in his office when Marianne called. Her speech was slow and flat. Only the most important words were uttered but I got the message: Tony had taken her to the ranch, and she would spend the day there with Gigi and Sari.

"You sure you're feeling well enough?"

"Jus fine," she answered unconvincingly."

"I told her I would pick her up at 6 PM, and we would drive back to Santa Rosa.

When I arrived, I found her out among the elephants at the Sarasvati. As I approached, I could see them throwing mud and dust at each other and Marianne. Marianne was getting the worst of it, but giggling.

"Funny, huh?" she declared after Gigi landed a pie on the

back of her head.

Marianne retaliated by trying to throw a handful of mud that only could have struck an invisible elephant. It was an uncoordinated effort that showed how much muscle control she had lost. She smiled and laughed causing Gigi to trumpet and spray both Sari and Marianne with water. Her eyes followed Marianne closely almost protectively, and then she sprayed her again gently.

Nimba was nearby, not quite sure what to make of this.

I wanted to freeze that moment and forever imprint it to memory. It seemed to capture the essence of Marianne's spirit and her love of these amazing creatures who were the vessels of memory, emotionality and self-awareness. That night back in Santa Rosa after dinner, Marianne asked if I would tell her about my own life in India.

"It's not a good story," I answered. "In fact, it's a cliff-drop."

"I know," she answered, "don't care. No hiding," she intoned.

"No hiding," I answered.

So over the course of an hour, I told her most of what happened after the death of Deli, including the story of *Lucknow Textile* and the *Lucknow Mail Disaster*. She pressed for more, so according to agreement, I filled in with the story of the Hamsa Swans and my futile dives into the river to save Amita and Arundhati.

She broke into tears, and I told her that over so many years I had pretty much cried myself out.

At the end, she kissed me and declared, "Wonderful gift... Amita and Arundhati...Dad too."

I sighed dismissively.

"No," she answered. "Be grateful."

I thought about it. "Yeah, you're right."

"Look forward to be with Amita and Arundhati."

I chuckled. "In the great Hindu after-life."

"Yes."

She said something about the Buddha, and I had to unscramble it: "Did I grow up near the Buddha's home?"

She nodded.

"Within 100 miles of Kapilavastu, and about the same from Lumbini where the unredeemed busy themselves at the archaeological digs trying to prove his place of birth."

"Teach me...please."

"The stories about the Buddha are pretty apocryphal. I could tell you the story of India but it might make your headaches worse—about what happened to elephants, about what happened to the forests, about sewage in the rivers, about rape and kidnapping, about spirituality run amok."

"Just tell good parts—like swans."

I smiled and kissed her forehead. "For you and the elies, my love."

From then on, every night for a week, just before sleep, I would spin gossamer to Marianne about Siddhartha, the dharma, the *Mahabharata* and stories of Tibetan masters. I even prepared for the performances by paging through dusty archives of what I had first heard from my father, pre-*tin can*. Some of it came from the notes in *The Book of Elephant* that now was never far from Marianne's night-time reach.

I told this curious wonderstruck spirit the story of how Buddha was born—about Queen Maya's dream of the white elephant with a lotus in its trunk entering her side; I spoke of the Buddha's visions to become a renunciate *sadhu*, and then Siddhartha's discovery of the Middle Way. I related what he learned as a ferryman on a great river and the arrival of the *Four Noble Truths* to solve the problem of suffering.

She was unsated so I recapitulated the *Lotus Sutra* and the story of the Buddha's supernatural powers as he penetrated *maya*. I described the visit of the Bodhisattvas traveling from distant planets to rain down rare flowers upon the earth. I described the lotus as the pure flower of rebirth, arising from swamp muck at Dal Lake and other fertile wetlands.

Of all that I related, it was the story of Srinagar and the Hamsa Swans that she loved most, just like Amita. She was mesmerized by images of the weightless White Ones winging over the Himalaya to the lake, and then with unwetted feathers hovering above the surface among the lotuses.

Reading her enchantment, I spoke of the legendary musical instruments making music on their own in powerful serenade, and then I noticed that the song from those invisible lutes and drums had quelled the shaking of her hands, and the throbbing of her brain, and delivered her to the cradling, comforting embrace of the Buddha. For the first time in my life I was grateful to India for what she had given me.

At the end of the week, Marianne called me at *The Barb* and with words that took forever to form asked if I would join her and the elies in the evening for a ritual. She wouldn't elaborate, but then again she wasn't talking as much as before.

I arrived and she beckoned me to the Sarasvati where she was surrounded by Sari and Gigi. On unsteady trembling legs, she waded into the pond holding a large white tuber. I wasn't sure what she was up to but knew that in her present condition she was seconds from a fall. Gigi seemed concerned as well and reached out with her trunk as if to prevent the collapse.

I caught her just as she lost her balance. I carried her to the bank clinging to her plant as Gigi trumpeted over the drama. Marianne held her plant out toward me with intoxicated, unblinking joy.

Suddenly it hit me that this was an Indian lotus, and she was planning to do the work of the Buddha by seeding birth, redemption and the great turning of the wheel.

"Where did... you get this?"

She couldn't quite get the words out as her arms trembled. But I didn't have to hear them or get her to verbalize her wish. I stripped to my waist, took the lotus from her arms, submerged and embedded it in the muck.

"Do you think 10 inches is enough?"

She nodded. And then Gigi sounded. I was sure she wanted in on this, but Marianne shook her head suggesting that this wasn't a game of fetch and eat.

"Why do I think Gigi will be having lotus salad tomorrow?"

If Marianne was concerned, there was no sign of it.

The next day I took her to the ranch in the early morning, noticing nothing peculiar about her manner or dress. About all that was different was that her eyes were a little more watery than usual, and she seemed to be mooning over me abnormally.

"Careful, slim. You're looking a little love-struck to me. We don't want to make the elies jealous."

She smiled, and I kissed her. "I'll be back for you at 6 PM, okay?"

She nodded, and when I hugged her she didn't seem ready to let go. I could hear her sniffling and realized she was crying.

"Back as soon as I can, sweetheart. No worries."

I arrived at the ranch just after 6 PM, stopping first at the bunker-house because Marianne usually met me there. Rae-Ron and Nimba seemed to be out on the acreage for a walk. I turned and Sari came rushing toward me obviously agitated, crying out in the same way she had the day that Hansa died. Right away I was alarmed.

I raced off toward the yurts and noticed Gigi at the opening of the yurt that Marianne usually occupied. Horrific howling filled the air that I recognized instantly as death song. Gigi's head was just inside the yurt, and now I realized her trunk was wrapped around something. My God, it was Marianne's limp body.

Gigi spotted me and met my eyes mournfully, beseeching me to do something. I knew at that moment exactly what had happened.

I took Marianne's lifeless body from her embrace and fell over it, crying inconsolably. Only a few feet away on the ground were empty bottles of morphine and barbiturates. Lying on open pages of *The Book of Elephant* was the following note:

"Time to go, Pankaz, dearest. Be waiting for you and family among swans at Srinagar. So very precious Love."

The day we interred Marianne's body at the edge of pond, all gathered to pay their respects. The family included Tony, Roger and Darrell, Rae-Ron, Vincent, Red Bill and Truman. Tony noted that he had passed the word to Alex and was quite sure that respects would be paid by all the conjures and parrots of Telegraph Hill.

There were no wordy elegies or gaudy poetry. We simply held each other in a common grief, aware of what she had done to enrich our lives and make us more loving and caring about the natural world. All the while, Gigi and Deli rumbled a deep and heartful evensong that no doubt was being conveyed through ley lines all across Mastodonia that the Patron Saint of Elephants had been delivered from suffering and had joined Airavata and the Hamsa Swans on their return to Srinagar.

Epilogue
Sun City Million

On the night that Tony and I flew out of San Francisco International for Hopetown, I authored the following story for *The Barb*:

Local Pigeon Homes in on World Crown
by Pankaz Panday

A local pigeon trainer claims to be on a mission from God or at least "the Patron Saint of Elephants" to win the international homing pigeon contest in eight weeks in Hopetown, Africa, and to support a sanctuary for abused elephants.

The trainer in question is Tony Amato, who was one of the last US Army Signal Corps "pigeoneers". Trained by the famous Colonel Clifford Poutre, whose couriers saved countless lives in WW II and the Korean War, Amato gleams with pride over the prowess of his star pigeon, Rosy, who shares the same bloodlines as G.I. Joe, a courier who saved a British brigade in the Italian campaign during WW II and delivered messages to George Patton in Tunisia.

"Rosy is sweet and friendly," declared Tony with a twinkle in his eye, "But don't let this deceive you. She flies like the wind with a homing instinct like McArthur for the Philippines. I think she'll mop the skies with these other birds."

The competition will draw champions from all over the world, including a star named Goya, who won the celebrated Tenerife European for the third-straight year...

Two months later, I gave my eye-witness account of the race:

Rosy Cops World Crown
Dusts Pigeon Rivals in Hopetown Million
by Pankaz Panday
Special Report to *The Barb*

You would have thought that the alien African landscape alone would have been enough to scramble the inner navigation of Rosy, the San Francisco homing pigeon competing in the Sun City Million. If not that, the difference in Southern Hemisphere magnetism, sound transmission or whatever mysterious forces of nature explain the navigation of homing pigeons. But Rosy had to cope with much more—unusual winds off the Veldt, unrecognizable predator birds and even poachers.

She survived it all, soldier that she is, just like GI Joe, her great ancestor of WW II fame, and today won the esteemed and lucrative crown as the World's Fastest Long-Distance Pigeon.

The race began in the Veldt, 400 kilometers northeast of Hopetown. Here at 10 AM local time race officials "liberated" 300 pre-qualified champions, including the illustrious Goya from Tenerife who went off as a 2-1 betting favorite. Rosy was considered one of the longest of long shots, posted at 60-1 by bookmakers, despite an untarnished record in lesser state-side competition.

But Rosy possessed at least two advantages on Goya and the other birds—schooling by Tony Amato who had learned his craft in the US Pigeon Corps under the famous Colonel Clifford Poutre, and what Tony describes as "an extraordinary passion to be home sipping a beer." According to Amato, Rosy enjoys rhythm and blues, popcorn and "an occasional taste of Guinness."

Those who witnessed the "liberation" claim that Rosy shot from her open "basket" and only circled once before gaining her bearings on Hopetown which lay on a compass reading of 20 degrees south-southeast. For a bird like Rosy that read had to be immediate and instinctive.

According to Tony, "She's a bird trained to fly to Kashmir if necessary. My only worry was that a hawk might nail her."

It was no casual worry. The Veldt liberation point was natural and forbidding. Off in the distance hawks and carrion birds were circling some kind of carcass at a watering hole. The pigeons had to negotiate that to arrive at Hopetown.

Four hours, four minutes and twenty seconds later, at the grouped lofts in Hopetown, Rosy dropped from the sky and landed on her perch. With high-powered binoculars, Goya could be spotted about one kilometer behind. In characteristic fashion, Rosy bobbed several times, fell into her usual circling, self-satisfied moonwalk, then disappeared inside her home-loft. You could hear Amato's exuberant cry from afar—"You did it girl. You did it for Gigi, Sari, Winkie and Marianne."

If you enjoyed *Saddam's Parrot* consider Jim Currie's *In Dire Straits: Keeping Spirit Alive When the Wheels Come off* (Savant, 2011)

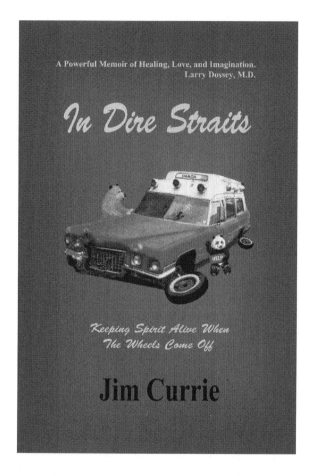

IN DIRE STRAITS is a healing memoir about the challenges of coping with and recovering from an incapacitating rheumatoid disease. Told from the perspective of a solo world traveler, it reads like a travel book, full of edifying adventures and quirky discoveries. Each encounter prompts reflection on self-empowerment through greater mindfulness, curiosity and imagination.

About the Author

Jim Currie is a Seattle writer and ecologist whose credits include fiction, screenplays, non-fiction, and over twenty publications on natural resource management and ecology. He holds an honors degree from Harvard and a masters from Berkeley. His writing and teaching reflect wide-ranging curiosities in the arts, science, humanities and philosophy. His fiction is playful and original, involving memorable characters struggling with defining dilemmas.

His published titles include IN DIRE STRAITS (Savant, 2011) and THE MINDFUL TRAVELER: A Guide to Journaling and Transformative Travel (Open Court, 2000). Jim writes about ecology, elephants, conservation and climate action at http://www.SydneysThumb.com

See @SaddamsParrot for latest squawks by Alex on state of the planet.

Jim Currie

If you enjoyed *Saddam's Parrot,* consider these other fine books
from Aignos Publishing:

The Dark Side of Sunshine by Paul Guzzo
Happy that it's Not True by Carlos Aleman
Cazadores de Libros Perdidos by German William Cabasssa Barber [Spanish]
The Desert and the City by Derek Bickerton
The Overnight Family Man by Paul Guzzo
There is No Cholera in Zimbabwe by Zachary M. Oliver
John Doe by Buz Sawyers
The Piano Tuner's Wife by Jean Yamasaki Toyama
Nuno by Carlos Aleman
An Aura of Greatness by Brendan P. Burns
Polonio Pass by Doc Krinberg
Iwana by Alvaro Leiva
University and King by Jeffrey Ryan Long
The Surreal Adventures of Dr. Mingus by Jesus Richard Felix Rodriguez
Letters by Buz Sawyers
In the Heart of the Country by Derek Bickerton
El Camino De Regreso by Maricruz Acuna [Spanish]
Diego in Two Places by Carlos Aleman
Prepositions by Jean Yamasaki Toyama
Deep Slumber of Dogs by Doc Krinberg

Coming Soon:
Beneath Them by Natalie Roers
Chang the Magic Cat by A. G. Hayes

Aignos Publishing | an imprint of Savant Books and Publications
http://www.aignospublishing.com

as well as these other fine books from Savant Books and Publications:

Essay, Essay, Essay by Yasuo Kobachi
Aloha from Coffee Island by Walter Miyanari
Footprints, Smiles and Little White Lies by Daniel S. Janik
The Illustrated Middle Earth by Daniel S. Janik
Last and Final Harvest by Daniel S. Janik
A Whale's Tale by Daniel S. Janik
Tropic of California by R. Page Kaufman
Tropic of California (the companion music CD) by R. Page Kaufman
The Village Curtain by Tony Tame
Dare to Love in Oz by William Maltese
The Interzone by Tatsuyuki Kobayashi
Today I Am a Man by Larry Rodness
The Bahrain Conspiracy by Bentley Gates
Called Home by Gloria Schumann
Kanaka Blues by Mike Farris
First Breath edited by Z. M. Oliver
Poor Rich by Jean Blasiar
The Jumper Chronicles by W. C. Peever
William Maltese's Flicker by William Maltese
My Unborn Child by Orest Stocco
Last Song of the Whales by Four Arrows
Perilous Panacea by Ronald Klueh
Falling but Fulfilled by Zachary M. Oliver
Mythical Voyage by Robin Ymer
Hello, Norma Jean by Sue Dolleris
Richer by Jean Blasiar
Manifest Intent by Mike Farris
Charlie No Face by David B. Seaburn
Number One Bestseller by Brian Morley
My Two Wives and Three Husbands by S. Stanley Gordon
In Dire Straits by Jim Currie
Wretched Land by Mila Komarnisky
Chan Kim by Ilan Herman
Who's Killing All the Lawyers? by A. G. Hayes
Ammon's Horn by G. Amati
Wavelengths edited by Zachary M. Oliver
Almost Paradise by Laurie Hanan
Communion by Jean Blasiar and Jonathan Marcantoni
The Oil Man by Leon Puissegur
Random Views of Asia from the Mid-Pacific by William E. Sharp
The Isla Vista Crucible by Reilly Ridgell
Blood Money by Scott Mastro
In the Himalayan Nights by Anoop Chandola
On My Behalf by Helen Doan

Jim Currie

Traveler's Rest by Jonathan Marcantoni
Keys in the River by Tendai Mwanaka
Chimney Bluffs by David B. Seaburn
The Loons by Sue Dolleris
Light Surfer by David Allan Williams
The Judas List by A. G. Hayes
Path of the Templar—Book 2 of The Jumper Chronicles by W. C. Peever
The Desperate Cycle by Tony Tame
Shutterbug by Buz Sawyer
Blessed are the Peacekeepers by Tom Donnelly and Mike Munger
Bellwether Messages edited by D. S. Janik
The Turtle Dances by Daniel S. Janik
The Lazarus Conspiracies by Richard Rose
Purple Haze by George B. Hudson
Imminent Danger by A. G. Hayes
Lullaby Moon (CD) by Malia Elliott of Leon & Malia
Volutions edited by Suzanne Langford
In the Eyes of the Son by Hans Brinckmann
The Hanging of Dr. Hanson by Bentley Gates
Flight of Destiny by Francis Powell
Elaine of Corbenic by Tima Z. Newman
Ballerina Birdies by Marina Yamamoto
More More Time by David B. Seabird
Crazy Like Me by Erin Lee
Cleopatra Unconquered by Helen R. Davis
Valedictory by Daniel Scott
The Chemical Factor by A. G. Hayes
Quantum Death by A. G. Hayes
Running from the Pack edited by Helen R. Davis
Big Heaven by Charlotte Hebert
Captain Riddle's Treasure by GV Rama Rao
All Things Await by Seth Clabough
Tsunami Libido by Cate Burns
Finding Kate by A. G. Hayes
The Adventures of Purple Head, Buddha Monkey and Sticky Feet by Erik Bracht
In the Shadows of My Mind by Andrew Massie
The Gumshoe by Richard Rose
Cereus by Z. Roux
Shadow and Light edited by Helen R. Davis

Coming Soon:
The Solar Triangle by A. G. Hayes
A Real Daughter by Lynne McKelvey
StoryTeller by Nicholas Bylotas
Bo Henry at Three Forks by Daniel D. Bradford

http://www.savantbooksandpublications.com